"Tessa."

This time Noah whispered her name—as if their shared past drew his breath from depths she hadn't known she'd reached. His gaze washed her with the same insatiable need she felt. A yearning that had nothing to do with sex.

They were two people who'd lost everything. Seeing him brought it all back. The joy as well as the pain. Joy scared Tessa more. She didn't want to remember that much happiness now that she'd lost it.

"I don't want you here." What she meant was she never wanted to need him again.

His grimace acknowledged what she couldn't say. "Who did this to David? Are you all right?"

"I'm fine." She wasn't. She wanted to cry—for David, for his daughter, for herself and maybe a little for this empty-eyed shadow of Noah.

Dear Reader,

Imagine that the loss of your beloved baby girl has broken your marriage. You've taken refuge in a small Maine town, working with your best friend in a law practice that drags you back into life. But then you find your friend murdered, leaving you as his daughter's guardian—and somehow as the prime suspect.

Only the threat of losing another child would make you call your ex-husband for help. That's what happens to Tessa Gabriel when she becomes Maggie's guardian. She calls the best homicide detective she's ever known, her former husband, Noah—and he comes because he believes clearing her of the charge might make up for letting her down in the past.

I hope you'll enjoy finding out what Maggie has to teach Noah and Tessa as they discover the killer who's still threatening Tessa and their future.

I'd love to hear what you think. You can reach me at anna@annaadams.net.

Best wishes,

Anna Adams

Books by Anna Adams

HARLEQUIN SUPERROMANCE

Don't miss any of our special offers. Write to us at the following address for information on our newest releases.

Harlequin Reader Service
U.S.: 3010 Walden Ave., P.O. Box 1325, Buffalo, NY 14269
Canadian: P.O. Box 609, Fort Erie, Ont. L2A 5X3

Maggie's Guardian
Anna Adams

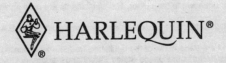

HARLEQUIN®

TORONTO • NEW YORK • LONDON
AMSTERDAM • PARIS • SYDNEY • HAMBURG
STOCKHOLM • ATHENS • TOKYO • MILAN • MADRID
PRAGUE • WARSAW • BUDAPEST • AUCKLAND

ISBN 0-373-71082-8

MAGGIE'S GUARDIAN

Copyright © 2002 by Anna Adams.

This edition published by arrangement with Harlequin Books S.A.

® and TM are trademarks of the publisher. Trademarks indicated with ® are registered in the United States Patent and Trademark Office, the Canadian Trade Marks Office and in other countries.

Visit us at www.eHarlequin.com

Printed in U.S.A.

To the ones who were there and to those who could only watch. We continue to survive September 11.

CHAPTER ONE

ICY RAINDROPS PLUMMETED out of the gray sky to pound on homicide detective Noah Gabriel's head. He planted one foot in front of the other, hoping to reach District C6's station door before he dropped to his knees. He'd stayed out too late, drunk too much and recounted each second of his broken marriage too thoroughly last night. His ritual for the past eighteen months.

He kept meaning to put Tessa and their lost baby girl out of his mind, just as Tessa had turned her back on him. But he never drank quite enough. And the next day, he always battled a hangover that felt like an anvil player composing inside his head.

He reached the sidewalk in front of the station just as two female patrol officers burst through the glass doors. Their high-pitched voices sliced through his scalp, excising the last functioning sections of his brain. Ducking around the women, he skidded on an empty soda can and rammed his shoulder into the building's dirty brick wall.

Laughter at his expense actually raised the women's voices to a more lethal tone. Noah dragged the door shut behind him to escape the pain, but once he was inside, the disgruntled swearing and shouts that grew louder as the afternoon progressed battered him.

Suck it up, he told himself, taking the stairs two at a time. By the top, he considered passing out. Fighting dizziness and unfamiliar pangs he faintly recognized as hunger, he followed the squares of gray— once white—tile floor that led him to his desk.

"Gabriel," his commander, Captain Larry Baxton, barked.

Noah concentrated on not looking as if he wanted to kill someone before he let himself focus on the other man. Baxton brandished a fistful of pink telephone message slips.

"Glad you could make it—why don't you let these people know I'm not your secretary?" He slammed the messages on Noah's desk. "We have two from your ex-wife, and I've lost count of the rest—from some police chief in Maine. I especially don't want to talk to that Podunk crossing guard again. Got it?"

Baxton pivoted toward his own office. From their respective desks, Noah's fellow detectives eyed him. They weren't idiots, and they couldn't know he'd made sure his vices hadn't begun to compromise a gift for catching bad guys. They seemed to think he'd forgotten this group of men and women were a homicide *team*.

With their stares like stilettos in his back, he dropped into his torn leather chair. His body weight butted it into a stanchion that bounced him forward again. He ignored the knowing snickers that insinuated he'd come to work under the influence. Why try to prove he was sober?

He scooped up the scattered messages. From the top slip, Tessa's name leaped off the "who called" line.

His mouth tightened, a painful, involuntary response. As "Tessa" whispered inside his mind, angry grief stirred to a boil. Not content to raise hell in his off-duty head, she had to sabotage his working hours, too?

He held the pink paper square over the garbage can beside his desk and then opened his fingers. Not bothering to watch it flutter away, he concentrated blurring eyes on the next message. Left by Chief Richard Weldon.

The chief was from Prodigal, Maine. Noah glanced back at the garbage can. Tessa had moved to Prodigal after the divorce. It'd be one hell of a coincidence if she and the chief of police in her new hometown wanted to talk to him about something different.

He searched for Tessa's other message. Beneath her name, he read the words, "She said never mind."

Never mind? She called him out of the blue after eighteen months, and she thought "never mind" was enough explanation?

He stared at the stack of Weldon's messages. Baxton had just slashed the word "urgent" across each of the slips. Urgent must be an understatement. Tessa wouldn't have called him for anything less vital than the end of the world.

He toed his chair in a circle until he faced his desk again. The divorce Tessa had demanded gave him an excuse to ignore her summons.

But if she was in trouble? He reached for the phone, his body a drum that vibrated in time with his pulse. The sight of his own shaking hand made him back off. He shrugged out of his black leather jacket. He'd started to sweat.

Get a grip. He closed his eyes and faced truth in the darkness. A grip on what? Pressing his fingertips hard against his throbbing temples, he fought wave after wave of pain. Nothing put Tessa in perspective. And her "never mind" hadn't let him off the hook. She wouldn't have called if her problem was something she could handle by herself.

He stared at the phone again, dreading the rejection in her voice, disillusionment that had swallowed any softer feelings she'd had for him. He'd survived the eighteen months since his daughter's death, by learning to make himself numb. Opening his eyes again, he swiped his hand across his mouth.

What kind of man let a woman do him this way?

"If you're sick, go to the men's room."

Noah turned, an answer ready for the smart-ass colleague who'd offered such sound advice, but the Ann Landers with the big mouth was actually a suspect being booked.

Noah planted both palms on his desk. He could either sit or clock the guy. And clocking the guy might impinge on their case against him. They didn't get jaywalkers up here. Just scum who'd killed one or more innocent human beings.

Breathing deeply, he stared at Richard Weldon's name. He'd talk to Weldon first, and maybe he wouldn't even have to call Tessa. He snatched up the receiver and then punched in the number. After one ring a man identified himself as the police chief.

"Noah Gabriel, returning your call."

"I've tried to reach you all day."

He took enough of that tone from Baxton. Noah eyed the stack of messages. "Yeah?"

"It's about your wife. I don't know how to tell you—I'm not even sure I should tell you, but I've put her in an office in my station."

"So?" An office—that was Tessa's big crisis?

"Look, buddy, when your wife called you, I heard her ask for 'Detective' Gabriel. As a professional courtesy, I'm letting you know I have her."

"For what?" He wasn't holding her for anything big if he'd only shut her up in an office. Noah almost smiled as he pictured Tessa's reaction to being "held" at all. Five feet four inches of trained lawyer, dogged independence and, if you crossed her, notable fury. He remembered how he'd crossed her, and his urge to smile passed. He swallowed hard, his throat muscles contracting.

He'd been the one to find their baby daughter in her crib that hellish morning. Her name stole across his thoughts, too. "Keely," a body blow that caught him unaware. He usually tried not to let himself think her name. He hadn't said it out loud since her funeral.

Not since the moment he'd realized Tessa blamed him. He'd checked the baby last the night before she'd...

But SIDS gave you no warning.

He hadn't known he should plant himself beside his infant daughter and listen to her breathe all night. He hadn't even known he should have kissed her cheek one more time, stroked the downy black hair off her warm forehead before her skin grew cold. He shook his head and swallowed, trying not to get sick at the memories that raked him.

Rage, his abiding companion for the past year and a half, clenched his hand around the receiver. He saw himself throwing the telephone through the nearest damn window—but he didn't do it.

Civilized men held on. For what? How the hell was he supposed to know?

"What did you say, Chief Weldon?" Even to himself, he sounded as if he were strangling.

Weldon hesitated a lengthy moment. "I'm letting you know your wife may be in deep trouble."

"I'm not married." He'd said it so many times he'd learned how to make it sound as if it didn't hurt.

"Your ex-wife, then. Man, I don't know what's wrong with you two, but you'd both better listen to me. She found her partner dead in his office today, stabbed. At least she says she found him, but we have no witnesses, and I've heard some ugly stories about her and Mr. Howard. I'm not holding her officially right now, but I thought you'd want to know I plan to question her again."

"David? Stabbed?" One more death shouldn't shock him. It did. The pounding in his head built up steam until Noah suspected his brain must be all veins, no gray matter.

"David Howard, that's right."

Grief for his friend and for David's small daughter overtook him, until instinct intervened and he stopped himself from feeling anything. He focused on the small-town policeman's crazy accusation. "You think my wife murdered her best friend? With a knife?"

He forgot the "ex" part of his relationship with Tessa. "She couldn't lift a finger, much less a knife, to hurt anyone, and especially not David. They've known each other since kindergarten. David and their law firm—'' He broke off. David and Tessa's firm had dragged her out of the ashes of the divorce.

"I'm not sure what I think. Mr. Howard's wife hasn't been dead a year yet. We know he and Mrs. Gabriel were close, and we heard your marriage broke up about five months before Mrs. Howard passed away.'' The chief's wary breath wheezed in Noah's ear. "Their receptionist tells me they argued lately. Frequent arguments. I have to wonder if they were lovers' quarrels.''

"You're nuts.'' This guy was implying Tessa had killed David because of what—unrequited love for her best friend? "Tell my wife to shut up until her lawyer comes.'' Standing, Noah yanked his jacket back on, one-handed.

"You're not married anymore, remember?''

"I'm on my way, Chief, and I'd advise you to go by the book with my wife. That includes letting her out of your two-bit station house.''

"She's resting. We're doing her a favor.''

Noah swore into the phone before he slammed down the receiver.

SHE WASN'T AFRAID, but the moment the office door began to open, Tessa Gabriel swiped tears of grief off her face and eased around the desk. She brushed against musty dime-store drapes whose stink washed her in a wave of nausea. She covered her mouth briefly, determined not to show Weldon the least sign of weakness.

"Mrs. Gabriel.''

She searched his gaze for some sign he'd heard

from Noah. He stared back, challenging her with his suspicions but not with rage. Illogical relief swept her. Noah would have fired him up.

She'd called her former husband out of habit—the last remnants of once-upon-a-time days when she'd believed she could depend on him—before he'd proved he wanted nothing more to do with her. When she'd come to her senses, she'd called back and told him not to come, but who knew which message he'd pay attention to?

Forget Noah. She'd deal with the cops on her own, and she'd call Child Protective Services and get Maggie out of whatever home they'd put her in. Planning for Maggie made her think of David, and she almost cried again.

She forced a little steel into her spine. She knew how to honor his memory—by taking care of Maggie, making sure his and Joanna's love for her figured more strongly in her life than their deaths.

"The sooner you talk to me, Mrs. Gabriel, the sooner we'll finish."

She hadn't realized she'd gone silent. Her throat hurt as she held back grief. "I've told you everything I saw. What more do you want? I didn't kill David." And she couldn't believe he thought her capable of plunging that huge knife into David's body again and again and again.

But she took a leaf out of her ex-husband's book. Don't let them see you care. They can't touch you if they don't know how bad it hurts. Her sorrow might even make her look guiltier to this half-blind police chief.

"I think David must have disturbed a burglar." She

tensed as she pictured his body among the bloodied papers on the darkened rug. "You saw the office. It's a mess. Obviously, someone was searching for money, or something."

Weldon just looked at her. And looked at her, until his pale blue eyes and tired, hound-sad face were all she could see.

She knew this game. If he didn't talk, she'd have to. She role-played, too, to get the effect she wanted in court. This game didn't interest her.

She used every muscle in her body to shake the chair in front of her. "Where's Maggie Howard? You tell me where that little girl is right now."

Officious jerk—he looked pleased with her outburst.

What did she care? She'd lost her best friend. She could only help David now by keeping her promise to take care of his child if something happened to him and Joanna. "Even you must see Maggie will be terrified in a stranger's home."

"A foster home," he said, as if Maggie, at nine months, would know the difference between foster caregivers and strangers. "And, Mrs. Gabriel, I want to talk to you about that baby girl."

His tone hinted at more trouble. He terrified her, and she leaned toward him. "She's not hurt, too?" If someone could do...that...to David, what might have happened to Maggie?

He narrowed his eyes, looking for guilt, as Noah would have done. "She's fine, but tell me, do you believe in coincidence?"

"What coincidence?"

Weldon smoothed a perfectly shaped eyebrow. "Your daughter died, didn't she?"

His soft question tossed her into the past. Tessa tried to breathe and not see the persistent image of Keely's face as she'd lain in her crib that morning. Add that to her gore-filled last memories of David, and she could barely speak. "What does my daughter have to do with Maggie?"

"You lost her and then your husband divorced you. How desperate are you to replace your family? Maybe you think a new child will bring Detective Gabriel back to you."

Struck dumb, she stared at him. She couldn't think of the family she and Noah and Keely had been if she wanted to deal with the life she was trying to build. "Even if you think I'd hurt David, why do you suppose my ex-husband would come back to me for someone else's child?"

"You want the truth? I think the whole damn bunch of you are sick. I believe you were sleeping with David Howard, and his wife found out. To deal with his cheating, she relapsed into taking hard drugs and she was high when she wrecked her car. I think Mr. Howard knew he'd caused his wife's death, and guilt made him move heaven and hell to persuade the power in this town to help him hide her drug use. And then he cut you off. But what do you want more than anything? You want to start over with what you lost—a husband and a baby. You may even love Maggie Howard, but if you couldn't have her father, why not kill him and start over with your ex-husband and your lover's child?"

"You're the one who's sick." How had he discovered so much about Joanna? In a miasma of postpartum depression, she had only imagined an affair, but she *had* started using drugs again. And when Tessa discovered the truth after Joanna's death, David had begged her to keep quiet. He'd loved Joanna deeply, and he hadn't wanted Maggie to find out her mother had died under the influence. He'd bribed or pressured some powerful men to keep Joanna's secrets, and Tessa tried to lead the chief away from his suspicions.

"David was my friend—and only my friend. He should be alive and raising Maggie. The last thing Noah or I would want is to love another child."

Weldon narrowed his gaze, as sidetracked as she could have hoped for. "I don't understand you," he said. "Why did you agree to take custody of Maggie Howard?"

Because she'd never dreamed she'd have to.

She gathered her wits. Since she'd joined David in the law firm, she'd represented a few clients facing misdemeanor charges. And she'd lived with Noah long enough to understand how single-minded the police were on the trail of a criminal. Pushing away from the desk, she fired another defensive shot. "No one can replace my daughter. That's all you need to know."

She didn't bother to tell him she was leaving. He'd probably figure it out.

He said nothing as she opened the door and then carefully closed it behind herself. In the overly bright hall, she flexed her fingers against the wall. It was the light that made her falter, not the torment of a past she'd buried deep enough to keep it from touching her anymore.

The door opened at her back. Declining to turn, she forced herself to straighten up and stride toward the reception area. A deputy stood as she drew even with his desk.

"Mrs. Gabriel?"

Let Weldon explain where she was going. She had to find Maggie.

"Mrs. Gabriel, your husband is on his way from Boston." At the chief's quiet announcement, she stopped.

She didn't need Noah to rescue her from this police station or her grief for David. She should have chopped off her hand before she'd let herself dial his number.

"Please tell him I changed my mind. Send him back to Boston." She faced the man who'd virtually held her prisoner. "Good evening, Chief Weldon."

"Call me Richard. We'll be seeing a lot of each other."

His jaded amusement all but brought Noah into the room. Police cadets must spend hours in front of their mirrors practicing that look.

"Why don't you search for the real killer instead?"

She grabbed her dark green overcoat off the rack by the door and then hurried into the snow-spotted night. The wind snatched her breath out of her mouth as she pushed her arms into her sleeves and pinched her lapels together beneath her chin. She fumbled for the cell phone in her pocket.

Stopping beneath a feeble streetlamp, she dialed Information and asked for Child Protective Service's number. While the operator connected her, Tessa leaned into the light to read her watch. Barely after six in the evening, it was already nighttime according to the January sky.

Tessa's heart thudded as she made her way to her car. After four years of practicing family law in Boston, she'd turned all such cases over to David when they'd pooled their resources. She'd no longer wanted to deal with children or families. However, when the representative on duty answered her call, her old instincts took over.

"I'm looking for Maggie Howard," she said. "She was put in your care today, but I'm her legal guardian, and we both know she'll be better off seeing a familiar face."

"I don't think we need to disturb her—"

"I'll be at your office in—" Tessa gazed up at the snowflakes falling out of the black sky. "I'll be there in about twenty minutes."

She hung up without waiting for the woman to answer. She pushed her phone and both hands into her pockets with such force her coat went taut over her shoulders. She'd never stopped believing she should have been able to save Keely. The mere idea of loving another child made her feel guilty, as if she were forgetting her own daughter, and afraid that the worst could happen again.

NOAH'S POST-HANGOVER headache had turned into a full-fledged migraine by the time he turned onto Prodigal's typical New England town square. City buildings and small brick-and-glass shops closed around a wide lamplit, snow-covered lawn.

From spring through fall, the school bands would practice on that grass. Citizens would stroll to the gazebo where bird feeders of every size rocked together in the snowy night. If it was anything like the village where Noah had grown up outside of Boston, a farmers' market and the local craft merchants would set up their stalls on the lawn on nice days, hoping for business.

He parked in front of the police station, opened the door and lifted his face to the snow. The icy flakes on his face relieved some of the pressure that had only intensified with each mile he'd driven on his four-hour trek. A sound of wood hitting against wood drew his burning gaze to the bird feeders on the gazebo.

He dragged himself out of the car and concentrated on walking as if he wouldn't rather pass out. A deputy met him at the station's glass doors.

"Can I help you, sir?" Suspicion colored his offer.

"I'm looking for Tessa Gabriel." As soon as he said it, he wondered if she'd stopped using his name. But the deputy backed up, and his eyes went carefully blank.

"I just came on duty, but I can tell you she left about two hours ago. Are you her attorney?"

"Does she need a lawyer?"

The younger man's slow blink made him look more like a kid wearing a toy badge. "We let her go. That's all I'm able to say."

So they hadn't cleared her yet. Noah turned away, bent on getting back to the car before the anvil player in his head worked up to a new crescendo. "She went home?" he said over his shoulder.

"I guess."

He guessed? Yet she was still a suspect? Even the Prodigal police realized they didn't have evidence to charge her, or they'd be watching her.

Outside, Noah opened his car door and lowered himself to the seat. By the dim interior light, he worked out the way to Tessa's house on his map.

Ten minutes later, he pulled to the curb in front of a Cape Cod on a quiet street. Light, like two lasers beaming from the cheerful lamps attached to either side of her door made him sick. He tried to blame his weak stomach on the migraine, but deep down, he knew exactly what was wrong.

Tessa's was the one face that brought back their baby's death and the grief that he beat down twenty-four hours of every day.

Maybe he couldn't have saved their little girl, but he had let Tessa down. He'd had nothing left to give her, no comfort to feed her needs.

With a groan, Noah rested his head on his finger-tips. Motion in the night dragged his gaze to the left. A dark car flowed past and then edged to the curb in front of him. Almost immediately, Tessa rose from the driver's seat.

Noah exhaled, a sound drenched in agony that startled him in the silence of his car. Ashamed of his own weakness, he rubbed the misted windshield clear and leaned forward to see Tessa better.

Wind and snow lifted her straight blond hair from the collar of her dark coat. He couldn't see her face as she leaned into the back seat of her car. She moved as if she were wrestling with someone inside, and then she straightened, holding something in her arms.

Her stance scourged him with memories that refused to fade.

His blood froze, slowing the beat of his heart. He'd seen her cradle their child exactly the same way, but he'd never realized he should imprint that image on his brain. And now she was holding someone else's baby.

She had to be David and Joanna's daughter.

Clutching a shopping bag in her free hand, Tessa hurried up the steps and propped the bag against her leg as she opened the door.

He resented her for daring to care for another little girl. How could she hold another baby in arms that would never hold their daughter again? But then he remembered what David's child had lost, and his resentment shamed him.

He turned his car key in the ignition. He had to get out of here. He wasn't the man to help Tessa now.

He stomped the accelerator, but he hadn't put the car into gear. The engine roared, but he went nowhere.

CHAPTER TWO

AFTER SHE KICKED THE DOOR shut behind her, Tessa dropped the shopping bag at her feet and shrugged out of her coat. As she laid Maggie on a wide ottoman, the baby woke, scrunching her small face in displeasure.

Breathing in the scent of baby and snow, Tessa tugged the pink knit mittens off Maggie's tiny clenched fists and then unzipped her snowsuit. At once, Maggie gripped Tessa's index finger and clung unquestioningly.

Tessa's heart raced with panic, her gut reaction to such humbling trust from David's daughter. Sure she'd carried a sleeping infant from a foster home in the middle of the night, but she hadn't quite realized she was starting a lifetime of caring for Maggie. In the year since she'd left Noah, Tessa had built herself a safe, solitary existence, a life raft she'd ridden out of the wreck of her marriage. David's baby girl threatened her security.

She closed her eyes, tensing with shame. She'd been reluctant before, in the early months of her pregnancy with Keely. She'd always meant to have children, but she'd wanted them according to *her* time frame—when she was ready to be the best mother who ever undertook childrearing. She'd planned a perfect life for her family, a mom and dad wildly in love, a doting home, good schools, and at least one parent available to provide unfettered devotion.

She'd spent so many days alone while her own father had built his reputation as a plastic surgeon and her mother, the ultimate Junior Leaguer, had paved his social path and waited for Tessa to grow up and become interesting.

But she hadn't grown interesting. She hadn't even grown out of being too short and too round to make a less-than-embarrassing Junior Leaguer in training. And she hadn't mastered the fine arts of womanhood her mother modeled so flawlessly—studied helplessness, perfect decorum in the face of disaster and the all-important ability to set a perfect table with an ideal dinner for an impromptu party of six or more.

Her father, who could fix anyone, and her mother, who'd never needed to be fixed, still didn't understand that their absences and their disappointment had taught her to make sure it would be a glacial day in hell before she'd parent by their examples.

She'd intended to build her career first. She wanted no success as an attorney at anyone else's expense, but eventually, she'd planned to have time to work from home, or to take a break from her career, to make sure her children knew how dearly she and Noah had wanted them.

Pregnancy had smashed her plan, and her early reluctance now seemed like a red flag she'd waved at fate. Quickly abandoning her idiotic ideas about time frames hadn't saved her daughter. She hadn't even managed to save Keely with love deeper than she could bear to remember.

She squeezed Maggie's hand. This baby needed love, too, and Tessa had learned not to taunt fate. What if curses were real, not the product of her grief?

She gazed into Maggie's tear-damped blue eyes, smiling through a tremble that hurt her mouth. She lifted the baby in her soft terry sleeper. Need sliced through her. She shifted Maggie to her shoulder so she could hide her face as she gritted her teeth. Her arms ached for Keely's warmth.

She breathed deeply. In...out...in...out. Maggie needed her now.

When the baby shifted, ramming her fist into her mouth, Tessa recognized the gesture with a start. Despite trying with all the willpower she possessed to forget the past few years, she remembered how to care for a baby.

"Are you hungry?" Thank God, she'd stopped for bottles and formu.a and baby food.

But as she reached for the shopping bag, something moved outside, breaking the line of porch light that spilled across her pine floor. She straightened, staring through the small panes of the bay windows.

Nothing else moved.

Then she remembered she was holding a baby whose father had been viciously killed. What if someone had acted on a grudge against David? Tessa shot to the wall beside the door, slamming her hand over the switch to turn off the living-room lamps. Easing Maggie onto her other shoulder, she leaned across the door and yanked the cord that dropped blinds over the nearest section of the bay window.

Footsteps crunched the snow on her porch. Tessa gasped, and Maggie started to whimper. Smoothing her hand over the baby's head, Tessa forced her breathing into a regular pattern.

Good guardians tried not to terrify children in their care. She'd given Weldon her honest best guess about what had happened to David. Nothing else made sense.

All the same, unexpected company scared her tonight.

Fear drew images of David, sprawled on his office floor. Trying not to sob, she turned toward the kitchen—and the closest phone. With Maggie here, she couldn't take chances. She should have asked Weldon to send someone to watch the house until he caught the killer.

Tessa veered toward the keypad beside the kitchen door and tapped in the alarm code she barely remembered. She'd hardly ever used the thing. Nothing that had frightened her before went bump in the night.

Just then the doorbell chimed, and Maggie tugged her little fist out of her mouth. "Da?" she demanded. It had been her first word, and David had crowed proudly.

Tessa pressed a kiss to the baby's silky hair. "I'm sorry. It's not Daddy." She stroked Maggie's back as the little girl whispered another call for her father. Tessa pulled her even closer, trying to share her own body heat as comfort.

She reached for the wall phone and started to dial 911, but Maggie yanked the receiver from her hand. The baby's playful grab gave her a moment to think. Was she overreacting?

The person on her porch might be another friend of David's, coming to pay his respects, to check on

Maggie. Why tell Weldon she had a prowler if she didn't? He'd love an excuse to search her house.

She inched back along the living room wall to the door, angling her body to protect the baby. Supremely indifferent to Tessa's little dance of fear, Maggie attacked her own fist with another hungry cry.

"Hold on a minute," Tessa whispered. "I'll feed you." As soon as she made sure a maniacal killer hadn't come to call. She parted two of the slats to peer through the ice-encrusted glass.

The stubbled chin at eye level triggered alarms all over her body.

Noah. She recognized the faint dimple beneath his bottom lip before she raised her gaze to his shadowed dark brown eyes. He tipped his head in an unspoken *let me in,* and Tessa sprang back. The blinds clattered into place, keeping time with her erratic heartbeat.

She went hot and then cold, and then warmed again with frustration.

"Open the door, Tessa. You need help."

Her name sounded unfamiliar on the ragged edges of his raised voice. She should have called Larry Baxton one more time and begged him to burn her message.

She studied the living room's shadows. She'd felt safe here because she didn't have to avoid images of her broken family in these rooms. This house contained no memories of Noah or their own baby.

But now she had to think of Maggie. In a few hours, the baby had grown more important than Tessa's worst fears. She had to learn to love Maggie and make new memories. And she couldn't teach David's little girl to be afraid of love or of facing a painful past.

Something heavy slammed into the door at her back. Noah's fist, no doubt.

She must have lost her mind when she'd called him. She hadn't been able to depend on him after Keely—after... He'd disappeared inside his job, finding more comfort with the murderers he was so good at catching than with her.

The door shuddered under his fist again. "Open up or I'll shoot the damn lock."

She didn't like being pushed around. She bit her lip, curling her toes inside her shoes as she refused to walk away. Responsibility for Maggie pinioned her to the floor.

"Just let me in." His strained patience was anything but familiar. They'd long since stopped trying to bear with each other. "Give me a chance to help you. And David's baby."

Tessa opened her mouth to answer. At the same time, Maggie sensed anger in the air. She teared up, puckering her lips.

Damn.

Tessa turned to a second keypad by the door. She didn't want him in her house or anywhere near her life again, but Noah would help her keep Maggie safe. He'd turned away before, but he wouldn't have driven all the way from Boston to turn his back on her now. She tapped out the code that disarmed the security system.

The moment she opened up, Noah pushed inside. She'd forgotten his scent. All male, it tugged at her, slipping between memories too intimate to face, too insistent to ignore. She hated the need that absorbed her in his drawn cheeks and the lines she'd never seen before, at the corners of his eyes. Emotion she couldn't understand and certainly didn't trust thinned his mouth.

"Tessa." This time he whispered her name, as if their shared past drew his breath from depths she hadn't known she'd reached inside him. His gaze washed her with the same insatiable need she felt. A yearning that had nothing to do with sex.

They were two people who'd lost everything that mattered most. Seeing him brought it all back. The joy as well as the pain. Joy scared her more. She didn't want to remember that much happiness now that she'd lost it.

"I don't want you here." What she meant was she never wanted to need him again.

His grimace acknowledged what she couldn't say. With shaking hands, he dragged his hair away from his face. Black strands stuck to his scalp, and moisture clung in drops to his fingers. He shut the door and turned the dead bolt. "Who did this to David? Are you all right?" His eyes looked like holes in his face. "Is someone trying to hurt you?"

"I'm fine." She wasn't. She wanted to cry—for David, for Maggie, for herself, and maybe a little for this empty-eyed shadow of Noah.

Somehow she'd managed to forget the ghost who'd walked out long before she'd left him. She'd been angry with the Noah she'd loved, the husband with whom she'd planned at least one brother or sister for Keely and a future as long as forever.

Another reason to forget about counting on life being fair or normal. She'd better just tell Noah what had happened and hope he'd be able to help before he vanished again.

"David must have interrupted a burglary. Whoever—" She stopped. David's death grew more real each time she had to talk about finding him. She wiped her mouth. She had to function for Maggie. "Whoever hurt David also tore the office apart."

"You—" He sounded scared, except Noah didn't get scared. "You found him?"

His question confused her. "Didn't Weldon tell you? Why are you here?"

Noah shook his head, as if he realized he didn't sound coherent. "Weldon told me, but I hate thinking of you seeing him like that."

She backed up a little, distancing herself from his concern. If David was still alive, she'd be planning to tell him about this crazy conversation. David had been the one she could rely on. She clenched her teeth to keep from crying out loud.

David would never come back again, and Noah hadn't come to comfort her. Better count her blessings he was such a good cop. Closing her eyes on her tears, she turned away, but Noah caught the arm that wasn't clutching Maggie.

"You're not all right."

She stared at his hand until he let her go. "I was better until I had to ask you for help."

"I know you called back and changed your mind, but I couldn't pretend I didn't know." One step brought Noah closer. "And I know why you don't want me around. You don't think about...her, until you see me."

She resented him for never saying Keely's name. "Do *you* forget her?"

Maggie cried out at Tessa's hostility, but Noah didn't have to answer. Grief hollowed his eyes and his gray face made him look like the walking dead.

Tessa scaled down her anger. She wasn't being fair. "I shouldn't have called you the first time."

She shifted the baby against her breast, and Noah stared, mesmerized by Maggie. When he looked slowly back at Tessa, he staggered. At first, she thought he was upset, maybe even drunk, if the rumors she'd heard from their Boston friends were true. But he reached behind himself, grasping for anything solid.

"You're sick." He'd had so many migraines after Keely died Tessa had begged him to see a doctor. He hadn't.

With a grimace, he ignored her. "How can you take on that child?"

He'd gone to the heart of her doubts. She wasn't certain she'd make a good substitute parent for Maggie. "What choice do I have?"

"Are you being fair to her? You can't just give her up if it doesn't work out. You won't."

He shut his mouth in lines of pain. After Keely, they'd forgotten how to love each other, but he did still know her, and she knew him well enough to recognize his anguish.

He backed unsteadily into the wall, and she forgot to be wary of him.

"I'll make it work, Noah. She needs me." She slid

her free arm around his waist. His muscles tensed against her, from her shoulder to her thigh.

Feel nothing, she warned herself. He's temporary here.

"Migraine," he muttered.

"I guessed. Come sit down."

Noah shrugged off her helping hand. "Carry the baby. I'll manage."

Shadows intensified the paleness of his cheek where his beard grew more sparsely. Tessa swallowed, trying to wet her dry mouth. She'd forgotten that small patch of skin she'd kissed so many times she could feel its texture now against her lips.

"How did you get out of the police station without an attorney, Tessa?"

"I don't need an attorney."

"Weldon hinted you did, and you should pay attention when a cop talks like that." He enunciated each word too carefully. "Don't tell me you're representing yourself."

With sudden impatience, Maggie brought the fleshy part of Tessa's thumb to her mouth. Sharp baby teeth grazed Tessa's skin, making her draw a deep breath. Leaning down, she grabbed the shopping bag and then headed for the kitchen. "Let me feed her and I'll drive you to a hotel, Noah. We can talk tomorrow."

She switched on the kitchen light, but Noah, who'd driven at least four hours in excruciating pain, gazed at her through slitted eyes, trying to filter out the brightness. "What hotel?"

Maggie's protest at the lack of anything filling in Tessa's hand left little time to argue. "You can't stay here."

"Why? We don't love each other anymore. I can't hurt you."

"You know why." She wasn't about to admit how long she'd worked at sleeping in a house where she couldn't even hope he'd be coming home. "We got divorced. We didn't part on good terms. I called you because with David...gone...I didn't know who else to turn to." She pushed the shopping bag onto the kitchen counter.

"I'm sorry about David."

"Me, too." She couldn't keep moisture from gathering at the corners of her eyes, but she used her forearm to wipe it away. Better get Noah out of here before the shock of David's death finally wore off.

She kept remembering how painful "never" was when you realized you wouldn't see someone you loved again. Saying goodbye to David would feel something like letting Keely go. She couldn't do that with Noah watching her.

He'd been unable to share her pain for the daughter they'd both loved deeply. She wouldn't expose herself to his reserve again.

Fortunately, he had his own concerns, and he seemed oblivious to hers. "You don't seem to understand how angry someone must have been to stab David like that," he said. "It could have been a client. It could have been a friend. It had to be someone who knew him." Noah's investigative instincts were so strong he'd trained half the detectives on Boston's homicide force. "I don't care how you and I split up, I'm not leaving you alone tonight when someone killed David in your office this morning."

"What use would you be?" She softened her

voice. She wasn't out to get him, just to remind him he wasn't at top strength. But she was used to helping him when he had a migraine. Keeping a tight grip on the baby, she eased Noah toward a chair. "You can barely stand up straight."

"I could throw you my gun."

His wry tone threw her off balance. Maggie began emitting an "aiyiyi" sound that apparently meant she was ravenous. Tessa peered from the baby to the man. Maybe now wasn't the time to prove she didn't need him. She just might.

"For tonight," she said. "Until we're sure no one has a grudge against David that includes Maggie."

Unexpected wistfulness colored his exhausted gaze. "She is kind of cute."

"You could have met her at the christening."

"No." In response to the invitation David and Joanna had sent him, he'd simply scrawled "I hope you understand" on the RSVP card. "I couldn't," he said now.

Tessa wanted to think badly of his weakness, but she remembered how she'd sweated outside the church, furiously trying to force herself through those doors. Only her friendship for David and her growing concern for Joanna, whose second addiction had begun to show itself, had pulled her inside.

The last of Maggie's temper went up in a shrill cry that whitened Noah's already pale skin. Tessa reached into the bag and pulled out a baby monitor. Noah stared at it, and she stared at him.

They'd left Keely's monitor on that last night, but it hadn't helped. If she had to strap this one to her hip and turn up the sound until she heard ice forming on the windowpanes, this baby would survive.

"I'll wait in there," Noah said, and departed the field for the safer confines of the living room.

Tessa nodded, taking out the formula mix to refresh herself on the recipe. Maggie drank most of a bottle before her eyes drifted shut, but Tessa waited to make sure she was sound asleep. She backed through the kitchen door, clutching the baby and the monitor.

She tried not to wonder where Noah would turn up. Had he scouted out a bedroom? Hardly seemed likely.

She had to cross the living room to reach the stairs. Noah sat hunched forward on the sofa, resting his head between splayed fingers.

"Did you take anything?" she asked in a low tone.

He looked up. "The medication knocks me out. I was waiting for you to finish in there."

"We don't have to talk tonight."

"You found a murder victim today, and Weldon wants me to believe he suspects you. Think of Maggie if you can't see you're in trouble."

"I'm not afraid. I didn't hurt David."

"You'd better be afraid. You know how many people have been ruined because the police falsely suspected them, and you know someone hated David enough to kill him. Put the baby to bed and come back down here."

When he reminded her Maggie was her priority, she had no choice. She had to give in.

She carried the baby up the stairs at the far end of the room and turned onto the gallery that led to the three bedrooms. She managed not to look down at Noah as she took Maggie into hers.

Mentally preparing herself to make their talk quick, she recounted each second of her morning. Noah had despaired more than once about witnesses who'd kept "inconsequential" case-breaking information to themselves.

She glanced at Maggie, who suckled in her sleep. "We'll find the guy who did this to your daddy. I won't let you forget him and your mom. I promise you." Her voice broke under the strain of holding on to her grief, but she kept her mind on getting Maggie to bed and seeing Noah once more tonight.

She searched her room for a safe bed for a nine-month-old. The armchair wouldn't do, and neither would her bed. She wasn't used to sleeping with a baby, and she didn't want to risk rolling over on Maggie. Maybe a dresser drawer?

Tessa positioned pillows on the bed and eased the baby into the center. Then she opened her dresser's bottom drawer and emptied it. She fished a quilt out of her closet and lined the drawer before adding a blanket. Then she checked Maggie's blessedly dry diaper.

The baby whimpered when Tessa laid her in her makeshift bed, but after one strong stretch, Maggie burrowed into the little nest.

She might manage to crawl over the side, but she'd only slither onto the floor. Just in case, Tessa surrounded the drawer with a comforter from the hall linen closet and then set up the monitor by the baby's head. Tomorrow she'd find a crib, but for tonight, Maggie would be safe.

Tessa took a scarf from another drawer and settled it over the lamp shade to dim the light. Cupping the monitor's receiver in her hand, she tiptoed from the room. She paused to pull the door, but when she leaned over the gallery rail, Noah seemed to have fallen asleep.

With one arm angled over his eyes, his other hand flattened on his belly and one knee bent so his foot rested on the floor, he looked peaceful.

Sleep was the only sure cure for his migraine. Why wake him when they couldn't solve anything tonight? She reached for her door again, but stopped, swearing under her breath as she stole another look at him. He might get cold if he slept there till morning.

She snatched another comforter and a pillow from the linen closet and negotiated the quiet stair treads. She set the pillow and the monitor on the floor beside her former husband and then made herself spread the comforter over his long body.

He shifted one lean leg, and the past exploded in her head like Fourth of July fireworks. Noah's legs, naked and strong, wrapped around hers, his back curved protectively as he covered her.

Tessa bit her lip, trying not to whimper the way Maggie had. She'd better forget those days. And the nights. The lovely, loving nights. They were all over. Lost. Unshared grief had destroyed her marriage.

"I'm not asleep."

She jumped back, tripping over the coffee table, but Noah caught her hands.

"Don't break your neck. Sit down beside me."

He still looked pale enough to pass out at any moment. Those treacherous memories tempted her to curl her body into his and pull his head onto her shoulder, but she perched on the opposite arm of the sofa. He didn't suggest she come back.

"Tell me what you saw." He pushed the comforter off. "From the moment you stepped inside your office."

Horrible images flooded back. She tried to distance herself. She'd had enough practice, getting through the days after Keely's death. "The main door was locked. I had to open it with my keys. I didn't notice anything at first. I worked for half an hour in my own office." She shuddered. If only she'd gone to David's office. Had he still been alive? "Whoever—the killer must have already gone. I left my door open and anyone who tried to leave would have had to walk past."

"You have a receptionist?"

"She comes at nine o'clock, but I got there around eight because I had to finish some research for a meeting today." She'd never called to cancel that appointment.

"You changed your routine so you could go in early. That's why Weldon thinks you arranged to meet David. He thinks you might have killed him and then pretended to find him."

She began to breathe fast. She hadn't taken Weldon seriously.

"Are you all right?" Noah leaned forward and cupped her nape. While she stared at him, startled that he'd touch her, he made her bend down. "Put your head between your knees before you faint."

She put her head down because goose bumps radiated from the place where he'd pressed his fingers against her skin. "You think Weldon really suspects me?"

Noah didn't speak, so she looked up as he considered his answer. He'd become a cop because he'd seen his father die making an almost routine traffic stop. His intuition had been born that day, and Tessa trusted it.

"I don't know." Weariness strained his tone, and he looked more haggard by the second. "He even mentioned Joanna's accident. He said she was using drugs because of you."

"What?" Her promises to David meant more than her own reputation. She'd vowed she wouldn't let anyone else find out about Joanna. "Weldon got his training at the movies. Joanna had an accident."

"Weldon thinks you wanted David for yourself."

She sprang to her feet, flustered. No matter where they stood now, she didn't want Noah thinking there'd been something between her and David. It was hard enough to live with the fact Joanna had thought so. "He was my friend."

Noah drew his mouth into a brief, tense line. "I have to ask you—as much as I don't want to—did your feelings for David change after you left me and Joanna died?"

The man had to be blind. She hadn't left him until he'd made sure they were living separate lives in the same house. And David had welcomed her here. They'd always been close, but their losses had created a shorthand that had strengthened their friendship until Joanna became ill. "We were friends, the same as always."

She couldn't explain the truth about Joanna without betraying David. She looked down at her hands. A tear splashed just above her thumb, horrifying her. The last thing she needed was to cry in front of Noah.

She tried to clear her throat. "If anything, we weren't as close after Joanna died. David was distracted with Maggie." And they'd both felt guilty that their innocent friendship might have hurt Joanna.

"Weldon said you'd argued."

"Who told him that?" She couldn't explain to Noah. He'd want to get all the way to the bottom, and she couldn't tell him the truth about Joanna. "I thought David was preoccupied, raising Maggie alone."

"But now?"

"Now? Nothing," she said. "He was preoccupied with Maggie. We had a couple of troublesome clients, one who sort of harassed me."

"What?" Noah was instantly razor sharp.

"David and I handled it." She felt and sounded defensive, but she couldn't help it.

"The guy what—called you?"

She nodded. "Last time was about two weeks ago."

"Did he ever come here? To your house?"

She blinked in surprise. It was odd to hear him talk about *her* house. Once, she'd assumed she'd always share a home with him. "Once or twice. I never encouraged him."

"You should have told me about him the second I arrived. Did you tell Weldon?"

His brusque question sealed their new, impersonal relationship. In Noah's eyes, she'd become a witness.

"I only told him what I saw this morning." Her

quavering voice gave her grief away, but again Noah didn't notice.

"Someone wanted David to suffer. The rage that kind of murder takes—who knows if it's dissipated? When you found him you must have been—"

"I *was* terrified," she admitted.

"This guy you're talking about—do you think he'd be capable of stabbing David?"

"I don't know." She truly didn't. "He also thought David and I were more than friends." She denied it again with a shake of her head. "Eric gives me the creeps, but I can't imagine anyone doing what I saw."

"Eric?" He reached inside his pocket for a note-pad, but Tessa held out her hand, mindful of his pain.

"Don't. I'll write it down for you in the morning."

He nodded a terse thanks. "Your other clients— the ones who were unhappy—did you solve their problems?"

"Yes, or we're in the process. Hugh Carlson was rebuilding his factory after a fire, and we argued with him about following code. We're also defending a lobsterman's daughter against a breach of promise by her former fiancé." She thought about his assumption that the killer's rage might spill over to someone else in their office or onto David's child. "Do you really think someone might try to hurt Maggie?"

"Or you." He rubbed his temples. "When I thought about it, I was almost glad Weldon wanted to keep you. I stopped at the station."

"I walked out," she said. "I haven't done a lot of criminal law, but I knew he couldn't keep me." She lowered her head again. "Wouldn't I know if some-one were that angry with me?"

"Did David?"

"He never said anything." Because of the distance that had crept between them? "I keep thinking he'll call, that I'm baby-sitting for him tonight."

Noah dropped his police persona. "You baby-sat?"

"Occasionally. More over the past few months. As I saw less of David, I saw more of Maggie." She shook her head. "You've got me suspicious of every conversation we had."

"Could he have been afraid something was going to happen? Maybe he wanted you to be comfortable with the baby, and today was what he expected."

"He would have told me that, Noah."

"I'm wondering why he didn't." He glanced up at her room. "You seem comfortable with her."

She'd felt way out of her depth. "She was David's daughter before now. I could *like* her, but I didn't have to give her much of myself. You know?"

"More than anyone." His gentle tone offered the kind of comfort she'd once needed, but then he detached his feelings and became a suspicious cop again. "Where are Joanna's parents?"

"I haven't heard from them yet, but Weldon called them." She glanced toward the phone. "They might have tried to reach me." Taking a deep breath, she plunged on. "I wonder if they're going to change their minds about leaving Maggie with me."

"Why did they agree in the first place?"

"They're both in their late sixties. I'm young enough to be a mother figure to Maggie, and that was what David and Joanna wanted for her. We drew up the papers just after Maggie was born, and Joanna asked them to sign a consent, but I don't know how I'd fare in court.''

"They're probably concerned if they've heard David was murdered at the office.''

Her breath caught, but she made herself think of good times with David—when they'd dangled off her roof, cleaning the gutters, the way he'd hounded her about not using the alarm system. He'd been her best friend. "Maybe I should call the Worths.''

"Yeah. David wasn't so much killed as slaughtered.'' At his blunt statement, she pulled back from him, and he grimaced. "They've lost him, too, Tessa.''

"You're right. I didn't think of that.'' She stood, already looking away. "I'll call from my bathroom. I can take the phone in there without waking the baby, and I know you need to sleep. Can I get you some water?''

"I'll get it.'' He rose, too, apparently as anxious to have her out of his way as she was to leave him on his own.

"I have a guest room upstairs.''

"I'll take a look at it later.''

At his rueful tone, she picked up the monitor and left him. This was the way they should be together. Except for those first few moments, when they'd absorbed each other like two lost souls who'd wandered in from a desert, they'd treated each other as acquaintances.

She put their first reaction down to unfinished business, but she was happier being Noah's acquaintance. He'd guide her through any pitfalls the Prodigal Police Department could throw in her path. He'd keep her from making a mistake that would hold their attention on her.

Upstairs Tessa carried the phone into the bathroom and eased the door shut. She called Information for Eleanor and Joe Worth's phone number. Eleanor answered on the first ring.

"I'm so glad you called," she said as soon as Tessa greeted her. "Where's Maggie? That idiot police chief said he'd had Child Services pick her up from day care, but they wouldn't tell us—"

"I have her." Tessa waited for Eleanor's reaction.

"Thank God." Her gratitude sounded heartfelt. "Why don't you bring her to us? She needs familiar faces around her, and we'd love to have you both."

"Thank you," Tessa said, a touch uneasy. Maggie knew her face. "But I have to arrange for the funeral and take care of the office." And Weldon might not let her travel forty-five minutes beyond his jurisdiction until after he had cleared her.

"Oh." Eleanor's voice faltered into silence.

Her disappointment pricked Tessa's conscience. "You could come here." The second she offered she wished she'd kept her mouth shut. Now was not the time to confuse Maggie about who would be taking care of her. Eleanor and Joe might not be able to keep themselves from interfering if they had any second thoughts about the guardianship.

"We should come. Maggie's too young to go to her father's funeral. We'll look after her."

Eleanor's excitement felt inappropriate at a time when Tessa couldn't get David's broken body out of her head, but the other woman and her husband were all the family Maggie had left. Tessa didn't want to alienate them. Maggie would need her grandparents, and naturally, they wanted to see her.

A squeak in the floor made her glance toward her bedroom door. Noah must have decided to use her extra room.

Used to old habits, she stood, on the verge of asking what he thought about having the Worths stay, but she came to her senses.

"Let me tell you how to get here from David's house. It's on your way." Again she held back sorrow to take care of business.

"We have a few things to do first, but we'll drive over late tomorrow morning."

CHAPTER THREE

HOURS LATER, Tessa lay staring into the darkness. A bony limb scraped at her ice-etched window. Wind seemed to lift the eaves with each sudden gust. The house settled, making familiar snaps and clicks. The only thing she couldn't hear was the sound of Maggie breathing.

And at last, she couldn't stand not knowing. She turned on the lamp and knelt beside the baby in her makeshift bed. On her side, with one small hand across her face, Maggie looked ridiculously older than she was. Her terry sleeper lifted and sank with lovely regularity over her chest.

Tessa eased a relieved sigh between her lips. She slid to the floor and cushioned her own elbow beneath her head.

Before long, she began to shiver. The pine floor transferred the cold, despite being insulated by another layer of house downstairs. She crawled back and yanked down a pillow and her own comforter. Then she burrowed into a warm nest beside Maggie on the floor.

Tomorrow night, maybe she'd be able to sleep in her bed. If she found a crib and pulled it near enough.

She closed her eyes. Maggie's rhythmic breaths became her own. She felt each in-and-out exchange of oxygen that fed Maggie's blood and hers. Until finally, by some miracle, she stopped thinking at all and fell asleep.

NOAH OPENED ONE EYE to the morning sun. The anvil player in his head had slowed the tempo enough to make life bearable. He turned over, but the familiar scent of the sheets beneath his face startled him. He lifted his head.

Until this second, he hadn't noticed his own sheets no longer smelled like this, fresh and something floral that made him remember lying with Tessa. He pressed his face into the bed and breathed in.

In the scented darkness, he could almost pretend the past eighteen months hadn't happened. Any second now he'd hear his baby cooing the odd, off-key songs that had tugged at his heart as Tessa sang back to her.

Punching a hole in his fantasy, a sharp screech erupted from the next room. Noah pulled a pillow over his head, but it couldn't muffle Tessa's confused response.

He'd never known her to face the morning with pure joy. Maybe if he'd had twenty years with her, he would have gotten sick of her bad humor in the a.m. He'd only lived with her five years, just long enough to find her morning temper endearing. She'd hidden it from their baby, and even now, she spoke lovingly to Maggie.

He shoved the pillow away. Tessa had less reason than ever to welcome a new day. Memories of finding David's body would probably hit her harder this morning.

She'd never seen such violence. Tessa's family tended to be detached. She'd grown up on her own for the most part, in a nice safe, upper-middle-class environment. But her parents had protected her from anything resembling David's death.

A sudden spurt of anger surprised Noah, twisting out of the depths of his apathy. Loss of life pissed him off, but David's death mattered even more. After his and Tessa's divorce, he'd backed away from his friendship with David in case the other man felt he had to choose between them.

Since then, they'd shared exactly two beers on two separate occasions when David had come to Boston for business. They'd never talked about Tessa, and they'd never discussed David's personal life. Noah figured David had chosen which friend he wanted to keep.

But he'd be damned if he'd let anyone get away with killing David Howard, and he'd be damned again if he'd let anyone think Tessa could hurt their friend.

He got out of bed, and a whole anvil chorus tuned up for a more complex piece. Pressing his fists to his temples, he staggered to the chair where he'd left his clothes.

He dressed and then opened the door just in time to stumble into Tessa, carrying small brown-haired Maggie. His ex-wife's glance flickered over him. Despite the percussion in his head and his need to maintain a professional distance, interest rode his nerve endings along the path Tessa's gaze had taken.

He stepped back into his borrowed room, realizing

a retreat probably exposed his response to her innocent gaze. Fortunately, she had her eye on Maggie.

"I forgot how often they want to be fed." She
broke off, looking stricken.

He knew. She didn't want to forget their baby, even
the small, everyday functions of caring for her. He
lifted his hand to comfort her, but second thoughts
held him back.

He'd come to make sure no one charged her with
murder, not to resurrect a relationship they'd failed
at. Nevertheless, he cleared his throat and tried to
sound like the kind of man she'd once needed him to
be. "It's all right to talk about our daughter. Maybe
we'd both be happier now if we'd talked about her."

Over Maggie's head, Tessa's green eyes lit with—
reproach? Anger? He couldn't tell which.

"I feel guilty when I think of being happy, and you
can't even say her name."

Obviously she still blamed him. He took a stern
grip on his temper when he really wanted to hurt
Tessa back. Maybe he'd chosen a touchy word, but
something was sure as hell wrong with both of them
after eighteen months of grieving. How was he supposed to say their child's name when thinking of her
tore him apart? If he said her name out loud, that
morning would unfold all over again.

And now, since Tessa seemed to be saying his pain
wasn't as bad as hers, he eyed her, unable to put the
truth in words.

"What?" She stepped up, small and furious, spoil-
ing for a fight.

Being angry got them nowhere. He concentrated on
his own failure. She'd suffered, and he'd let her. He

hadn't meant to, but he hadn't known how to bridge the gulf between them. "It's too late to say this, but I wish I'd been a better husband to you."

All emotion drained from her face, and she walked away. "It is too late to talk about our marriage." The baby's head bobbed over her shoulder as they reached the stairs. Even Maggie seemed to accuse him.

He stared at Tessa's hair sprouting from an untidy ponytail, at the wrinkles in the short, tight T-shirt that hugged curves he'd loved and she'd loathed. The left leg of her sweats climbed halfway up her calf, and she should have looked a mess.

With her stiff neck and her disinterest, she just looked as if she didn't want him here.

"I have to drive back to Boston and pick up some clothes. I came without packing." His only thought had been to straighten Weldon out about Tessa. He forced himself to march down the gallery behind her. He matched her indifference. "First I'll check around here, see what I can get out of Weldon. Maybe one of the traffic cops noticed someone hanging around David's house. Will you need help with the arrangements?" For David's funeral. He didn't have to specify. Tessa would know what he meant, and she was the only one left to set it up. David's parents had passed away years ago.

Still, she didn't look back. "I'll take care of everything. He wanted a memorial service."

At the bottom of the stairs, he caught up, taking her elbow to make sure he had her attention. "While I'm gone, I want you to be careful, Tessa."

She shrugged lightly to release herself. "I won't take chances."

She was thinking of David's daughter, not of her own safety. "I'm not just talking about the baby. You might be in danger, too."

"I get it." She made an obvious effort to keep her tone civil. "I won't go out after dark, and I'll set the alarm. The second I see anything suspicious, I'll dial 911."

"Keep your cell phone in your purse or your pocket, wherever you can get to it in a hurry. We should ask Weldon for protection until we're sure whether David interrupted a robbery."

The baby muttered, a slight edge to her voice that even Noah already recognized.

Tessa turned toward the kitchen. "I don't want the police tossing my house."

He almost laughed. "The police search. Criminals toss." He followed them, and when Tessa turned, he nodded at the baby before he went on. "Remember you have her before you turn down protection."

Again she relented. "If I had to let them in because of Maggie, I would, but couldn't Weldon leave someone outside?"

Truth was, neither he nor Tessa had charmed Weldon so far. "We'll be lucky if I can browbeat him into having someone drive by."

"Which does us no good unless the cop and the bad guy happen to show up at the same time. Let's drop it." As the hungry little girl arched her back and mouthed a furious complaint, Tessa soothed her with the same sounds that had calmed their own baby.

She took a bottle from the fridge while Noah watched and marveled. Every step she took was sure.

"Joanna's parents are coming over." Tessa put the

bottle in the microwave and set the timer. "They're staying here, so if you need to take care of business in Boston…"

"How far away are they?"

"Only about forty-five minutes, but they want to see Maggie, and she needs all the love she can get. I don't mind if they stay."

"I'm glad someone will be here with you." He'd remind Weldon that no matter how annoying he found Tessa, she remained his best witness. That should insure some extra police interest, and three adults ought to be able to work dead bolts and the telephone.

As for him, he needed clean clothes, and Baxton would force him to fill out paperwork for a leave of absence. They needed to talk about a case the two of them had been working in their free time, an abusive husband who seemed to be on the verge of hurting his wife and children.

However, that old saw about murderers showing up at their victims' funerals was sometimes true, and Noah intended to get back to Prodigal in time to attend David's service.

Tessa took baby cereal and a small jar of fruit from a shopping bag on the counter.

"Do you have everything you need for her?" He should offer to hold the baby, but he couldn't move the impulse from his mind to his mouth. He didn't want to hold her, to risk being reminded of the child who'd been, along with her mother, his greatest joy.

"I don't have anything," Tessa said, unaware of his cowardice. "Do you think Weldon will let me go to David's house to get her clothes and her crib?"

A crib? He hadn't even thought about one. "Where did she sleep last night?"

"In a drawer." The last word came out around the baby's fingers as Maggie tried to plunge her hand into Tessa's mouth. Laughing, Tessa ducked out of the grinning little girl's reach. Their smiles made the floor drop from beneath Noah's feet.

He grabbed the table's edge, wanting, needing, craving one more impossible second with *their* baby. One morning spent just this way, preparing her breakfast, enjoying the destruction she'd wreaked in their kitchen with her curiosity.

"How's your head, Noah?" Tessa planted the baby-food jar between her arm and her body and twisted off its lid. "You don't look as if you've recovered yet."

"I'm fine." Dizzy with unexpected sorrow, he looked anywhere except at her and pretended his most vital interest was the growth of beard on his chin. "Do you mind if I take a shower before I visit Weldon?"

She stared at him over the baby's head as if she heard something in his voice. She might not want to care for him anymore, but concern cut a frown across her forehead. He had to be more careful. He faced her until she turned back to her task.

"The guest bath is next door to your room." She spooned some of the fruit into a bowl. "Toward the stairs. You can take a disposable razor from the cabinet beneath my sink."

Right. He was dying to rummage through her personal belongings. Annoyed daily at the sight of his own bare bathroom counter, the last thing he wanted to see was the face cream and toothpaste and perfume he still expected to shift out of his way.

"Why don't you take out a razor after you finish with her and leave it by the guest bathroom door?"

"Don't be ridiculous." His pathetic need to maintain their separate lives made her laugh. "Just get a razor. Everything else you'll need is either in the bathroom or in the linen closet. That's the door between our rooms on the gallery."

Her apathy taunted him. His life should have grown easier after she'd left. He no longer owed her the emotional outlay loving required. Facing the back of her head, knowing she considered him a failure at emotional outlay, he wanted badly to prove he could still make her feel anything at all.

But what if he couldn't? He'd learned enough about his weakness from Tessa. Why risk any more self-knowledge?

He pushed away from the table and exited the kitchen, slowing only as he all but burst through her bedroom door. The clutter pushed him back a step.

Her room was a muddle of her clothes, Maggie's makeshift bed and stacks of books. To hell with perfume. He swallowed a groan as the books took him back eighteen months in less than a second. He knew Tessa's stacking method as well as she did. Just looking at the piles, he knew to the book which ones she'd already read.

A bone-deep ache drove him into the small bathroom where Tessa's sweet, sexy scent pervaded everything, the curtains, the shower, the cabinet whose door he yanked open.

Sweat poured off his face as he fished out a razor

and then dug a bar of soap from a cellophaned pack of six. Why the hell did a woman on her own buy soap by the six-pack?

He straightened, meaning to grab what he needed and beat it. Instead, he stopped to inventory the rest of Tessa's things. Nothing that belonged to a man. He wasn't terribly surprised, except at the relief that flooded him.

This was ridiculous. She'd left him. He hadn't asked her to go. He wasn't the kind of needy jerk capable of mooning around Tessa's room.

He slammed the cabinet door, pretty sure he'd lost his mind. Fortunately, the past eighteen months had taught him he didn't need certified mental health to catch a killer.

TESSA HAD BARELY SUNG, cajoled and bribed Maggie to take a nap in her brand-new crib when the telephone rang. She grabbed the receiver and then buried it in her sweater, trying to keep the ringer from waking Maggie as she grabbed the baby monitor and bolted from her room.

Please let it be Weldon. She'd dialed his office after breakfast to ask if she could pick up some of Maggie's belongings.

When he hadn't returned her call by the time Maggie ate her second meal and began to scrub at her eyes with weariness, Tessa had gone out to buy a new crib. By some miracle she'd managed to set it up in her room while Maggie slept on a pile of quilts on the living-room floor.

At the bottom of the stairs, Tessa pulled the phone

out of her sweater and whispered a hello, but instead of Weldon, her mother's voice breathed her name.

"Are you all right? My neighbor just called to tell me about David. Why didn't you call?"

"I'm fine, Mom." How did the neighbor know the number of the bed-and-breakfast they were staying at in England? Amanda and Chad Lawlor, her parents, hadn't left the number with her.

"Mrs. Hawkins said you found his body."

"I'm fine," she said again. Most of her conversations with her mother went this way. She tried to say whatever might be least likely to spawn a melodramatic reaction. Her mother drove forward.

"You have bad luck, Tessa. First you marry a guy who works with dead people. Now your best friend's husband dies and you find him."

Why argue that Noah tried to keep people alive, and David hadn't gotten killed on purpose? Despite the fact the entire family had known David since he and Tessa were in kindergarten, her mom still couldn't remember she'd met Joanna through David, not the other way around. Ladies didn't have male best friends, unless they were hoping to date them.

"I blame it on Noah," Amanda said.

"Mom, you like Noah, remember?"

"I'd like him better if he'd taken that lieutenant's position. It was a much more respectable job, and I'll bet you'd still be together if he'd stopped chasing unkempt, unfit criminals and devoted himself to you."

"Mom, he's here." And who would be a kempt, fit criminal? "He came to help me because the police think I know something about David's death."

"What?" At her mother's shocked bleat, Tessa scrambled to backtrack. A suspected murderess might find herself designated persona non grata in the Lawlor family.

"I don't know anything, of course, but I was his partner, and because of Maggie, I'll have indirect access to his assets."

"Why ever would you not? You agreed to take care of little Megan. Why is Noah there again?"

"Maggie, Mom. David's daughter is Maggie. And Noah came because he didn't like the way the police treated me. I don't want you calling here and saying something ugly to him."

"As you said, I like the man. He's gorgeous, after all. I just think he might have done better by you."

"What happened between Noah and me, we did to each other." Tessa changed the subject. "How's Dad?"

"At a seminar at some hospital. That reminds me, dear, I have to get his tux cleaned. We have tickets for *Madame Butterfly* on Friday. Do you think this David thing will get you and Noah back together?"

"Mother, my friend was killed."

"What happened anyway? Someone shot him? A robbery, honey?"

Her mother, a blasé citizen of Boston, obviously imagined a nice, clean death, a bullet that served its purpose with little or no trace. "No, Mom. He was stabbed."

"Do you need us to come back to the States for the funeral?"

"No." Noah was enough to face for now. "But thank you."

"We want to be there for you."

"Thanks, but too many people might confuse Maggie. Every time someone opens the door, she asks for David."

"She's another good reason for you and Noah to try again. You're too fragile to take care of her by yourself."

Fragile? She was anything but. "Thanks for the advice."

"Call me after the funeral. Your father will want to know you're fine, too."

"All right, Mom."

"I love you."

"Me, too, you."

She clicked the phone's off button and dropped her arm. As she turned, Noah seemed to rise out of the floor. She hadn't heard him come in, but he crossed the room in three steps.

"Was that Weldon?"

"My mom."

"Oh. Amanda." He lifted one shoulder, and for a moment they read each other's thoughts. He turned away.

"She means well." She'd always tried to pretend her family was "normal."

"You know exactly what she means. You know who they are, Tessa, and what they are. Why do you waste time protecting them?"

"They're not your problem any longer."

"Did you talk to your dad? Are they coming here?" He managed to make it sound like the last straw.

"They're in England. He's at a seminar."

"Good. Their comfort is the last thing you need." At her affronted glare, he shoved his hands into his pockets. "My mother always asks me if you're ever going to speak to her again."

She'd avoided Lucy Gabriel since the divorce. Not that she was mad at Lucy. She just hadn't wanted to poach on Noah's property. Lucy, whose independence was her greatest possession, next to her son, would be annoyed that Tessa could consider anyone property, but that happened during a divorce.

"She blames me," Noah said. "She thinks I told you to stay away from her."

Tessa planted the baby monitor on one hip and the phone on the other, forgetting she had them in her hands. "I never said so. I just didn't want to come between you. She was your mother first."

"But you still belong to her, too. She doesn't like to lose anyone she loves."

His unaccustomed frankness made her feel contrite. And that bugged her. "Why don't you handle her? Tell her not to worry about me."

"Handle my mom?" His eyes crinkled, making the irises seem darker than she remembered.

"I don't know how to be friends with her now." She wasn't about to admit Lucy reminded her too much of Noah.

His gaze intensified. Palpable unease and one of Maggie's breaths filled the silence. He tossed his coat at the couch. "Don't tell me to 'handle' her. You care more for her than that."

"I do." Hot shame raced across her skin. "But she tries to talk about you. I know I hurt you both, but I had to go. I couldn't stay in that house when we were both so alone.''

He spoke through tight lips. ''Why did we have to be alone? We lived together.''

''We didn't.'' Her solitary grief swept her with familiar emptiness. ''You wanted nothing from me, but I needed someone to make me want to live again.''

He tilted his head, eyeing her with an incredulous question. ''How can I make you want to live?''

''I don't know.'' She cleared her throat. ''And I don't need that now, but I couldn't get through to you. We left each other, and then I finally moved out.''

''Why didn't you tell me you were leaving?''

''I told you over and over, but you refused to hear.''

He nodded suddenly, and the light picked out silver strands in his black hair. ''I didn't want you to go. I think—I thought—you should have given me another chance.''

As if she owed him? They looked back at the end of their marriage just the way they'd lived it—miles apart in perception.

She glanced toward her future, asleep behind her bedroom door. ''Maggie's the last chance I have in me. You and I stopped owing each other anything the day our divorce became final. I just have to do right by her now.'' She twisted the kinks out of her shoulders. ''About your mom, what do you say to her?''

''That you'll call when you're able to talk to her again.''

Which made it sound as if there was something wrong with her. She started to get mad again.

He saw. ''Just call her.'' His tone, almost defeated,

reminded her he rarely recovered from a migraine in only twenty-four hours. "Mom keeps insisting she didn't need to deal with a divorce."

She'd spent a lot of time trying not to miss Lucy. Noah's mom had made her believe in unconditional mother's love. With bright copper hair, bloodred faux nails and a legion of suitors, Lucy had been the worst example Amanda could imagine for the daughter she'd considered a failure as a woman. Amanda had admired the quantity of Lucy's suitors, but she'd lectured long and hard that a woman should more subtly display her attributes.

To Tessa, Lucy had always been...Lucy. What you saw was what you got. She'd only turned her back on her borrowed mother because she'd loved her so much. She'd sworn she wouldn't come between Noah and his mom.

"I'll call," she said with dread. Lucy probably still considered the divorce a temporary measure because Noah had told her he didn't want it. His signing the papers hadn't convinced her he'd lied, and Lucy would never stop trying to piece her family back together.

"I don't mean just for today. Call Mom because you're a daughter to her, as much as I'm her son."

Tessa walked around him. "Don't take yourself too seriously in this ex-husband-to-the-rescue role. I need you because you understand the way Weldon thinks, but I've learned how to run my own life again."

"Maybe I'm more worried about my mother than about you." He said it so quickly she knew he meant it, that he hadn't planned the one answer that would make her wonder if she'd made a mistake.

Surely he knew her well enough to see she still loved his mom. "I'll call her," she said again. Continuing toward the kitchen, she tried to step back onto last night's impersonal footing. "Did you talk to Weldon? What are you doing back here anyway?"

"I wanted to check in before I left town." He followed her lead. "Weldon has nothing on you. He just doesn't have any other suspects. I talked to the patrol officers who work David's neighborhood." He paused as she took out bottles and the formula mix. "What are you doing?"

"Making formula for later. She'll be hungry again any second. How much longer do you suppose she'll drink this stuff?" She made a mental note to schedule an appointment with Maggie's pediatrician.

"I don't know. Can I help?"

She nearly slammed the formula onto the counter. A cozy suggestion, but unthinkable. "No, thanks." She tried to sound as if his help didn't matter in the least. "What did the patrolmen say?"

"No one's been hanging around David's house, or here, either."

"Good." She hadn't wanted to believe she and Maggie might be in trouble.

"Weldon wants you to search your office records again to make sure nothing's missing."

"I'll have to ask Emily, our receptionist, to help." She glanced at him. Bracing his hands on one of her kitchen chairs, he looked big and completely at home. As soon as they switched to business, he shucked off the discomfort that felt like her second skin. "Emily does a lot of the filing."

"I'd like to talk to her, too. She might know more about David's office than you."

He was right. "Does Weldon want to see me again?"

"He didn't say so, but he knows I'm on your side, and I'm afraid I all but called him a small-town idiot."

"That should help." He didn't answer and the silence stretched. She began to spoon formula into tonight's bottles. "Noah?"

"Yeah?"

His voice warned her he was coming around the table to look her in the eye. "Why are you so sure I'm innocent?" Following his earlier approach, she asked it quickly. A healthy divorced woman didn't care what her ex-husband thought of her.

"Are you kidding? I know you."

"Not now. You knew me before." As in before she'd lost him and Keely.

"Nothing we've been through turns a loving woman into a murderer."

She nearly dropped the bottle again. If he thought her loving, why had he said no to the divorce but then signed the papers?

"Why are you helping me?" She turned to watch his expression as he answered her.

He looked away. "I let you down. And maybe I should have been able to save our daughter."

Terrifying compassion swayed her toward him. "Don't say that."

"You don't believe it's true?"

"Not at all." She couldn't force her voice above a whisper. She'd felt the same guilt all this time.

"Then why did you leave?"

"Because you didn't love me anymore, and I had to learn not to love you." She brushed away her tears. "Why are you helping me now?"

"Because I owe you."

Rage flashed up and down her nerve endings. He owed her? She set Maggie's bottle on the counter and reached for him. He lifted one thick eyebrow, and his shoulder flexed beneath her palm. He felt real and warm and alive, and she wanted to shake him.

"You feel sorry for me, because you couldn't love me after Keely—after she—" She couldn't say it. Eighteen months later, and she still found it hard to say the words.

"I have to make up for the way I let you down so I can get on with my life." His raspy tone, the warmth of his breath on her face, reminded her she'd been his wife. She'd been much closer to him than this.

"So if you help me now, you'll make up for everything that happened before? I'm your penance?"

"If I'm doing what you need, why do you care about my motives? You only called me out of habit."

"I hope you're right." She struck back, unable to stop herself. "I don't want to need you again."

He tilted his head away, as if her anger ricocheted off his face. She hadn't known she could still hurt him. She hadn't realized how badly she still wanted to make him pay because she'd hated living without him and Keely.

Most of all, most painful of all, she didn't want to be a debt he owed.

The doorbell rang, and she spun away from Noah, accidentally elbowing the bottle off the counter. Powdered formula sprayed her floor, and she strode through it.

She pressed her hands to her chest, trying to slow her pounding heart. Behind her, sounds from the kitchen told her Noah was cleaning up. If she were as self-sufficient as she'd tried to be, she would have thrown him out of her house. He didn't belong here.

The bell rang again, and Tessa hurried to open the door. A tall woman, who seemed much older than when Tessa had last seen her, spilled over the threshold.

"Where's Maggie?" she demanded.

On her heels, her husband carried a single large suitcase. He hadn't changed as much as his wife. Tessa hadn't seen them since they'd last driven down to visit David and the baby.

"She's asleep." Tessa closed the door and turned to her guests. Her heart danced a vicious tango as Noah joined them from the kitchen.

"You remember my husband—" She passed her hand across her mouth and then tried again. "My ex-husband, I mean."

CHAPTER FOUR

ELEANOR AND JOE LINGERED in the doorway, both staring over Tessa's shoulder at Noah as if he shouldn't be there. The older woman's animosity startled Tessa, but then her mouth trembled, deepening the lines in her shocked face. Tessa felt for her. She'd been through too much, starting with Joanna's accident.

"Mr. and Mrs. Worth." Noah came so close his body heat surrounded Tessa. "Good to see you again." He curved his hands around her waist and eased her aside to make room for the other couple. "Come in, out of the cold."

Tessa glared over her shoulder, annoyed that Noah had touched her possessively to mark himself as the host in her home.

Eleanor managed a tight smile. "We didn't expect to see you, Mr. Gabriel." Faint welcome warmed her voice. "I mean, Detective Gabriel—I'm sorry—I just don't know how to treat policemen since my daughter's death last year. After Chief Weldon took office here, he came out to our house. He tried to make us believe she was under the influence of drugs that night she died."

Tessa started. Did the Worths know? David had told her about Joanna's depression soon after Maggie's birth, when he'd begun to back away from their friendship. She'd only discovered Joanna's drug use when she'd caught David flushing his wife's stash after the accident. He'd sworn Tessa to secrecy, to protect his family. He would never have told Eleanor.

Noah took the older woman's hand, unexpected compassion in his gaze. Surprised again, Tessa watched him comfort Joanna's mother.

"Police are naturally suspicious. You have to make allowances," he said. "I'm sorry about David. He was a good friend to my—to Tessa. She counted on him."

Tessa felt her eyes widen. An expert at reading character, he'd failed at tending frayed relationships. Had he changed or was he merely offering the Worths appropriate responses?

She rubbed her temples, trying to avoid old resentments before they bubbled to the surface. After Keely's death, Noah had maintained his phenomenal success rate at work. Murder had claimed the largest share of his attention, as if he couldn't be both a good cop and a good family man. He'd steered clear of the pain and regret that had swallowed her as their marriage withered, but his empathy for Eleanor now obviously touched the older woman.

Tears welled in her eyes, and pink color stained her thin face. "We'll miss David," Eleanor said. "I don't know what Maggie will think, after her mother and now this."

With heartbreaking tenderness, Joe Worth stroked his wife's back. "We'll make sure Maggie remembers her mother and father, and she'll still have us and Tessa."

Noah looked suddenly uncomfortable. Tessa knew what he was thinking. He was only a temporary part of the picture.

"Noah's on his way back to Boston." She'd grabbed for her hard-fought sense of detachment. Easier to do with Noah out of the way.

He obliged by moving toward the door, and Eleanor and Joe sank against the wall to give him room. But Joe grabbed his sleeve.

"You're satisfied the police here can handle the case?"

Noah opened his mouth, but he waited too long to be convincing. "Chief Weldon and his men are qualified."

His bland tone reminded Tessa of what he'd called the first rule. The initial twenty-four hours after a homicide were key. Almost thirty had passed.

As if his uncertainty went over her head, Eleanor changed the subject. "When do you think Maggie will wake up? I won't feel the world is a safe place again until I can hold her in my arms."

Tessa stiffened. Surely David deserved a moment's remembrance. But Eleanor had lost two members of her family. Naturally she needed to see Maggie. "She just went down for her nap—"

"I'm not leaving for good." Noah interrupted, making them all look at him.

He pinned Tessa, his gaze dark and intense. "I'll pick up my stuff at home and talk to Baxton about a leave of absence. Maybe you should give me a key so you don't have to wait up for me tonight."

Hand over a key to her home? "I'll wait up."

Pigs would fly before she'd invite him to come and go at will.

Clenching his jaw, he flicked a quick look at the Worths and then grabbed his jacket off the sofa. His broad shoulders stretched the leather as he wrapped himself in control. Skimming her face with a glance that came nowhere near her eyes, he held out his hand to Joe Worth.

"Nice to see you after so long. Mrs. Worth, again, my condolences."

Joe shook Noah's hand, nodding while his wife mumbled thanks. They wore the stunned smiles of the living who've lost a loved one. Noah opened the door, but Tessa caught it to ease it shut so they wouldn't wake Maggie.

"Wait." Noah grabbed the heavy door again, his greater strength shoving the cold wood against her palm. "I know you can't get into your office to access the files, but I want you to write down everything you remember about any client who's complained at any time in the past year."

"I can't, Noah. I'm their attorney."

"Don't start that. I'm not official, and we'll find a way to protect privilege if we have to, but I have to know what went wrong here. I'm especially interested in the guy who wanted you to be his own private attorney."

"I'll just bet you are." The words slipped out, echoing the last contentious days of their marriage.

Noah curved his mouth and the seductive fullness of his lower lip rattled her even more than his pleasure in provoking her. He spun on his heel and sauntered down the steps, in charge again, damn him. She hadn't learned his kind of control, and she was still mad as hell at him.

She watched him walk away until she realized divorcing him hadn't cured her addiction to the loose, sexy swing of his stride. Without another thought she slammed the door. And then cursed herself, waiting for Maggie's shrill cry.

Which came right on schedule.

"Let me get her," Joe said.

Tessa wavered, already used to having sole responsibility for the baby. But she had to assure Joe and Eleanor they were still important to Maggie. She might be afraid of loving enough to get hurt again, but she'd make herself trust a little for Maggie's sake.

"She's in my room." She pointed up at the gallery. "That door. I'll get a bottle in case she's hungry."

"I'll come with you, Joe." Eleanor followed her husband to the stairs. "But, Tessa?"

With her hand on the kitchen door, she looked back.

"Are you sure you don't want us to go to a hotel?" Eleanor asked.

"You're welcome here." Maggie knew them, loved them and needed them. "Noah's already taken the room closest to mine. You can have the one nearest the stairs, but I've been using it for storage. I'll clear it out for you later."

As simple as that, she began to transform her haven for one into a family dwelling. Her safe days of owing nothing to anyone were over, but she'd held Maggie without screaming in agony because she couldn't hold

Keely. Maybe she was turning a corner. Maybe she'd learn to treasure her memories instead of avoiding them.

Some of her memories anyway. The ones that featured Noah still spelled danger. He might be the one man who could find the real killer quickly, but afterward, he'd retire to his self-sufficient life. A hint of unease snaked down her spine, making her shiver.

She didn't want to need Noah again.

"BAXTON, I HAVE TO TAKE the time." Noah shifted in the cracked leather chair across from his angry commander. The other man glared at him from beneath bushy brows that looked more gray than Noah remembered. When had Baxton started to look his age?

More to the point, when was the last time he'd noticed anything except his own work? For eighteen months he'd made himself numb while he'd functioned on the job. He used that same detachment to focus now.

"You know Tessa's innocent. I can't let those village clowns nail her for something she'd never do."

"You're divorced. You haven't forgotten that in some drunken stupor?"

Noah passed on responding to Baxton's sneer. Taking a punch at his superior could end this negotiation badly, and if his boss had really thought he was coming to work drunk, he'd have been off the job months ago. "I haven't forgotten the divorce." He never forgot, but maybe if he did something right for Tessa, he'd learn to let her go.

"How well do you know her after all this time? When did you last see her?"

Noah wasn't about to admit he'd sat pathetically outside her parents' house on Thanksgiving, knowing the hour she'd walk up their steps to the door.

"We haven't seen each other since she left me—until last night."

Baxton rocked slowly back and forth in his chair as a clock ticked behind him. "How much time off do you want?"

"I'm not sure."

The commander seemed to think it over, as if he had a choice.

Noah reared out of his chair. "Look, Baxton, I'm not asking—I'm going to Maine to help my ex-wife. Fire me if you have to."

"Damn you, man, you know I can't fire you. I'd be explaining until my successor was planning his retirement party. Go, but you'd better make this fast. Let's go over your caseload."

"We'd better start with Della Eddings."

Della's was a case they'd worked on together outside of office hours. Abused by her husband, she'd arrived in the squad room in the early hours of a rainy morning, begging them to save her and her two children. Frank Eddings remained just outside the reach of the stalker laws, but Baxton and Noah, both sick of cleaning up after killings, had gone out of their way to protect her.

"My wife will thank me for spending double my usual time with Della," Baxton said.

"We're keeping her alive."

"I won't forget to check in with her."

Noah nodded. "I'll let Della know she should try you first if anything happens."

They covered the rest of Noah's cases, and he got up to leave. Baxton swung around in his chair as if a great idea had suddenly struck him. "If you manage to train one of those hicks well enough, send him back here instead of coming yourself. He'd have to be less trouble."

"Thanks." Noah gripped the doorknob, just a little ashamed of the pain in the ass he must have been in the past year and a half.

Baxton dropped his loose fist on the desk. "Don't forget to fill out your paperwork. I don't want to come up there after you to get it right."

"You're a warm guy, Baxton."

"Damn straight." Picking up a pencil, he prepared to move on to his next point of business. "You know you got no jurisdiction up there?"

"I don't need jurisdiction. I can dial 911 as well as anyone else." Noah pulled the door shut and met the accusatory stares of the detectives working their cases from the office. A single thought on so many minds was easy to read.

Eighteen months of grief he hadn't handled looked like reckless behavior to them. He'd long since removed himself from the team. And now they thought Baxton was giving him special treatment—time off to indulge in yet another phase of his dysfunctional family life.

TESSA SHARED a tense afternoon with Eleanor and Joe and Maggie. The moment Noah left, Eleanor opened all the blinds with a hearty welcome to the healthy sunshine for Maggie. Acutely aware that a killer might be on guard from the snowdrifts that dotted her yard, Tessa was hard-pressed not to shut the blinds as fast as Eleanor opened them.

She kept busy moving her stored things from the room the Worths were going to use to the attic. As she worked, she mentally sorted the firm's client list.

But picturing each case, she remembered discussing the files with David. She rubbed tears off her face, knowing she'd never again trade work with him or share a late-night dinner or even the goofy jokes they'd made about their exceptionally exciting after-work lives.

He'd been her best friend, her refuge from grief. She couldn't deal with her loneliness. For now, she had to make Maggie's grandparents comfortable and arrange for David's service.

He'd asked for cremation and a church service. After Tessa finished clearing the room for the Worths, she went to her own and called David's minister. She finished the preparations with haste that made her sad. As each step fell, like a domino, she sensed a horrible moment of finality, looming. How was the baby to do without her father?

Tessa washed her face and tied her hair back with a thick band. She shut her bedroom door at her back and tugged on the hem of her sweater, trying to make herself look untouched by loss. She could hear Eleanor and Joe's low voices threaded with Maggie's. Tessa hurried down the stairs. They came through the kitchen door as she reached to open it.

"We thought we'd give Maggie a bath," Eleanor said. "And then dinner?"

"Sounds good." Tessa touched Maggie's cheek,

and the little girl gurgled, tugging Tessa's hand toward her mouth.

"She's happy, isn't she?" Eleanor looked satisfied as she rescued Tessa from another baby bite. "You don't want a hand in your mouth, love bug. You'll be all right now."

Tessa gazed at her in confusion. "Now?"

Joe pulled the baby into his arms. "Now that we're all together. No one can get through all of us to hurt her."

Tessa nodded. They didn't seem to feel for David as she did, but like her, they must be putting off their pain.

Alone in the kitchen as night fell outside the windows, Tessa snapped to attention at each unfamiliar sound in her settling house. She hated being afraid. Worrying that someone might be outside, she wanted Maggie with her.

She tried to concentrate on David. To make this family real, she had to help discover who'd killed him. Scouring her memory for a hint of anyone who might have had a grudge against him, she realized how much less open he'd been with her in the past few months. Parts of his life looked hazy in retrospect. They'd both felt bad about hurting Joanna, even though they were innocent.

When she asked if he wanted to take Maggie to the zoo, he'd claim he'd made other plans, never saying what they were—and then he'd call from home to ask her a work-related question, or to tell her about some television program he was watching.

Tessa stirred Maggie's unappetizing cereal, seeing the past instead. What if she'd been wrong about David's motives for drawing back? What if he'd changed his mind about her having Maggie?

She'd heard of blood running cold, but she'd never felt it before. Shivering, she shoved the cereal box back into the long oak cupboard and picked up Maggie's bowl. David would have told her if he'd wanted to change their arrangement. Maggie had been his first concern, too.

Tessa was about to push through the kitchen door when Eleanor came back, cradling the baby. "I'll hold her while you feed her," the older woman said. "We should get you a high chair."

Tessa smoothed the damp, shiny strands of Maggie's hair. "She has one at home."

Eleanor's gaze clouded. "I keep forgetting. I guess it's easier than facing the truth."

"None of this should have happened," Tessa said.

"Starting with Joanna," Eleanor's said vehemenctly. She noticed Maggie's wary gaze, and pressed a kiss to the baby's cheek. "Better eat, sweet."

Maggie grunted softly and then turned toward her cereal. Tessa spooned a bite into Maggie's mouth and then scooped up the overspill. The baby's gummy grin softened her heart.

"With all that oatmeal sloshing in your mouth, you should look disgusting." She curved her finger beneath the baby's chin, and Maggie tried to bite her again. "She's accepted the changes so easily."

"Sensing she's loved probably matters most just now."

Tessa disagreed. "You don't think she misses David?"

Eleanor blushed. "I don't mean that. Obviously she does. She asks for him, but I'm looking to the future. We didn't know how Maggie would be with you."

Already she cared deeply enough to feel protective of the baby. "We want the same things for her, Eleanor." She offered juice from a sippy cup, but the liquid trickled down the side of Maggie's mouth.

"You don't think David started her on the cup too early?"

Tessa wasn't sure if she was defending Maggie or David when she answered. "She's getting more adept. About two weeks ago she spewed apple juice all over David's shirt, and he forgot to change before he took her to day care. One of our clients asked us if we'd had some apples go bad in the office."

"He was distracted lately," Eleanor said.

"You noticed, too?"

Eleanor nodded, but she offered no ideas. Tessa waited so long, Maggie yanked the cereal spoon to her mouth. Wondering what Eleanor might know but not want to share, Tessa finished feeding the baby. No need to push Maggie's grandparents. They'd loved David and lost him. They'd all have to get used to their new family ties.

The second Maggie lost interest in eating, Eleanor stood with her. "I'll take her upstairs to clean the cereal out of her face and hair, and then Joe and I can read her a couple of bedtime stories."

As Eleanor made for the door, Maggie howled in protest, reaching over her grandma's back for Tessa. Surprised, Tessa hurried after her.

"What's the matter?" she asked, and the baby girl

caught her face for a moist kiss, redolent of cereal and apples. It was messy, but oh, so sweet.

"Let's go find Grandpa," Eleanor said softly.

Tessa caught Maggie's hand and kissed the fingers the baby curled around hers. "I picked up some books for her while I was buying a crib. They're in a basket beside the dresser."

She let Maggie go, waving as Eleanor carried her away. Maggie must carry a little bit of magic in her fist.

Listening to footsteps overhead, Tessa started a load of infant laundry. She remembered the limited time a baby left for mundane things, like cleaning a kitchen or folding the baby clothes Eleanor had washed earlier. She was folding Maggie's things on the living-room couch when Eleanor and Joe slipped out of her room.

"She's asleep," Joe said.

Tessa looked for the monitor, but neither of them had it. She picked up a stack of towels and started up the stairs.

"She was tired." Eleanor patted her husband's arm. "So am I."

"Aren't you hungry?" Tessa asked. They'd shared a late lunch. Maggie had distracted the Worths, and Tessa had been so busy cleaning none of them had remembered to eat until about three o'clock.

"I don't think I could stay awake long enough to choke something down," Joe said. "What about you, honey?"

"Same here. Night, Tessa."

"I'm glad you came." Tessa stopped on the landing in front of them. "Maggie needs you."

They smiled at each other and then at her. "Don't you worry," Joe said. "We'll work this out together."

"In the morning," Eleanor added dryly, and the older couple went inside their room and closed the door.

An astounding amount of tension receded with them. They were good for Maggie, and she obviously made them happy, but Tessa couldn't resist sagging in relief against the linen closet door.

Then she looked downstairs at the open blinds and the lights that put the room on display. She stuffed the towels into the closet and eased into her room to retrieve the baby monitor. She checked on Maggie, gently pressing her fingertips against the baby's belly. Maggie smiled in her sleep, and Tessa smiled back. She couldn't help it. She brushed Maggie's hair off her forehead and backed out of her room, gently closing the door.

She hurried down the stairs and jerked the blinds shut, almost feeling eyes from outside looking in on her. She finished off at the window over the kitchen sink and then stood back, pressing her fists into the small of her back. As the kinks began to ease, she felt safe.

The rest of the laundry called, but she pushed it aside in favor of going through the client files on her computer before Noah returned. She hit the machine's power switch and sat at the living-room desk. While the computer powered up, she turned on the baby monitor and fished a notebook and pen from the drawer in front of her.

At the top of the first sheet of paper, she started

the notes Noah wanted. Almost without noticing, she began to relax. When she worked, she was in charge of her life.

Immersed, interrupted only by the snuffles Maggie made as she slept, Tessa wasn't prepared to hear a light tap on her door. She jumped. In a protective reflex, she glanced at her room upstairs.

David's little girl already seemed to be taking a firm grip on her heart. Tessa crossed the living room and reached for the doorknob, but then remembered she'd promised to be careful. She backed up to peer through the faint gap in the blinds over the bay window.

Noah's car sat behind the Worths' on her driveway. She opened the door and he blew in with a gust of icy wind and a shower of snowflakes that dotted both his black hair and her pine floor.

"It's snowing again?" She peered into the night, but Noah pulled her back.

"Don't stick your head out there." He shut the door, pushing her in front of him. "Who knows if someone's watching the house?"

His caution made her fear look less like an overreaction. His large hand, familiar and yet impersonal against her stomach, quickened her heartbeat.

Noah turned away from her to brush the snow out of his hair. She searched for something to say that wouldn't expose her susceptibility to his touch.

"I don't think anyone's out there. We had the blinds open all day." His sharp glance made her even more aware of the tremble in her voice. She tried again. "Are you hungry, or are you ready to work?"

He shucked off his jacket and a worn pair of leather

gloves she'd given him on their first anniversary, five years ago. "Do you have any aspirin?"

She'd forgotten the migraine that would hold him in its loosening grip for a day or two. "Will aspirin do the job?"

"For now. You know how it is—headlights in your eyes—and the way the snow shines against the wet black road." His husky tone held her still. His pained grimace reminded her how it had been to care for him. Before, she would have rubbed the tension from his neck. "I'll get the aspirin," she said.

He caught her elbow, his touch zinging up her arm and down into her fingers. "You don't have to look after me. Just point me at the medicine cabinet and a glass of water."

Without comment, she eased away and got him the water and aspirin. It was little enough to do when he'd put his life on hold to help her and Maggie.

She retook her seat at the desk. Try as she might, she couldn't resist watching as Noah knocked back the tablets like a man gulping his favorite brand of whiskey. As a stream of water trickled down his neck, she averted her gaze.

"I've started a file on the computer, but I also wrote some notes longhand."

"I'll read it, but first tell me what it says." Noah's voice was muffled. He must be wiping up the spilled water.

She opened her mouth, but no sound came out. She swallowed. "First up is Hugh Carlson of Carlson Knitting. He hired us when he was rebuilding his textile factory after a fire. We acted as advisors, rounded up 'the players,' as Hugh called them, the architects, engineers, an expert on environmental code. But then the town didn't want the factory rebuilt, so some of the powers that be raised zoning issues. Hugh complained about environmental safeguards—''

''And he wanted you and David to go around the rules.''

''I can't say that.'' She picked up the log she and David had kept during the project, records of phone calls with a brisk transcript of each conversation. Attaching those pages to the sheet of notes she ripped off her pad, she passed the thin stack to Noah. ''This is everything I know.''

''Look at me.''

She did, reluctantly. He liked to think he could read minds, and with her, he'd had occasional success.

''He wanted to fire you when you wouldn't let him bully you into breaking the law.''

She hesitated, but a terrifying memory of David's body on his office floor decided her. ''He's a funny guy. I think he means well, but he sees himself as some big-city operator. He can be vulgar and rude, but he respects his employees. He got so tired of us hounding him about code, he said he'd close Howard & Gabriel if he had to use his last breath to do it. But then he recommended us to a friend of his who runs a fish-processing plant in Portland.''

''Is Carlson the one who wanted to date you?''

She laughed. ''Hugh has a wife who's a lot more impressed with his power than I am.''

''Tell me about the one who considers himself in love.''

''I'm coming to him.'' Eric seemed harmless to

her, except for his unfortunate habit of popping up on her doorstep. "But I don't think he's a killer."

"Most murderers hope you won't think they're capable of killing." He said it gently, as if he were trying to remind her, not insult her intelligence.

She preferred his detective-size ego to his unexpected warmth. She couldn't look at him. He might be right about his ability to read minds. He read more in a person's eyes than most human beings could find on a printed page.

She turned back to her nice, safe list. "Next, a breach of promise. Ned Swyndle's daughter was supposed to marry Jon Fevre. Ned changed his daughter's mind when he walked in on Jon and his female first mate."

"Having sex?"

David had soft-pedaled that aspect of the suit. Noah was the blunt type. She nodded. "Jon and Ned are both lobstermen, but Ned has a fleet of boats, and Jon's just starting out. Ned withdrew both his daughter and his boats, and Jon filed for breach of promise."

"So much for a last fling." With a brief grin, he reached for the second stack of notes, and the tips of his fingers bumped hers.

She tried to smile back, but sharing even a sense of humor with Noah alarmed her. She'd missed him so much, living without him had been like learning to breathe again.

"You don't have to be angry with me all the time," he said. "We can still find the same things funny."

Tessa drew as far back as she could from him. She'd open herself to Maggie like a flower seeking the sun, but she'd be reckless to forget Noah's first line of defense. When he couldn't face their lives without Keely, he'd turned from her to his job.

"I'm grateful you came to help," she said. "But let's not get confused about what we're doing together."

He twisted his head, as if his neck still ached. "I've had two long drives today, and they gave me time to think of the mistakes I've made."

"What do you mean?"

"I wish I'd been a better friend to David. I tried to allow him to choose between us, but now I wonder why I thought he had to." Straightening, he stared at her, his gaze holding her so she couldn't look away. "Why did you and I make such a clean break? I don't know how many times I thought about you. I just wanted to know you were all right, but I never picked up the phone to ask."

"I don't want to be that civilized," she said. "We didn't fight our way out of a mess. We just faded into mutual, deafening silence." She should have said this before she left. "It's over, and we can't go back. After we find out who killed David, you're going home and I'm staying here."

Anger licked at the back of his gaze. "Don't panic. I'm just saying you and I lost a lot more than each other in the divorce. You gave up my mom, and I lost Joanna and David."

"What were we supposed to do?"

Impatience sharpened his nod. "I thought I couldn't help it, either, but I'll regret losing them for a long time, Tessa." With lines around his eyes and creases at the corners of his mouth, he looked as tired as he had last night.

"We should get back to work," she said.

"We have to resolve what happened between us sooner or later."

Resolve. The pragmatic word had nothing to do with the despair and the hope and the final defeat she'd had to endure before she could leave him. "We don't have to fix the past, Noah. We've both moved on."

Turning her back on him to change the subject, she printed a brief file that covered several less important complaints. "This set of notes, you can read. Minor annoyances, but you always said the most insignificant facts could change a case."

"I'm not finished." Despite his inflexible tone, he obviously hated continuing. "Our past isn't over." He shifted in his chair. "Maybe you gave up my mother and our friends without regret, but I counted on David, too. I wanted to talk to him about losing you and—"

He broke off, and she knew the name he couldn't say. She turned toward him, trembling with resentment.

"Keely." His inability to speak her name had denied Tessa the comfort of mourning their daughter with the one human being who'd loved her as much as she had.

He met her gaze head-on. "Keely." With his voice in hoarse shreds, his anguish caught her by surprise and opened a well of her own remembered agony.

Her stomach clenched. Instinct told her to walk

away. A smart woman who'd fought to be whole again wouldn't offer Noah her hand.

But she reached for him, and he was a bare millimeter too far away. Until he caught the tips of her fingers and then wrapped his hand around hers, gripping her as if she were all that held him in the sane world.

Maybe he pulled her toward him. Suddenly she was kneeling beside him, vaguely aware of the cold, reaching from the pine floor through her jeans. Knowing she shouldn't, she wrapped her arms as far as she could reach around his broad shoulders.

"I didn't mean to be cruel," she said.

"You weren't. I don't know why I can't—" He sat stiffly aloof.

She didn't care. In her head, his ragged voice repeated Keely's name, and she couldn't bear hearing it.

His grief made her honest. "I don't know who I am to blame you. I ran, too, but I know you hurt for Keely."

Slowly the stiffness left his body, first buckling his shoulders, then easing his hard chest against her, so that she almost felt his heart pounding in her body. "I loved Keely." Without warning, he caught her so fiercely against himself he squeezed the breath from her.

Just this side of pain, she found solace in holding him, in letting him hold her as tightly as he needed. She swallowed her own tears, intent on easing his unhappiness. His raucous breath shook her as their bodies met from chin to hip, and he buried his face in her throat.

He shook against her, and she felt afraid. This wasn't the Noah she'd known, and he certainly wasn't the Noah she'd left. That man hadn't known how to need.

But now he trembled in her arms, and she held him, stroking the silky hair he'd never worn long enough to curl around his nape before. The killing distance between them eased as they held on to each other.

Half the night might have passed before Noah leaned back. She half expected to see tears in his dark blue gaze. He looked back at her, his face oddly naked but dry-eyed.

"Thanks," he said.

She almost laughed. Thanks was enough. She climbed to her feet and took her chair again as if nothing had happened. But all she could think was how good it had been to hold him again, to be held.

"Tessa, I have to tell you one more thing."

She stared at him, positive he could see what she was trying to hide, that she still wanted to be in his arms.

"If you need me, for Maggie—for anything, you just have to call me, and I'll come."

"I don't think that's a great idea."

He curved his mouth in a reluctant, Noah-like smile, and she dwelt on the curve of his lips. She remembered his kiss so well.

He braced his shoulders and slipped back inside the cover of his aloofness. "You may meet someone else and remarry someday. Until we figure out what to do then, I'll be the friend I should have been before." He cleared his throat. "For David's sake and for Maggie's. If you need me."

David. God, how she missed him. He was the one she was supposed to talk to about her problems with Noah.

"You were going to tell me about Romeo?" he said.

She looked at him, distracted. Noah pointed at the screen.

"The guy who wanted you for his private lawyer?"

His quick change would have annoyed her before, but tonight he'd done her a favor. Maggie needed to be raised by a woman who wasn't afraid to love, and he'd showed her she could feel again. She simply wanted the cure in safe doses.

She focused on Eric's file. "You make it sound as if he was stalking."

"Was he?"

"I don't think so." She firmed her voice. "His name is Eric Sanders. He showed up in Prodigal after a messy divorce. He's one of the New York Sanders who fell out of politics after the Depression. But they kept their money, and they run a shipping company that all but monopolizes the East Coast. Rumor is, they exiled Eric to Maine. He never told us why, and no one else seems to know. The first thing he asked me to do was change his will."

Noah leaned forward. "He's a man who holds grudges?"

"Against his family, not against David."

"How did David end up with his case?"

"Because he kept asking me to meet him for drinks and yet another will change. Nobody gets along that badly with his relatives. One day, he'd put in his aunt, but take her husband out. The next week, he'd decide

to disinherit his sister. One night I made the mistake
of agreeing to meet him in a restaurant. Over Cos-
mopolitans he grabbed my thigh.'' She showed him
how high with her hand. ''I couldn't make him let
go, and I thought he was going to drag me out leg
first.''

''David warned him off?''

She shook her head, smiling faintly. ''You'd 'warn'
him. David tried to keep it professional, but Eric insisted he'd only work with me. He refused to talk to
David.''

''Why didn't both of you tell him you didn't want
his business?''

Noah's flat gaze, a dark lake with no ripples, neither accused nor threatened revenge on the man
who'd inappropriately touched his ex-wife. But Tessa
recognized his iron control, and she was glad he cared
if a client groped her.

''Look how small the town is. We couldn't afford
to turn away work. I was lucky David was willing to
share with me.''

''Is that why you took these cases? In Boston, you
only handled family law.''

''I stopped taking family cases after Keely.'' Adop-
tions had made up most of her caseload back then,
but when she'd come to Maine she couldn't face
working with children.

Awareness broke the surface of Noah's gaze.
''When did Eric last come to this house?''

She thought back. ''The past two days feel like a
month. Maybe two weeks ago? I left the chain on the
door, but he shoved his foot inside like a villain in
some B movie. I said I'd call the police if he came

back, and I mentioned his dad would probably be the one changing his will if he got put away for harassing me."

"He might be our best bet."

"Isn't he too obvious? Wouldn't he have waited until he wouldn't seem like the logical suspect?"

"Not if he's unbalanced. He might not have been able to help himself, and sometimes a suspect looks obvious because he is."

She didn't argue. In the end, Eric's single-mindedness had scared her. A thin wail from her room dragged her to her feet. "I wish I knew if she was sleeping through the night before."

Noah didn't answer, but she was already halfway up the stairs. Maggie, bouncing on her toes in her crib, stretched out her arms, crying for her "Da." Spontaneous tears, still too near the surface, burned Tessa's eyes, but she swiped them away for maybe the twentieth time that day and made herself smile at the sobbing baby.

"You're supposed to be asleep, you know."

Wailing, Maggie flailed her arms, and the second Tessa lifted her out, applied a full nelson. Laughing in surprise at her strength, Tessa hugged Maggie and hoped affection would ease her loss.

"Let's get you something to drink."

Still watery around the eyes, Maggie rammed her fist into her mouth and Tessa carried her downstairs. Noah stood, all in shadows now, away from the lamp-light. Catching sight of him, Maggie jumped.

"Da," she said again, and then wept harder than ever.

At the same time, moisture crept around the edges of her diaper. Poor little thing. Tessa had lost the hang of cradling a baby, grabbing water and laying her hands on a clean diaper and clothes, all at the same time.

She headed for Noah. He straightened, clearly seeing she was about to hand him Maggie. His wide gaze exposed curious fear. If he'd been born in the right place at the right time, he could have put Jack the Ripper away, but an infant girl struck him dumb with panic.

"Here, hold her, but you'd better watch out. She's soaked."

"Wait." Yet he held out his arms, and Tessa eased Maggie into them. Immediately the baby turned to look at him and stopped crying.

As she climbed the stairs, Tessa glanced back. Maggie had snatched a handful of Noah's lip. It must have hurt, but he didn't move a muscle.

She was tempted to laugh until she realized he probably hadn't held a baby since he'd taken Keely out of her crib that horrible morning.

CHAPTER FIVE

WITH HIS ARMS FULL of a baby who wasn't Keely—could never be Keely, didn't even remind him how he'd felt holding Keely, Noah suspected time had stopped ticking by.

His heart pounded at his rib cage so hard he was surprised his ribs didn't crack. He had the nightmare sensation of being too sluggish to run in the face of certain danger. He was going to fall. His arms, his head, his whole body had grown too heavy to support.

He inhaled and a second passed. His legs must have turned into stanchions. They were so stiff they wouldn't let him fall, but he couldn't move, either.

What a night. First, he'd all but blubbered on Tessa's shoulder because she'd challenged him to say their daughter's name. He took another breath, ashamed to have clutched at her.

Maggie tugged on his lip, and he realized no one had clipped her nails recently. While he welcomed the physical sensation of pain, he uncurled her fingers and eased her hand open.

Something about mauling his mouth made her giggle, and she sprayed his face with her warm, damp breath. He hardly remembered how to smile at a baby. He was surprised when his hard-fought effort didn't terrify her into another screaming frenzy.

He made himself say her name, to prove he could. "Maggie."

She twisted her mouth with adorable concentration, as if she were copying him. She managed a buzz and a string of drool that ran down her chin onto his fingers.

He hadn't minded Keely's drool. Must have been something to do with their genetic link. He seriously wanted to wipe Maggie's saliva off his hands.

"How'd you calm her down?" Tessa spoke from the gallery.

He hadn't heard her come out of her room. A few minutes with a baby in his arms, and he was already losing his edge. "I must remind her of David."

"You don't look anything like him."

"She's probably used to spending most of her time with a guy."

Tessa's quick look of alarm startled him. "We can't let her get attached to you."

That hurt his feelings. Obviously he wasn't part of Tessa's family anymore, but he'd meant what he'd said about showing up if she needed him. Maybe she didn't want him underfoot all the time, but did she need him to disappear again?

And if she wanted him to vanish, how would he stay away? In two days Maggie and Tessa had reminded him of what he'd hoped for from his marriage—an end to the fear that had dogged him from the day he'd witnessed his own father being gunned down by a drunk driver.

All those years, he'd secretly believed he'd caused his father's death, because his dad had been distracted, knowing he was in the car. Noah had believed he didn't deserve a family. Marrying Tessa had seemed like the biggest chance he could take, but they'd loved each other and when their healthy baby girl was born, he'd thought he'd beaten the odds.

Until Keely died. And then his whole past started to replay in his head on a looping reel. It began the moment his father had warned him to stay in the car that day. They'd been on their way to the zoo. His dad had only stopped the drunk driver to keep the man from killing someone. He'd walked to the guy's window and met the barrel of a gun.

And Noah had never admitted, even to Tessa or his own mother that he'd felt guilty, as he'd felt guilty for not saving his baby girl. As a child, he'd pushed his mom away, and after their baby had died, he'd pushed Tessa until she couldn't cling to the edges of his life.

"Noah." Tessa's tone demanded his attention.

He'd forgotten she was there.

"What are you thinking?" She glanced at the Worths' door and then hurried down the stairs. "I don't like that look on your face. I know it's strange to hold a baby and not fall apart, but don't get any risky ideas."

"About not letting you down again?" If he hadn't run from her like a spineless bastard, they could have salvaged something of their relationship.

"We didn't leave each other because of what happened with Keely." Standing just out of his reach, Tessa plunged her hands into her hair and raked it off her shoulders. "Don't fool yourself. We didn't share our lives before we had her. You went your way with your job, and I went my way with mine. We loved

Keely, and we both made time for her, but you and I worked our relationship around our other priorities.''

"We accepted each other's ambitions." God, that sounded stiff. "You're saying you could have lived differently?"

Color flooded her face, and he imagined the heat he'd feel on her skin if he dared trace the sharp line of her cheekbones.

"I'm not looking back at what I should have done." Her determination dumped a load of ice on his second thoughts. "We might be fine if nothing bad happened to us again, but we both deserve a chance to find someone who'll care for us in a crisis."

"You want someone else?" He sure as hell didn't want to picture her with another man.

Suddenly he faced the real truth. He'd never given Tessa up. He'd let her go, and he'd made a mistake. He'd thought, living each day, they'd find their way back to each other. He hadn't known he was supposed to do more. Was he capable of doing more?

Tessa shook her head as if she thought he wasn't sober or sane. She held out her hands for Maggie. "Give her to me, and if I were you, I'd stay away from babies. Look what they do to you."

For once, the picture that played in his head was not guilt, but scenes from their past, their marriage that Tessa seemed to feel had only gone skin-deep with him. Did he suddenly want her back because she seemed stronger without him?

Until he knew, he'd better be careful.

Forcing a smile, he held Maggie out to her, nodding at the huge wet spot that spread down the side of his shirt. "You're just in time." Maggie didn't want Tessa now. She reached around his neck, but she was too tiny to manage a good grip. He didn't have the heart to peel her off. "She's confusing me with David," he said.

"I'm doing everything I can to help her." Tessa tried again, but Maggie clung for dear life, bleating sharp sounds that cut into him.

"I'll hold her a little longer."

Tessa gave in with a wary glance from him to the baby. "Think of what you're doing, Noah. After we find out who hurt David, you're leaving."

He nodded, noting she'd said "hurt," not "killed." She wanted him to face the truth, but she couldn't yet. She needed him.

"You're probably right." This time he intended to do the right thing in his personal life, if only to prove his job didn't come first. He looked at Maggie, and the circumstances of "this time" nearly undid him. "Did you ever resent David and Joanna for having a healthy child?"

Tessa's eyes accused him. "That's why you stayed away from the christening?"

He nodded. "I know what kind of man that makes me, but I wanted—" He rushed a breath. "I wanted Keely."

"Firsts are always the hardest." Tessa spoke in a monotone, as if she didn't trust her own emotions. "I felt the same when I visited Joanna in the hospital, and then when I first went to their house after they brought Maggie home." Tears broke her voice.

He moved toward her, but the strength of his own need stopped him. He wanted to help her feel better. She'd helped him, but he didn't trust himself tonight.

As if she saw and somehow understood, Tessa set Maggie's things on the arm of the sofa. "Give her to me," she said. She managed to pluck Maggie out of his arms before he or the baby knew what she was doing. She pointed her elbow at his shirt. "You need a shower."

"I'm going."

"No, wait." She balanced the baby without managing to soak her own clothes. "Maggie can't change the past for us. I called you to help me with the police, not with her."

Talk about being obvious. Here he was trying to hold back until he felt sure he wouldn't make the same horrific mess of Tessa's life. But no need to worry. She'd warned him off.

"Let's talk about the police," he said. "You scheduled David's service for tomorrow?"

She pulled a baby blanket from behind a sofa cushion and laid Maggie on it. "His minister and I decided on a memorial service at his church at ten-thirty tomorrow morning. You don't have to come."

"I want to see who else attends, and you can bet Weldon will be among the congregation."

"Okay."

Silence fell, except for the baby, who twisted to gurgle at him while Tessa changed her diaper. He smiled at Maggie, stunned that he could return a baby's cute, spike-toothed grin. She was a charmer, pink-faced and active. Keely had looked just that healthy.

"I'm going upstairs," he said. "If you don't need help."

She didn't look up. "Good night."

In his room, he flipped his cell phone open and dialed his mother's number. She answered right away.

"Where have you been, son?"

The wonders of caller ID. "I'm in Maine."

"With Tessa? Thank—"

"Not the way you think, Mom. David Howard was killed." He couldn't bring himself to add the part where the police suspected Tessa. "I'm staying with her while she settles things."

"She's *letting* you stay?" Lucy Gabriel tapped something against the receiver. He pictured one of her long, fake nails. "Why?"

"She's upset." His mom might suspect he was lying, but Tessa would have to be the one to tell her the truth. "I just didn't want you to worry if you tried to call me."

"Which I have. I don't suppose Tessa would talk to me?"

"She's downstairs with the baby."

"I forgot about the little girl. Would I be intruding if I called Tessa?"

"Give her some time. She's not used to me being around."

"I'm not as much pressure for her."

"She doesn't seem to agree." He smoothed his hair over his forehead. "She has this idea she'll somehow come between you and me if she stays in touch with you."

Lucy scoffed, a strident denial that made him pull the phone away from his ear. "I have love enough for you both, but neither of you is willing to be loved."

Yeah, well, he'd heard enough about his reluctance to sustain a relationship tonight. He was a man, not a saint.

THE TEMPERATURE PLUNGED. Tessa woke to ice tapping at her bedroom windows. As soon as she sat up, Maggie clambered to her feet in a weary but determined hand-over-hand maneuver on her crib rail.

Bribing the baby to occupy herself with toys and a teething ring, Tessa sped through a shower. Afterward she bathed Maggie, and then they crept past the silent bedrooms.

All fed and content, they were enjoying a game of pat-a-cake downstairs by the time the Worths slipped through their door. Eleanor leaned over the gallery rail and then glanced at Noah's room.

"He's still asleep?"

"I guess."

"Have you eaten yet?" Eleanor whispered.

"I thought I'd make pancakes when you all came down."

"Let me make them."

Joe, already at the bottom of the stairs, made for the baby. "Here's my girl." He scooped her into his arms. "She could sleep in our room, you know. You don't have to act like David did, afraid to let her spend time with us."

Intrigued as much by his bitter tone as his words, Tessa stared at him. "David never said that. He thought of you as his parents, too."

Joe merely shrugged. Eleanor tsked at her husband as she reached him. "Don't start that again. David simply didn't have the time for us that Joanna made. Joe didn't understand that David couldn't drop everything to bring this little bit over to see us whenever we called.''

"You won't be like that, though, will you, Tessa?" Joe's steady gaze hid nothing of his fear that she'd put distance between Maggie and them.

"Not at all. And I'm sure Eleanor's right. David was busy. For all we know, someone might have threatened him before all this happened. He might have been wary of taking Maggie out.''

"He should have known she'd be perfectly safe with us." Eleanor stroked her soft cheek. "We'd be glad to have her sleep in our room.''

"Thanks, but she's restless, and I'm not sleeping well, either. She probably doesn't understand what's happened, but she misses her daddy." Tessa smiled at Eleanor. "And please don't worry about cooking or any other chores around the house. Take a break, and enjoy Maggie.''

"She definitely needs our attention." The older woman kissed her granddaughter's nose. "But she's mostly content, despite it all. David did a fine job with her. I'm surprised at how fine.''

Joe locked his arm around her waist. "Don't fret now." He pressed his lips to her silvery hair. The three of them made a family as Joe hugged his wife and cradled his granddaughter against his chest.

Tessa swallowed. They were so certain of themselves, but she still wondered if she was the right person to care for Maggie. Having David and Joanna's vote of confidence didn't seem to ease her doubts about becoming anyone's mother.

She'd never measured up as the daughter her mom and dad would have liked. And if she'd been good

enough for Keely, her own child might still be alive.
What made her think she knew how to be Maggie's
parent?

She shook her head. Last night's talk with Noah
must still be rattling around in her mind. He'd simply
asked her the questions she'd silently asked herself.
He'd obviously been vulnerable, and he'd gone too
far, even implying they might try to be together again.
Thank goodness she'd forced him to see sense, and
his moment of weakness had passed without too much
pain to either one of them.

She couldn't afford to make other mistakes. She
glanced at Joe and Eleanor, loving, responsible, long-
ing to help her make life right for Maggie.

Last night, she'd slotted her time with Noah firmly
into the past. Might as well face all her demons at
once. "I know you'd like to have Maggie full-time.
You wouldn't be human if you didn't. She must remind you of Joanna—"

"You don't have to explain why David and Joanna
wanted you to have her," Eleanor said. "Joanna told
us from the beginning. We were already in our forties
when Joanna was born, and Joe will be seventy next
spring. If Maggie lived with us, she might be facing
this same kind of situation in ten years or so. You
were family to my daughter and her husband, and
now we'll all three make a family for our beautiful
little girl."

Joe nodded. "Maybe we won't be the same as her
own mother and father, but we'll be the best backup
team in history."

Tessa hugged them both, surprised at the urge. Joe

and Eleanor glanced at each other, and suddenly the tension level rose again.

"I feel as if we're finally saying goodbye to Joanna," Eleanor said.

"Never," her husband denied.

Tessa began to feel like a fifth wheel, but Noah opened his door and stumbled onto the gallery. He stared at them, apparently oblivious to the older couple's distress. "I slept late," he said.

In jeans, bare feet and rumpled hair, he looked as if he'd slept badly. His long, muscled torso was leaner than Tessa remembered. Rubbing his fist through the thin trail of hair that arrowed toward his waistband, he opened the linen closet door and grabbed a towel before veering into the bathroom.

Tessa's mouth went dry. "He lives alone." She tried to find her voice, but it had mostly gone, stampeded by the memory of her ex-husband's satin smooth skin beneath her palms. "He's not used to making himself presentable."

"How long do I have, Tessa?" As if he wasn't sure she'd heard him, Noah leaned back out of the bathroom. "We need to leave by 9:30, right?"

"Plenty of time." Joe's frown disapproved of Noah's unkempt appearance. "You must have come home late last night."

Before Tessa could protest at the idea of her house being Noah's home, he nodded. "And then Tessa and I worked for a while. I'll take a shower and get dressed." Planting his free hand on the gallery rail, he focused on them. "Everything all right?"

It would be if he'd just drape that towel over the provocatively defined muscles of his chest. Who knew his half-nude body could send her priorities slithering out of control? She'd lived so long without wanting a man she felt compelled to act on wanting the one most dangerous to her.

"We're *all* fine." Eleanor planted another peck on her granddaughter's cheek. "Breakfast will be waiting when you're ready."

She headed for the kitchen. Noah lurched inside and shut the door at his back. Joe sailed away with Maggie safe in his hands, and Tessa forced herself to breathe again.

"I'll take care of little miss for a while," Joe tossed over his shoulder. "Why don't you dress for David's service?"

"Thanks." Climbing the stairs, Tessa tried to focus on the grim morning ahead rather than wanting Noah. But last night Noah had reminded her of the life she'd been wasting. As she neared the bathroom door, she trailed her fingers along the cool honey-colored wood, as if she were touching the man on the other side.

Water ran, splashing as it sluiced over his body. She rolled her shoulders, trying to unknot her own muscles. She stared at the door. What next? If the Worths weren't here, would she have dared to open it?

And what would she say? "Sorry, I made a mistake when I left you last night. I should have jumped on the hint of a chance to live with you again."

She hadn't made a mistake. Leaving him had saved her life, because he hadn't loved her. She pushed away from the door and headed for her own room.

She found a black dress and shoes to match and then fished a pair of black hose from her undies drawer. Distracting her despite her resolve, the sounds of a wet man moving beneath the shower spray traveled through the wall from next door.

When she should have been mourning David, she was remembering Noah, naked. Once upon a time, he'd begged her to share his shower, but she hadn't. She'd been too afraid to show him the body her mother had despaired of whipping into shape.

But Noah had never complained about the curves that had embarrassed her mother. Memories crowded Tessa, erotic images of loving that seemed unreal. She tried to elbow them aside as she dressed, but when she drew her hose over her legs, she remembered the play of Noah's passionate hands, the slide of his heated breath against her skin as he'd kissed her in ways that made her burn for the past.

She remembered the darkness, her friend. In the dark, she could pretend she was the slim woman she'd tried but failed to be. And when she'd been pregnant with Keely, Noah had traced the curves that had horrified her.

He'd touched her with love. She could remember that now without wanting to scream. Her pregnancy had changed her, almost made her believe she'd hold his love forever.

They'd both changed. They'd made time for each other, and they'd talked about life outside their respective offices. They'd planned their life with Keely, and when she'd come they'd taken joy in love that had surprised them both with its savage need to protect.

An attorney and a cop, they'd believed in law and

reason. They'd both used logic as a weapon. Keely had induced them to embrace their emotions.

Tessa had finally admitted to disappointing her parents with the extra ten pounds she never seemed to shed. She'd tamed her compulsion to stake herself in a job that meant she'd never have to depend on anyone for support again.

Noah had finally talked about the day his father had died. They'd sworn to protect their baby girl from guilt. Unconditional love for their daughter had begun to heal their childhood wounds. Healing had brought enough trust to believe they could fashion a safe, loving home for Keely.

But then they'd lost her.

Tessa slid the black dress off its yellow satin hanger. Who could have believed she'd have to attend David's funeral now? Hadn't he suffered enough when Joanna died? Hadn't he tried to protect her even after death? He'd been a good man, a loving father and husband who'd go to any length for his family.

Did fate have to be so damn cruel?

She unzipped the dress and scrunched up the material to slide it over her head. She mourned the friendship that had outlasted her marriage. Like a big brother on his best protective behavior, David had warned her off Noah at first, recognizing the other man's ruthless edge. But when he'd realized she loved Noah, David had gotten to know him, and Noah had good-naturedly jumped through David's hoops to prove himself.

Next had come the family dinner where David had convinced her mom and dad Noah was on the fast track to become police commissioner. As Tessa tried not to laugh, her mother had immediately begun planning a wedding fit for the top guy in Boston law enforcement.

Tessa laughed, remembering how she'd accused David of going too far. He'd sworn her mom would be Noah's friend for life, as long as she pushed her homicide cop to go for the top job. Even then, they'd both known Noah was always going to chase the killers.

As laughter turned to grieving tears, Tessa snatched a tissue from a box on her dressing table and dabbed at her mascara. Crying wouldn't help. She slipped a black silk blazer over her dress and braided her hair with compulsive neatness.

Then she applied makeup in sober shades of plum and faint purple and ran a matte lipstick over her mouth. Finally she slid her feet into the pumps she'd always worn for her most important interviews.

She had to find the person who'd killed her best friend. She owed David.

She glared at herself in her mirror. In case Noah was right about the murderer showing up at the service, she wanted to look like power.

NOAH HAD PLANNED to arrive at the service early and hang at the back of the crowd, but Tessa worried him. Dressed to kill, her eyes as cold as the snow blowing out of a blue-gray sky, she gripped his arm with Amazon strength and made him think of a bullet headed straight for a target.

At her side, he studied each dark-clad mourner. The men settled uncomfortably on the narrow bench seats and refused to look at David's photo, wreathed in greenery on a podium. The women, covered from chin to toe, exhaled icy suspicion as they watched Tessa.

He studied his ex-wife, too. Obviously, some fine citizens of Prodigal, Maine, agreed with Weldon's assumption that Tessa'd had an affair with David. Did she know? She looked away from no one. She challenged each mourner's gaze with her own questions, and she obviously didn't give a damn what they thought.

Good.

She finally understood someone in this town had killed her best friend. Something had awakened her from her shock.

"Any of your guys here yet?" he asked her.

She nodded toward a man in a faded navy pinstripe that might have been new two decades ago. "Mr. Swyndle, the lobsterman."

"Let's say hello." Working during the summers at the tourist towns along the Maine coast, Noah had heard stories about territorial lobstermen, but Fevre had taken advantage of Swyndle's daughter, not his lobster pots.

"Now? Couldn't we wait for a more appropriate time, Noah?"

"No." He took her arm and leaned into her shoulder, unable to avoid breathing the tempting scent of her hair. "We can't afford to be polite."

The fisherman stood as Tessa neared him. He offered his hand. "Morning, Tessa."

"Hello, Mr. Swyndle."

"Sorry about David. He was a good young man."

When she didn't answer, Noah slid a protective

arm around her shoulders. The fisherman eyed Noah speculatively.

"This is Noah Gabriel, Mr. Swyndle."

"I've heard of you." Ned Swyndle shook hands with firmness that reminded Noah of the strength it had taken to wield that knife. But the older man looked him in the eye as though he had nothing to hide, and in fact he was curious about Noah's presence.

"Pleased to meet you," Noah said, not satisfying the man's curiosity. "I'm sure Tessa's glad to have you here."

"I owed David my respects," Swyndle said. "And, Tessa, I'm still fighting my gold-digging prospective son-in-law, so you'll keep my business."

Surprise softened her voice. "Thank you, Mr. Swyndle."

"That's the best I can do for David, now," the fisherman said. "Keep my business in his firm."

"Who's this, Tessa?"

A man's sharp voice broke into their conversation from behind. High-pitched with barely held rage, the tone wakened all Noah's instincts. He turned, clamping Tessa to his side.

A tall, blond man took a step toward them, trying to challenge Noah with his jealous gray eyes. "I'm Eric Sanders," he said. "Who are you?"

"Tessa's husband." Not the precise truth, but Noah itched to show the guy who had rights to Tessa, and who'd better climb back into his family's bank vault.

"Noah," Tessa began with exasperation in her voice. She stopped when Sanders whipped his gaze to her. "I didn't expect you here, Eric."

"I wanted to see you. I know you'll need comfort now that David's gone. I'll be calling you."

The wheedling tone became a threat. Noah glanced at Tessa and was stunned to see her eyes brimming with tears. He moved, to block her from her stalker's view.

"I'm taking care of my wife, Sanders." He lowered his voice. "And I'll be taking care of you if you don't—"

"Noah," Tessa broke in. She grabbed Ned Swyndle's arm. "Maybe you would show Eric to a seat, Mr. Swyndle?"

"I think I should." The fisherman smirked. "He'll be sitting in the back with me today."

As Swyndle hauled the younger man to a pew, Noah clenched his fist. "I'll make sure he knows his place after today."

"Stop playing the jealous husband, and try to think of David. This isn't the place to square off with Eric Sanders."

"I know that guy, or guys like him." He brushed moisture from the corner of her eye. "He wants you, and he's not honest or honorable."

"Cut it out." She turned him toward the front of the church.

"This is why you asked me here. I'm doing my job. I'd have said the same thing to him if he'd talked like that to any woman." He and Baxton had been providing the same kind of protection for Della Eddings. How could he not protect Tessa?

"I'm begging you not to make this worse. I live in a small town, Noah, and I intend to go on living here for a long time."

Without answering, he took a seat beside her in their pew. No matter who the killer was, before Noah left Prodigal, he'd convince her Eric was dangerous.

"What was Swyndle's beef with David?"

"He thought we should have moved faster to destroy Jon Fevre."

Didn't sound like much. "Did you see the other guy? Carlson?"

"He's in front of Mr. Swyndle and Eric." She nodded over her shoulder. "Big guy, dark burgundy vest, leather cap. We're not going back there."

He looked. A large, florid man, wearing a dark reddish vest tautly stretched across a prosperous stomach, tipped his leather cap. Noah nodded and then leaned down.

"You can introduce me after the service." He tugged at his tie. "I didn't mean to make you uncomfortable with Sanders."

"This service is for David. I'd like to remember it with a small measure of dignity."

"I lost my temper. Sorry." He cared about their friend, too, but Sanders was a man who needed to be told he was being watched. He'd been too intent on Tessa.

After several minutes passed with no one else entering the dim, incense-laden church, the minister stepped up to his podium. "I'm sorry about the lack of heat, but we couldn't bribe a repairman to come this morning. Shall we start?"

Everyone nodded in answer to the rhetorical question. Tessa merely locked her delicate jaw. She was magnificent, so small her head barely reached his shoulder, but a hell of a fighter.

"David asked us to keep this brief," the minister said, "but I'm not sure he realized how many of you would be touched by his death. I'm glad you've come to pay your respects. Perhaps some of you will find comfort in telling us about your friendship with David before I wish him final farewell with a prayer."

New mourners entered in clumsy-sounding shoes that seemed to rock the arched rafters. Those shoes were police boots. The crowd stirred. Noah turned. Out of the shadows, Weldon seemed to materialize over a tall man's shoulder.

The young, uniformed kid who'd greeted Noah at the police station that first night hovered at Weldon's side. Another uniformed officer strolled to the last unoccupied pew on the other side of the aisle.

Had they come to make an arrest? He twisted his arm out of Tessa's grasp and pulled off his glove to link his fingers with hers. Over his dead body would Weldon or either of his henchmen take this woman from his side.

But they didn't seem to be interested in her. They searched each of the mourners' faces, just as he and Tessa had done.

"I have something to say." A young woman, maybe twenty if she was a day over eighteen, teetered to the podium, smoothing a too-short green skirt over her thighs. "I'm Serena Hope. I'm the teacher in Maggie's room at the Children's Cabin. I just want to say that whoever did this to David Howard ought to suffer the way he did. He was a good father. He loved his daughter, and it's just a damn shame what happened to him." She spun away, but then turned back. "Someone needs to swear when a good man dies."

Noah held back a cheer for Serena Hope's speech. She stared at Tessa, who slowly gritted her teeth. Serena clasped her hands to her own red face and ran, finding her balance on the heels.

Noah glanced at his ex-wife, who seemed unaware of icy tears streaking faint white salt paths across her cheeks. He let go of her hand and then slid an arm around her shoulders to pull her close. She forgot to resist.

Coughs punctuated the cold silence after Serena's belligerent speech. A burst of wind buffeted the church's stained glass windows. Rustling sounds betrayed the mourners' growing restlessness.

"Tessa?" the minister said.

She jumped, and Noah wanted to wrap both his arms around her and drag her back to the warmth and comfort of her small house.

She stood at their seat. "Many of you know David was my best friend and my law partner." She flicked a glance at the pews behind them. "What mattered to David was his family. He loved Joanna and he tried hard not to be lost without her because he wanted to be a good dad for Maggie. I can tell you he helped me survive my own daughter's death, and I'm sorry I'll never be able to make sure he knew what he and Joanna meant to me." She turned toward his photo, fisting her hands at her sides. "David, I miss you already. I wish you were here, because I need to talk to my best friend right now. I'd tell you I'll make sure Maggie knows how much you and Joanna loved her. Thank you for a friendship I refuse to mourn." Her voice broke. Her shoulders grew more stiff. "I love you, David, and I'll miss you. I'll never let Maggie forget you or her mom.''

Noah stared at her back, braced against all offers of comfort. He stared at his empty hands.

And he found himself on his feet. Taking a sharp breath that hurt his chest, he started talking. ''I'm Noah Gabriel. I have more to thank David for than maybe anyone else here. He worked at being my friend because he cared for Tessa, and when I wasn't the man I should have been, David and Joanna took care of her as I wanted to.'' His throat seemed to close. Public confession wasn't his best skill. ''I can't repay David for that, but I still have to say thank you.'' He stared at his friend's picture and silently wished he'd been a man to measure up to David Howard.

He dropped into his seat with a thud. His cell phone rang, completely out of place. He clapped his hand over it in his coat pocket and headed for the vestry, relieved he still had a job to do.

Away from the mourners, he opened the phone and cupped his hand around the receiver. ''Yeah.''

''Noah?'' The half-familiar voice jittered with agitation. ''Joe Worth. Noah, someone just fired a shot through the living-room window.''

''Maggie.'' Her name exploded from him.

''She's fine. Eleanor was rocking her to sleep upstairs. I was in our room, but we both heard the shot, and I came downstairs to check. I don't know much about guns, but it looks to me as if there's a bullet hole in the glass in that big curvy window by the door.''

"Did you call the police?"

"I called you."

Damn the man's doubts about the authorities. They didn't need to make Weldon think they were trying to maneuver around him. "Did you find the bullet?" Without ruining evidence, he prayed.

"Not yet. I'll find it by the time you get here."

"Don't touch anything. And call Weldon."

"What? We're not hurt. I don't trust those guys. If they knew what they were doing, they'd already know who killed David, and they never would have called Joanna a dope fiend. Eleanor and I think someone killed her, too."

Poor guy. Naturally, he didn't want his daughter's name smeared, but he might be risking his granddaughter's life. "I'll find out the truth about Joanna's accident, but you have to trust the police. I can't do anything without their help. I'm out of my jurisdiction, so you have to call Weldon."

"I—"

"Whoever shot at the house probably knew Maggie was there."

Joe gasped. Impatiently Noah counted his own breaths while he waited for the other man to face reality.

"I'll call, but you're coming?"

"As soon as I get Tessa." He whirled, inspecting the church for security weaknesses. The painted glass offered some cover, but what if the shooter didn't intend to content himself with potshots at a window? What if he liked threatening funeral parties, as well?

Slipping on the polished tile, Noah skidded into the church again. Only Tessa and the minister, intoning a prayer, didn't turn around. Everyone else stared. Somewhere a purse hit the floor.

Noah had no time to show respect. "Excuse me, sir."

The minister looked up, and Noah found he didn't want to frighten Tessa. He had no choice. "Joe phoned in an incident at your house. Someone shot at the living-room window." He veered his gaze toward Weldon. "Someone took a shot at Tessa's house."

"*Maggie—?*" Tessa asked.

"—is fine. So are Joe and Eleanor, but we need to go." He turned to the others. "I'd advise you all to go home, as well—at least to stay out of the open."

"This is a police matter!" Weldon shouted.

"Yes, but it's Tessa's house." Without a word, Tessa came to him. He held out his hand, and she took it. Together they were stronger than either of them was alone. He'd been wrong about her. She had nothing to prove about needing no one. She knew when to need.

Hand in hand, they were running down the aisle when Weldon's radio crackled. A near-hysterical dispatcher shouted his name. Joe must have dialed 911.

CHAPTER SIX

THE SECOND NOAH STOPPED the car, Tessa bolted into the house, where Weldon, who'd traveled faster with lights and sirens, met her at the door and all but pinned her against the wall.

"Naturally, you'll refuse to tell me who did this." He stood so close his bad breath and cheap aftershave turned her stomach.

Face the man, she told herself. She wasn't trying to hide anything from him. "I don't know who shot at my house, and I have to see Maggie."

"Don't touch that wall. We need to dust for fingerprints." He grabbed her wrists before she could flatten her palms against the cool plaster.

She forced herself to relax rather than fight, but Noah stepped between them, pulling her away from the other policeman. "Back off and hunt for a viable suspect. How was she supposed to shoot at her own house while she was at David's service with you and your officers?"

For once, Tessa took grateful shelter in the warmth of Noah's larger bulk. When she pointed out the obvious to Weldon, she sounded like any other suspect, trying to turn doubt from herself. Noah's experience spoke more convincingly.

But Weldon eyed him with a competitor's frustration. "You and I both know she could have hired someone to drive by and plug a window while she was out."

"And risk Maggie's life? You've lost your objectivity." With slight pressure on her hand, he urged Tessa farther into the living room.

She followed his direction. Her need to see Maggie screamed inside her head, and she was relieved to let Noah handle Weldon.

"Stop," the police chief said.

She took a deep breath. From upstairs, Maggie let loose with one of her excited giggles. Relief broke Tessa's tension, leaving her barely able to keep from dashing up the stairs as she waited for the police chief's next move.

"Don't touch any part of the house, and don't touch anything you don't have to in your rooms. Just pack clothes you'll need for tonight and maybe tomorrow. This house is a crime scene."

Noah turned her toward the stairs, and she let him. "You're using this as an excuse to search Tessa's home. The crime happened outside. You can search the property to your heart's content, but this house is off-limits until you produce a warrant."

"I don't need a warrant to follow the bullet's path," Weldon said, a bantam rooster trying to claim his barnyard. "I'm running an investigation in this house, and you know better than to sleep under a roof that's been shot up."

"Your job is to make sure we're safe. It's time you stationed a patrolman outside."

Tessa left them to battle it out and flew up the stairs to Eleanor and Joe's room. She knocked, and a deputy came out. Behind him, she saw Joe, red-faced and flustered on a straight-backed chair.

"We're busy here, Ms. Gabriel," the deputy said. "I need to find out exactly what Mr. Worth saw."

"Eleanor's in your room with Maggie," Joe said.

Tessa nodded, but she didn't move. "Joe—"

"I'm fine. Let's just get this over with, and maybe they'll start doing their jobs."

The deputy shut the door, and Tessa headed for her own room. Eleanor was sitting in the rocking chair with Maggie in her lap. They were passing a small blue ball to each other. Maggie looked up, clapping her hands as she saw Tessa, and Tessa scooped the little girl into her arms, trying not to squeeze her too hard.

"I'm so glad everyone's all right."

Eleanor nodded, reaching up to stroke Maggie's leg. "We happened to be up here. Lucky thing, I guess."

Barely standing on her weak knees, Tessa rocked the baby. "Was she scared?"

"Only when she noticed I was, but I've calmed her down."

Tessa sank onto the bed, which left her near Eleanor. When the other woman's hand smoothed her hair, Tessa jumped.

"You were afraid, too," Eleanor said. "Don't be. We'd never let anything happen to this little one."

Common sense almost forced her to remind Maggie's grandmother they couldn't have stopped a bullet, but Tessa bit her lip. Eleanor's kind touch offered an unfamiliar sense of peace.

Her mother tended to frown from afar and then

close in to pluck at her flaws. Hair that strayed from all semblance of style, an untucked blouse, skirts that fit too tight because her mom had purchased them a size too small, hoping the hint would take.

"What's going on?" Eleanor asked.

"Noah's throwing the policemen out, I think. One of the deputies is talking to Joe."

"Why do they want to search your house, Tessa?"

She straightened. Eleanor and Joe had been shot at. They were all in this mess together. It was time to tell the truth. "Weldon still hopes to find evidence against me."

At first, Eleanor didn't seem to understand. Finally comprehension dawned, widening her gaze. She began to rock in her chair. "They *honestly* think you—"

"I didn't. I loved David."

Eleanor grimaced as if she were in pain. Tessa reached for her hand where it rested on the chair arm. The other woman's fingers were chilled, and she jerked back.

"I'd never do anything to hurt David or his family."

"I know, dear." The older woman closed her eyes. "Joe and I know exactly how close you were to David and Joanna. This is just another instance of the police not knowing their own job. How do they expect—"

"Try not to get too upset with Weldon." Tessa's affection for Maggie now included Eleanor and Joe. She hadn't meant to upset the other woman. "Noah was offering him plenty of free advice downstairs, but

Weldon and his men aren't used to investigating murder."

"He's so desperate to say he's solved a big-city crime, he tried to make my daughter look like a druggie."

Tessa kept her mouth shut. Obviously David had tried to spare Joanna's parents, but the shot fired into her house changed things. A bad drug deal might explain David's death and the gunshot. Someone could have wanted payment or revenge for some perceived wrong Joanna might have done.

She had to stop feeling guilty because Joanna had misunderstood her friendship with David. And she had to remember Maggie's safety was more important than the promise David had extracted. She'd start with Hank Sloma, a dealer David had defended on a misdemeanor charge. Joanna might have met him.

"I don't know what Chief Weldon expects us to tell him." Eleanor twisted her mouth. "We were up here when we heard the glass break. It was probably a high school kid playing a prank. Someone who heard you'd already had trouble."

"In Prodigal?" As Maggie began to struggle in her arms, Tessa gave her back to Eleanor, and the little girl scrambled to retrieve her ball. "We don't have that kind of problem with kids here," Tessa said.

"No towns are that small anymore." Eleanor rocked a little harder. "Why is that man taking so long with Joe? He wants to talk to me next."

"Are you anxious? I'd be glad to stay with you."

"No, thanks. I just don't like Weldon. Noah may think he's capable, but I've begun to despair he'll ever find out who killed David. He's too busy making up stories about Joanna—and now you—to find a guilty party. And I have no idea who'd hurt David. It doesn't make sense.''

''To me, either.'' Tessa rose from the bed and began to tidy the room. She couldn't imagine why a drug dealer might have surfaced seven months after Joanna's death. Unless he'd been harassing David all along.

He'd pulled every string he possessed to persuade the town's former police chief to drop the drug evidence from Joanna's accident investigation. He'd said the whole family had gone through Joanna's first supposedly successful rehabilitation. He didn't intend to let them suffer through her failure, too.

Tessa clenched one of Maggie's sweaters in her hands. A drug dealer would have been as anxious as David to keep the truth quiet. But would he be after the Worths now? Could today's gunshot be a warning?

Would Eleanor or Joe know what was going on? Could they be so blind to the truth about Joanna that they would ignore a warning?

And would an angry dealer try to take revenge on Maggie? Tessa choked on her sudden fear for the baby. She'd like to whisk her away from this town where someone had killed her father and then shot at her new home.

She couldn't run. She had to find out what had cost David's life. She studied Eleanor, trying to peer through the other woman's grief to secrets she might be hiding. A warning only worked if she and Joe knew they'd been warned.

"I have to ask you an uncomfortable question,"
Tessa said.

Eleanor pressed her toe to the pine floor to stop
rocking, but she faced Tessa with a bland expression.
"What?"

"Has anyone tried to talk to you about Joanna?"

"I wish." Eleanor lifted her foot and the rocker
tilted forward again. "We can't persuade anyone to
listen to us. You're not starting to believe Weldon's
lies about her?"

Tessa tried another tack. "I mean, maybe Joanna
had bills that David didn't know about. Has anyone
talked to you about something Joanna might have
owed?"

"For what? She never had her bills sent to us. I'm
sure David paid everything."

She couldn't seem to get to the point with Joanna's
mother. Eleanor's wide gaze betrayed no doubt, only
confusion.

"Did Joanna borrow money from you, Tessa?"

"No." Talk about subtle—she'd managed to imply
Joanna had been begging money. Unless Eleanor was
a phenomenal actress, she hadn't known about
Joanna's relapse.

And Tessa suspected she'd watched too many TV
detective shows. Noah believed in his angry client
theory. Maybe she'd dismissed Carlson too easily.
And she had a feeling they'd be looking more closely
at Eric after today.

"What made you ask about Joanna's debts?"
Eleanor asked.

"I saw a piece of paper in David's office one day."
She snatched another of Maggie's blankets from the

pile on her bed and racked her brain for a believable story. "It was a note. I couldn't read the name at the bottom, but it showed an amount. Of money."

"You thought you saw Joanna's name?"

"A name that started with a *J*." She looked away. She was a lawyer for pity's sake. She should at least know how to apply spin. "I'd better go downstairs and start Maggie's lunch."

"Will you stop by Joe's door? I'd like to know what the police want from us." Eleanor rocked fast, tightening her grip on Maggie. "I hope they'll call me in soon."

"I doubt the police will open up and ask me to join them."

"I keep forgetting how inconvenient this is for you, but I'm glad we can all be together for Maggie."

"Me, too." Nodding reassurance at the other woman, she eased the door shut behind herself, and ran straight into the deputy who'd been guarding the reception area that first night at the police station.

She glanced over the gallery rail. Noah and Weldon were no longer downstairs. Tessa turned aside to pass the deputy.

She resented these men in her home. She had no faith anyone except Noah was trying to find the real killer. And letting Noah into her house went against everything she'd planned for her future without him.

She'd wanted nothing of her old life in this house—no memories, nothing that reminded her of her ex-husband or her baby. But she'd hungered for a real home, a place that belonged to her and welcomed her out of the cold.

She'd shopped each antique shop and garage sale

up and down Route 1 for every stick of furniture. She knew each curve in the plaster walls. She'd hovered as the chimney sweep had dragged tons of creosote out of her chimney. She'd searched appliance stores all the way back to Boston for a stove to fit in the large kitchen nook that had once held a wood-burning iron hulk.

It was her place, marked by her personality, branded with her choices. She hadn't even allowed her parents to visit, because her small place wouldn't meet their Back Bay standards. And now, because some nut with an arsenal had decided to launch an assault on David and his family and friends, she had to allow strangers inside.

She was mixing cereal when Joe and Noah came through the door, with Maggie on Joe's shoulder.

"The young guy's digging the bullet out of the wall above the fireplace hearth," Joe said.

"Where's Eleanor?" Tessa asked.

"She told us to leave her with the other two," Noah said.

"And you listened to her?" Tessa moved toward the door, carrying the cereal bowl in one hand, a plump-handled baby's spoon in the other. Someone had to protect Maggie's grandmother, and she might not have practiced criminal law, but she knew the rules.

"Stop, Tessa." Joe sounded certain. "She's no fool. She would have asked one of you to listen in if she was concerned about Weldon."

"I don't like having him in the house when he's so determined I had something to do with it."

"I wondered if you knew," Joe said.

"He's not exactly subtle."

"He's determined we saw something." Shaking his head, Joe reached for Maggie's hand, and the little girl clenched her grandfather's finger in her small fist. "All I could think was that we had to keep her out of harm's way. I all but shoved Eleanor and Maggie into a closet."

"I would have if someone was shooting at the house," Noah said. "You were lucky no one got hurt." He glanced at his watch. "How much time do you think we should give them?"

"Eleanor can hold her own."

Tessa glanced at Noah, and she was positive they shared the same thought. Joe knew a stronger Eleanor than they'd met.

Behind the men, the door opened again, and Eleanor sailed through. Her color ran high and her eyes looked too bright, but she was clearly satisfied with herself.

"They're getting ready to leave, Tessa. You might want to make sure they don't plant evidence from every crime committed in this town for the past year on your premises."

Tessa pushed the cereal bowl and spoon onto the counter, but she barely passed through the doorway ahead of Noah. They found Chief Weldon, overseeing his men as they measured from the window to a hole chipped into the plaster above the fireplace.

"Don't assume I don't know what I'm doing because I don't come from Boston, Detective. We don't plant evidence around here any more than you would."

"You won't find any evidence here, because I didn't do anything," Tessa said.

"Are you offering to let me search?" Behind him, one of his men held up the bullet in an evidence bag while the other began to gather tools.

"No," Noah said. "But I think you should remember you might be letting the real killer go with your concentration on my wife."

"Ex," Weldon and Tessa said together.

She'd said it unconsciously, her mind on the possible suspects they hadn't told him about. Noah's sharp glance made her regret her quick correction.

"I don't have to tell you not to leave town," Weldon said as his men left.

"And you will have your deputies patrol this road."

"We're watching this house." Weldon tipped his cap and exited on the line he might have been saving just for them.

Tessa waited for Noah to blow up, but he merely locked the door behind the chief and set the alarm. When he turned away from the wall panel, he must have seen her surprise.

"I don't care why he patrols. I just want to be sure someone keeps an eye on you."

"I think we should give him a copy of the notes I gave you."

"All of them?" He arched a dark brow. "I don't think you can if you want to keep your license."

"I mean an expurgated copy. So they'll know we had problems with some of our clients. If it's one of them, I want Weldon to find him before he hurts Maggie."

"You could talk to them and get their permission to give the information to Weldon."

She nodded. "And you could try them out on your suspect meter?"

He laughed. "Can't hurt. I think Swyndle's a non-starter, but Eric looks good for my bet."

"You haven't met Hugh yet, and I doubt Eric will agree to talk to you."

"I plan to deal with Eric the stalker."

His pleasure with the plan made her nervous. He never ran low on testosterone, and someone stalking his ex-wife clearly raised the levels, but they both needed to remember his role. "I'll handle Eric. You act more like a husband than a cop around him."

"I'm serious. I'm going to talk to him."

Why waste time arguing? She was no gothic heroine anxious to put herself or her makeshift family in danger just to prove her own strength. "I'll ask Eleanor to look after Maggie and we can schedule visits with Hugh Carlson and Mr. Swyndle and Eric."

"Eric gets a surprise visit," Noah said. "Otherwise, I think he'll suddenly fall in love with his family in Boston again."

"I'll go along with what you want. And by the way, thank you." She wasn't sure she'd said it before, and she found it hard to say now. "For coming, and for keeping Weldon in line. I'm so stunned I forget I have rights." She sputtered to a stop. Simple gratitude shouldn't be so hard to express. She'd fallen out of the habit of thanking Noah, just as she'd learned to stop loving him.

"It's natural," he said. "You're in shock. You've

lost your best friend, and you can't imagine someone would think you'd kill David."

He slid his hand around her arm. Gently massaging, he forced her to meet his dark brown gaze.

She saw more than she wanted to. Empathy and compassion, recognition of the past that had nearly driven them both out of their minds.

Suddenly he smiled. Lines crinkled at the corners of his eyes, and his mouth tightened. "I should have said you're welcome."

"Who knows what we're supposed to say to each other?"

He tilted his head back, as if he didn't want to see her or to let her see his face. "I'm glad we're working together, but I wonder why we couldn't after Keely died."

He'd said her name, finally, without stopping to think. "We loved her too much." The answer was so obvious. What he couldn't know was that she'd sensed the thwarted anger he'd tried so hard to hide from her. She'd just thought it was blame.

"How much do you love Maggie?" he asked.

She blinked. It was the last question she'd expected, but she answered honestly. "Not as much as I loved Keely yet, but I believe I'll feel that much for her, if I remember history won't repeat itself."

His eyes seemed to hollow. The pupils dilated until she saw only black. "Can you be sure?" He pitched his voice so low she had to move closer to him to hear. "How do you know you can love Maggie without losing her?"

"I have to make myself believe, or I won't be able to love her."

"Mind games." Noah crooked his finger beneath her chin. His skin felt warm and coarse and too damn familiar. His short almost-laugh lightly ruffled the hair at her temples. "When did you start playing mind games with yourself?"

"When the stakes became irresistible." She moved, not wanting him to see the pulse banging in her veins like a drum. "For Maggie's sake, I have to win."

She went back to the kitchen, where Eleanor had taken over making the baby's cereal while Maggie watched from her grandfather's arms.

"I told him again that Joanna wasn't using drugs, so we weren't about to find any evidence of it," Joe was saying.

"I don't know why he insists." Eleanor turned around, but jumped a little when she saw Tessa and Noah. "See, Tessa? You're not the only one he's determined to convict. He won't leave Joanna alone, and he can't get to her now."

"Do you know why he's so certain?" Noah asked.

A chill fingered its way down Tessa's spine. "He doesn't need a reason." She jumped in, to protect David's secret as always. "He lets his crazy ideas confuse him about reality."

"Thank you, Tessa." Eleanor beamed at her as she took Maggie's lunch to the table.

Noah didn't answer, but Tessa felt his silence. With all her might she tried not to look at him, but she couldn't help it. His speculative gaze nearly made her swear out loud. He knew something was up, and she'd confirmed his suspicions.

She turned from him, trying to breathe. All this

togetherness, his constant eye upon her—why had she ever wanted the lion's share of his attention?

Truth was, she hated lying. Even to Noah. She was starting to smother in the secret it might be foolish to keep. She wanted to tell him so they could clear it up.

She needed time to think about what to do next. She reached for the phone and punched in the number for the police station. A deputy gave his name and asked if he could help her.

"This is Tessa Gabriel. I still need to go by David Howard's house. Has the chief decided whether I can?"

"Just a minute. I'll have to ask him."

"Okay." She waited without turning around. She didn't want any of her guests to offer to go along.

After a second, the deputy came back. "The chief says one of us can meet you at Mr. Howard's house in an hour."

NOAH BIDED HIS TIME. Tessa had a secret, but she wasn't about to tell it. If the Worths knew, Joe looked like a better source. Eleanor's steel with Weldon had surprised him, and he didn't have time to wear her down.

After half an hour picking at a sandwich, Tessa pushed back her chair. "I'd better head over to David's."

"Let Joe and me go," Noah said.

She blanked her gaze, the way she'd always done before they'd had Keely, if he'd suggested she didn't have to go into her office on his one day off in a week. "You don't know what I need," she said.

"Clothes. Toys. Can't be that tough." He glanced at Joe, who also stood.

"Sounds good to me," the other man said.

Eleanor set her water glass on the table. "I'd feel better if the menfolk went. Since the police are so busy watching us, you can't know who might be there."

"Weldon's deputy, for one." Tessa was predictably hostile at the concept of letting the "menfolk" take the risks.

"Enough said." Joe jumped in. "We'll go. We both know what a baby girl needs."

Noah coughed, to cover up a jolt of pain at Joe's careless assurance. Memories of Keely came back at the worst times. She'd needed someone to make her breathe, but he'd shown up too late.

"You know the way, don't you, Joe?" This would be a good time to get to the bottom of all Weldon's drug talk.

"Sure." He leaned over to kiss first his wife, and then Maggie. "See you later."

Noah felt some remorse at Tessa's frozen gaze, but not enough to persuade himself he could extract the truth from her when she so obviously didn't want him to hear it. In the living room, he grabbed his coat and Joe's. They both put them on as they hurried out the front door. Noah put on his gloves as they walked through their own frozen breath beneath Tessa's spiny trees.

He unlocked his car and turned on the ignition while Joe went around to take the passenger's seat.

"Better let the engine warm a minute," Noah said. He didn't have much time. The drive to David's was bound to be short, and he couldn't talk to Joe in front of Weldon or his men. "I wonder if the chief will be at the house."

"Probably. He thinks we're all hiding something."

Noah made himself go slowly. He'd scare the other man off if he sounded suspicious. "You mean the drug thing with Joanna? What's that about?"

"I don't know. I guess it started because she was going so fast when she hit that tree. But they did an autopsy. If she'd been on something, they would have known. She was clean."

"You're sure?" He went for interest, not curiosity.

"I'd know, or Eleanor would have. We were her parents. We knew when she had the problem the first time."

"Did you see much of her?"

"After the baby came, she spent more time with us. We wondered if she and David were getting along. She swore they were fine and then the month before she died, she never came around at all. And after she died we saw David and the baby less."

"Why do you think that was?" What had changed Joanna? Drugs? Postpartum depression? A real problem with David?

"She seemed aloof from us, from David, though not from Maggie. She loved that little girl. I don't know what went wrong, and I have to live with not knowing every day of my life."

Joe's admission spilled out on a sheet of white-hot pain that blanketed the car. Noah rubbed at his chest. He knew exactly what the other man was going through.

He put the car in gear. "Regret doesn't let go of

you when you lose a child,'' he said. ''You'll always wonder what you could have done to save her.''

"Yeah.''

And that was it. Something had happened to Joanna. Noah had no clue what it was, and he wasn't sure Joe knew, either. Did Tessa know?

"David's place is that way.'' Joe directed him around the square where kids and their parents were building snowmen as if this were a normal day.

They passed traffic and people walking their dogs on shoveled sidewalks. They turned down a narrow neighborhood street just the other side of the tall, red-brick courthouse. Noah knew to stop when Weldon stepped out of his squad car in front of a white clap-board house.

Weldon nodded to them as they got out of the car. He led the way through David's wrought-iron gate, up the drift-covered sidewalk and onto the narrow porch. Joe produced a key.

"I have one,'' Weldon said. ''We took Howard's keys from his office.'' He opened the door and let them into the narrow entryway.

Joe took a deep breath that made Noah check to see if he was all right. He was an older guy, after all.

"You know which room is Maggie's?'' Noah asked.

Joe nodded. His face tight, he climbed the narrow staircase on the left side of the hall. He went slowly, as if he didn't want to go at all.

"We'll wait down here,'' Weldon said, wielding his small-town power to keep Noah in his sight.

"I'd like to see David's room.'' Noah saw no reason to pretend he hadn't come to investigate.

"I've checked it. Completely undisturbed," the chief said.

"I'd like a look."

"Sorry."

Noah ignored him and wandered from the sparsely furnished living room to the small butler's pantry, to the kitchen. Hardly any pictures hung on the wall, though Maggie, at different stages of growth, crowded the mantel over the fireplace.

Not one photo of Joanna or David.

"Detective Gabriel."

"Hmm?"

"I'm not interested in trailing after you."

"Do you notice how neat the place is?" To keep looking, he pretended they were searching together. "You and your men didn't clean up?"

"No."

"I can't remember if David was always this compulsively tidy. Even though no one's been here in two days, I don't see one fleck of dust. Where'd he find the time?"

Or where had the killer? Noah had seen stranger things in his time than a killer whose trophy was cleaning the victim's house, as if he could take the victim's last sign of humanity with him.

Joe came back down with a stack of clothing. "Why don't you see if you can find something to put this in? I'm not sure where David kept the luggage."

"I saw cereal and fruit jars in the pantry," Noah said. "And a box of garbage liners. I'll get them."

Weldon watched as they packed. Frustrated at not seeing upstairs, Noah nevertheless went along with the chief's plan to get them out of David's house. If the guy's sense of his professional dignity meant more to him than working together to catch David's killer—well, Noah had no time to retrain him.

They drove back to Tessa's in silence. Joe seemed more upset than at any time since he'd come. Naturally, seeing his son-in-law's empty home brought back memories. His own daughter had died only seven months ago.

Noah suffered a moment's remorse over asking him along so he could question him. But he'd come to Maine to find evidence. He didn't want to hurt anyone along the way, but Tessa and Maggie were his priorities.

When they got back, Tessa had moved her car from the driveway to the garage. The trunk and the car doors stood open, and Tessa's feet, in climbing boots, protruded from the back seat.

Eleanor met them at the house's front door, holding it wide so they could carry in the stuff they'd brought back for Maggie. "Shh," she said. "Baby's asleep."

Noah set his armload on the sofa and straightened. "What's Tessa doing in the garage?"

"She's cleaning her car."

Great. If Weldon's deputy drove by, he'd assume she was erasing evidence.

"I'll see if I can help her."

She must have heard them drive up. She was no longer hard at work. She'd shut the trunk and the doors, and she was sitting in the driver's seat, her hands folded on the steering wheel.

He got in on the passenger side.

Tessa looked at him as if she were exhausted. He had the feeling losing David was the last pain she could endure. "What did you fish out of Joe?" she asked.

"Why is Weldon so sure Joanna was using drugs?"

Glancing his way, she held her tongue. Not Tessa-like behavior, but he saw the pain she was trying to hide. He had to get to the bottom of it.

He offered the comforting smile he knew he'd withheld when she'd needed it most, when they'd lost their own baby. He hadn't known how to comfort her then. He'd been the one who'd left Keely alone too long. Tessa's profound, unwavering sorrow had made him feel more guilty for failing their daughter, for failing his family.

Dealing with grief had never been his best skill. After his father's death, he'd promised any power that might listen that if no one else he loved died, he'd grow up and catch all the killers he could find. That promise had dictated every decision he'd made since.

In return, he'd won Tessa for his wife, and together, they'd created Keely.

But after Keely—passed away, his old agony had reared up. Every glance at Tessa had reminded him their innocent, beloved baby had died while he wasn't looking. And that had to be his fault.

Instead of telling her he was afraid he'd lose her, too—simply because he'd loved her—he'd protected her with indifference. This was his chance to make it up to Tessa even if he had to force her to be honest with him.

"What did the coroner say after Joanna's accident? Was she using drugs again?"

She turned to him. Her scent, spice and cleanliness, taunted him with flashes of memory—her gaze, dark in early morning light, her arms stretched above her head as she'd welcomed him with a love-filled smile, her breasts firm against his lips as he breathed her in.

His head hit the back of the seat. He could hardly hear when she finally spoke.

"I don't know where Joanna was going, but she slid on a road during a thunderstorm and hit a telephone pole. They found no drugs."

Damn. He recognized her bland, careful tone. He closed his eyes. She knew more than she was saying. "Weldon suspects she was using. He doubts his own coroner?"

"Weldon's new. He ran in a special election when the previous police chief resigned after Joanna's death."

"The last chief resigned because of the way he investigated Joanna's accident?"

"No." Now she sounded too certain. "At least he didn't drop by and tell me so. He took a job up near Presque Isle."

So Weldon's suspicions might have arisen out of some odd professional jealousy. Weldon had his share. But what would he gain? His predecessor had already gone or he wouldn't have gotten the job.

Tessa had turned to stare out the water-streaked window.

"What do you think about Joanna?" he asked. "Was she using again?"

She didn't move for a moment. Then she seemed to make a decision, turning to him, her eyes as hard as the ice on her driveway. "I know her daughter and her husband were lost without her. I know her parents miss her the way I still long for Keely. I know you're following the wrong thread, and don't you dare interrogate me again."

He held her gaze with sheer willpower. She was too angry. A twinge of dread tightened his gut. She was lying to him. She'd always been the worst liar he'd ever known.

Once, he'd come home early from work, and they'd ended up in bed and stayed too late to go to a dinner party. On the phone to their hosts, she'd spun a yarn fit for the bestseller lists. But she always realized just too late that she was bound to step all over herself when she forgot the twists in her tale. Invariably she got this look of dread in her eyes when she lied. The rage was something new in her repertoire, but this lie was important to her.

She'd been his wife, and he'd never doubted her word about anything, but this was different. He already knew she was lying, and deep inside she already knew he'd guessed. She couldn't hide the truth from him.

"I'll find out for myself." And the answer would probably explain why Tessa was trying to hide it. She turned to get out of the car, but he caught her gloved hand. "Give me something, Tessa." She'd become someone new, a woman he didn't always know. "For old times' sake,'' he said, certain their old times meant nothing to her.

"Sloma." The name slipped between her gritted teeth. "Hank Sloma."

CHAPTER SEVEN

TESSA AVOIDED HIM the rest of the day, and that was all right with Noah. She'd given him plenty to think about with her half stories about Joanna.

He patched the broken window and then decided to change the locks and the alarm system code. Afterward, he called Baxton to check on Della Eddings, whose husband was still missing but no doubt hovering somewhere near her, out of sight.

Then he'd asked Baxton to look up Hank Sloma. The only information he'd discovered had been the misdemeanor possession charge David had defended him on. What would have made Sloma switch to capital murder?

As if they felt the undercurrents that flowed between Noah and Tessa, Joe and Eleanor wandered the house like ghosts. Maggie made the only noise, and she remained cheerful despite the tension. Occasionally she asked for her "Da," and the silence deepened for a short time, but they'd all grown adept at diverting her attention.

After dinner that night, Tessa started toward her room with Maggie, to bathe the baby and get her ready for bed. Noah followed her to the foot of the stairs. She turned on him, still reluctant to talk. He had to insist.

"I found Hank Sloma's misdemeanor charge, but that's all. Maybe you should tell me what else you think he might have done."

She flicked a glance toward the kitchen where Joe and Eleanor seemed most comfortable whiling away their time. "I just wondered about him, because of Weldon."

He hated to treat his ex-wife like a suspect, but he didn't believe her.

He nodded at Maggie. "Go ahead with her, and I'll wait for you. We need to go over your notes again, so we can arrange to talk to your clients tomorrow."

Tessa nodded, and Maggie eyed him with interest, gnawing on her fist. She opened her mouth. "Duh?" came out, the sound drowning in a puddle of drool.

Despite himself, Noah smiled. He tucked his hand under her chin, unintentionally catching the rest of her saliva.

With a mother's instinct, Tessa lifted the hem of her already spit-soaked sweatshirt and briskly dried his fingers and his palm. "Sorry about that."

Trying not to dwell on the glimpse of flat abdomen that opened a hole in his innocent intentions, he slipped his fingers into his jeans pocket. Her apology separated him from the growing familiarity between her and Maggie. He should have been happy, but he felt left out.

He stared from Tessa to Maggie, feeling their warmth, breathing the scent of baby and his wife. Temptation and loneliness put a crazy offer on the tip of his tongue. What if he could do it right this time? Could he be the kind of man Tessa might need? Could he convince himself he'd be able to keep Maggie safe?

Some promises were beyond his ability to keep. He stepped back, almost staggering out of his ex-wife's reach.

Tessa didn't even notice. "I think she must be teething." Tessa turned her back on him, her focus on the child. Maggie watched him steadily as Tessa climbed. "I'll come back down after she's asleep."

Tessa didn't wait for him to answer, but Maggie's gaze accused him of turning down a play date. He didn't move until Tessa closed her lacquered door. And then he sucked in the breath he hadn't taken as he'd watched her leave.

The moment he turned, the Worths emerged from the kitchen, their sudden appearance startling him. He must be losing his grip.

"What's wrong?" Joe glanced up the stairs. "You look as if you've had bad news. Did you talk to Weldon again?"

Bad news? He'd discovered he was a coward. Noah shook his head. "Just deciding what to do next." He pulled himself together. "Tessa's bathing Maggie."

"Wonder if she'd like company, Joe. Let's ask her."

Noah got out of their way.

"We'll just say good-night to the baby," Eleanor said. "And then I think we'll have an early night, too. It's been a long day."

On their way upstairs, Joe peered over his shoulder, distracted, his mind already on his granddaughter. "Good night, son."

Only his mother had called him son for nearly three

decades. It didn't feel right coming from Joe. He swallowed as the other man tapped on Tessa's door and then entered before she spoke.

Noah sank onto the couch, covering his eyes to ease the burning sensation he felt. Voices wafted through the house. He couldn't discern actual words, but he recognized the sound of increasing warmth and trust, especially between Eleanor and Tessa.

One deep concern bound the women to each other. Maggie. And Maggie had given Tessa courage that made him see how badly he'd failed his wife. Broken and guilty, he hadn't possessed enough strength for himself, much less an extra portion to offer Tessa when she'd needed it.

He forced himself to his feet. He was still a man, and he was trying not to be a coward about his feelings toward Tessa. He couldn't do more.

He hit the power switch on her computer and listened to the machine whirring to life, rather than the voices of the family group upstairs.

No good detective ever involved himself with witnesses or suspects. Tessa and Maggie had involved him, but it wasn't too late to keep his eye on the job.

He listed his tasks. Stop letting Tessa and Maggie distract him. Figure out how to manage the tenderness they engendered in him. Find the animal who'd killed David.

He pushed another chair close to the computer desk. No matter where she sat when she came back, he intended to see the files close up. Opening her word-processing program, he also opened the file she'd last used, on her clients. He sat in the desk chair and left the second one for her.

But she didn't come right away, and his eyes felt as if they were about to spring out of his head. He braced his elbows on the desk and lowered his face, resting his fingertips against the pressure points that ached most on his face.

At last, the Worths left Tessa's room. He didn't have to wait long. She opened her door, but when he looked up, she pressed a finger to her lips.

Gripping the baby monitor in one hand, she came down the stairs. Fierce concentration scarred her face with a frown. She avoided the desk, except to set the monitor down before she wandered the room, gathering a toy, a half-full bottle, her own buff-colored leather gloves.

She looked at him again as she scooped her purse off the sofa and tucked the gloves inside. "I always lose these," she said.

He'd once suggested they allow for glove-hunting time before they went anywhere together.

She tugged at the white turtleneck that hugged her slender throat. Instantly he could taste her, feel the soft texture of her skin against his lips, as if he'd kissed her mere seconds ago.

He swallowed a groan. She no longer trusted or wanted him, but her disinterest only fired his need for her.

With a lightning glance from her green eyes, she dropped one of Maggie's blankets on the end of the sofa and straightened. At last, she came toward him. His breath escaped his body on a gasp, and his legs straightened in front of him.

Reaching the desk, she lifted her hands behind her head and twisted her dark blond hair into a knot at the nape of her neck. Her long fingers made even the simplest action an exhibition of graceful movement.

How many nights had he held her hands to the moonlight as they'd lain in bed? Tessa's sure, sensual fingers had seemed to hold the key to every question he would ever think to ask.

She'd accepted his drive to be the best at his job. She'd loved him despite his occasional distraction. Until Keely had died.

Time had deepened the distance between them until there'd been no "them." Only divorce papers and Tessa's resolve to move to Maine and forget he and Keely had existed.

As she held her hair up with one hand and used the other to rummage through her things on the desk, he asked himself if he should have fought harder, if she would have listened if he'd insisted she stay in Boston and they try to work out their problems.

She stopped searching through the papers as if she felt him watching her. He looked down, but the lushness of her full breasts seduced him. He meant to look away, but her sweater hugged the indentation of her waist and so did his gaze. His palms remembered her hips, their gentle curves a constant source of frustration to her and her mother. He folded his eager hands across his stomach to stop himself from pulling her onto his lap.

Her legs, in faded jeans, conjured an image of the pale brown birthmark just above the bend of her knee, the small, leaf-shaped stain he'd kissed again and again until she'd sworn she couldn't bear the stroke of his tongue.

"What's the matter with you?" she asked.

Drowning in a rush of need, he licked his dry lips, but her taste was in his mouth and he couldn't speak.

"Excuse me," she said. "If you aren't going to move so I can reach, will you hand me that pen next to the phone?"

God, he needed a drink. He needed anything that would stop him from wanting her. He didn't have to take her hand, but he cupped her fingers and pressed the pen into her palm.

Her suspicious gaze cooled him a degree or two. She twisted out of his grasp and wove the pen through the layers of her hair to hold it in place.

"Nice 'do." He tried to tease her, to prove he could subsist on the detached relationship that came a hell of a lot easier to her.

But his voice gave him away, and she zeroed in on the need he couldn't hide.

She smiled, and the corner of her mouth trembled. "I'm hardly likely to care if I impress you, am I?"

Avoiding her eyes again, he noticed the smudge of baby carrots on her cheek and the formula stain on her sweater. He also saw the flutter of her heart beneath the thin knit material. None of Maggie's mess stopped him from needing Tessa.

But say she could still care, say he made her admit she could want him the way he wanted her tonight. What came next?

Who the hell knew?

Wrong answer.

Work was the right answer. He turned to her computer screen.

"Let's start a new file." He fought a nervous urge

to clear his throat. "We'll edit in the facts you can show Weldon without betraying confidentiality."

Turning his mind to the job at hand, he tried to ignore an unrelenting ache that started in his scalp and radiated through his body. It might be migraine. It might be loss, pure and simple. He didn't look closely enough to find out.

He still missed Tessa—his wife. In this house that was new to him, neither his nor hers in his mind, he'd forgotten he wasn't supposed to notice her as a woman.

"Let's start with Carlson again. As the head of a company, he'll be the busiest. I think we should see him first tomorrow."

"Then you don't remember how lobstermen work. Mr. Swyndle will be doing something on his boat before you're conscious in the morning." Her smile took the sting out of her comment. It made her seem approachable.

If she were a suspect, this would be the moment he took advantage of her weakness. He'd pry the truth about Joanna out of her before she knew he'd closed in.

He turned his chair toward the computer, the squeak emphasizing his foolish decision. He couldn't help thinking like a cop, but damned if he always had to act on it.

SEVERAL HOURS and a defined plan later, Noah tossed Tessa a distracted good-night as he went in search of more aspirin. Yawning, she climbed the stairs and slipped into her room. She eased across the floor to check on healthy, sleeping Maggie. Tessa tucked a blanket around the baby.

What a day. She'd started out lying to Noah about Joanna, or at least coloring the truth pretty hard. How long till he investigated the police chief who was hiding in his family's Presque Isle summer camp while he waited for Weldon to uncover the whole truth about Joanna's investigation? The former chief had allowed her cremation to go forward without proper toxicology results, and Tessa doubted David had paid him enough to make the crime worthwhile.

She wondered why Noah hadn't pressed her for the truth that morning. He wanted her help with her clients, and maybe he was more vulnerable to her than she'd ever understood. He cared, and he wasn't that good at hiding his feelings.

Fortunately, his own need seemed to upset him so much he hadn't discerned hers. Tonight she'd hovered at his side, dictating and editing what he'd written, and somehow she'd kept herself from stroking the hard curve of his shoulder. She'd barely managed not to bury her face in his hair. If he hadn't been so determined to avoid looking at her, she might have begged him to touch her.

Which would have been her most foolish mistake yet. For herself and for Maggie. Though she'd left Noah a year ago, she'd always wished she could have stayed. She'd forced herself to go, working on autopilot as she'd packed her things and started the divorce.

Back then, he hadn't wanted her.

He'd already wrapped himself in the life he'd made before he'd known her. She'd still lived in his house, slept in his bed, tried with all her might to remind him she was his wife. Until she'd finally taken the hint. Without Keely, he hadn't wanted a wife.

Shut firmly out, she'd made a life of her own, away from Noah and away from her parents, who'd told her freely they'd expected the divorce. Noah had measured up to their original expectations, no matter what her mother said now.

Tessa had learned to value herself, and she didn't intend to give up her hard-fought confidence. Not even for passion that had shimmered like an unsubstantiated promise between Noah and her all night.

She tiptoed to the navy-tiled bathroom to brush her teeth. At a first glimpse of her flushed cheeks in the mirror she groaned in humiliation.

Big surprise. No matter how bad he'd be for her, she still wanted the only man she'd ever loved. Her body responded, though she refused to waste more time on a man whose job had been her rival.

Her enemy had bested her. Why fight when she'd long since posted the flag of surrender?

She rinsed her mouth and patted her face dry with the yellow towel that had warmed all evening on a heated rail. She'd learned to enjoy other physical comforts. Only a fool would fight to keep Noah in her life.

Tessa hung the towel back where it belonged, carefully straightening the corners. She changed into the flannel pajamas that had seemed to materialize with her divorce papers. She checked on Maggie again and then restlessly switched off the lamp and opened the curtain to peer outside.

Snow covered every surface. Ice glittered on the

roof next door. None of it was cold enough to chill her thoughts.

Frustrated with her own weakness, she pulled back the bedclothes and clambered between sheets where the cold finally reached her. Shivering, she congratulated herself on making the right decision tonight. Life with Noah was a dance whose steps she was safer forgetting.

IN THE MORNING Tessa asked Eleanor to look after Maggie while she and Noah talked to her clients. Following behind her, Noah cautioned the Worths against venturing too far from the safety of the house.

Tessa nearly gave in to second thoughts. Leaving Maggie, even with Eleanor and Joe, felt risky, but it was the only way to check out the guys on her list.

While Noah warmed the car, Tessa gave her cell phone number to Eleanor who was getting breakfast for the baby. As Maggie gnawed contentedly on her fat spoon, Tessa hugged her again, until the baby whacked her on the head. Laughing as she rubbed her forehead where the spoon had thudded, Tessa kissed Maggie goodbye and then backed out of the room, all but positive she was inviting disaster.

Opening the front door, she battled frigid wind. Sunlight, too bright to stand, reflected off the ice and snow. She shaded her eyes. Steps and the short, sloping lawn separated her from Noah, who looked frozen in his ineffective bomber jacket. Beyond him, her neighborhood stretched—salt-splashed cars and morning papers, and children, wrapped up like small, colorful snowmen on their way to school.

Noah hunched his shoulders as he scraped snow

off his car. Wind kicked more snow across her yard, whipping Noah's hair and snatching her breath away.

At her short gasp, Noah turned. With one hand jammed in his pocket, he clutched something small and square between the black leather fingers of his glove. He barely nodded her way.

"What are you doing?" She crunched across the icy grass.

"I lost my scraper." He pulled his other hand, bare, out of his pocket to brush ice off the credit card he'd used to clear narrow lines on the windshield.

"Where's your glove?"

He looked up, his gaze testy yet self-mocking. "I guess I lose mine, too."

Tessa bit her lip, but the cold ached in her teeth. Noah hadn't forgotten or lost a single object since she'd met him. A memory like a movie that played in his head had been one of his major weapons against the bad guys.

She spun toward her car, digging keys out of her purse. Breathing hard, she opened the back door and found her scraper. By the time she took it back, Noah's car heater had softened the ice on his windshield. He reached for the hard yellow plastic in her hand, his body heat crowding her toward the car's hood.

"I'll do it," he said.

"I can. My hands are warm."

He didn't argue, but he didn't move, either. He lifted his hand to blow warmth on his reddened fingers. Tessa liked the way he held his mouth. Mesmerized, she almost felt the heat of his breath. She passed him her scraper.

"Was Maggie upset when you left her?" he asked.

"No, why?"

"Saying goodbye took longer than usual."

He hadn't been with them long enough to know "usual," but the past few days had begun to seem like the only past she could remember. Before was growing hazy.

"I'm a little afraid to leave her."

"But she's all right with Eleanor and Joe?"

She frowned. Beating around the bush wasn't like him. "You can see Maggie loves them."

"Did they have a problem with David?"

"No. They were his parents, too."

"But he saw less of them without Joanna?"

"How did you know that?"

"Joe told me yesterday on the way to David's house. Did David tell you why?"

"I assumed he had a hard time being around them because they reminded him of Joanna."

He looked doubtful. "Is that why he kept no pictures of her?"

"What are you talking about? She was in a lot of his pictures last time I was at his place."

"I didn't see one yesterday," he said. "We found photos of Maggie on the mantel, but not one sign of Joanna."

She lifted an eyebrow. "He was still trying to get over her, and you know grief comes back in waves. You don't have any photos of your dad, and he died when you were ten. Maybe it was the same for David, and he suddenly couldn't stand to look at her picture."

Noah grunted. He might agree, or he might think

she was crazy. She couldn't tell. He opened the passenger door, and heat blew into both their faces.

"What kind of a murderer would steal family pictures?" she asked.

"That's what I'm asking myself. Weldon wouldn't let me look upstairs, so you might be right. I didn't get a chance to see if David just put them away."

"Joe must have gone upstairs."

"He was so upset I couldn't make myself ask him. I'll have to if we can't get back in. Why don't you call Carlson?" he said.

She was dialing as he slid behind the steering wheel.

"You know his number by heart?"

She pointed left as he backed into the street. "I had to mediate every day for over a year." She pointed at the first right corner, sheltered in the bare limbs of an overgrown oak. "Turn there."

The phone rang in her ear. Carlson's secretary breezily wished her a good morning.

"Lynn, it's Tessa Gabriel. Is Hugh available?"

"Morning, Tessa, I believe I can fit you in one day next week. When would be good for you?"

This dance she knew well. "Today would be perfect, Lynn."

"You know Mr. Carlson can't see you on such short notice."

Oh, yes, he would. "I should have called yesterday for an appointment, but with David's death, I've been a little distracted."

"I'm so sorry about David. Mr. Carlson had me make a donation on his behalf. You should see the card in a few days.'' She hesitated a second. ''If they let you back in your office.''

Why would Hugh Carlson donate anything to anyone in David's name? The huge spray of flowers he'd sent had towered over her at the memorial. His scrawled name had screamed off the card. That was Hugh. He'd done the right thing, but he wanted to make sure everyone knew it.

''Lynn, why don't you go in and tell him I'm on my way with my ex-husband. Hugh's heard of Noah.''

''The homicide cop?''

''You've heard of him, too.'' Tessa was surprised. She'd never talked about that part of her life.

''Small-town chatter,'' Lynn said.

''If you get up and walk into Hugh's office, he'll yell and then get over it by the time we arrive.'' She pointed out the next turn.

The other woman hesitated. ''All right,'' she finally said. ''But I'd better put you on hold. I don't want you to hear him shouting at me.''

Not for the first time, Tessa wondered if Hugh thought the ranting between him and his secretary impressed their visitors with his power. ''Thanks.'' She turned to Noah. ''She put me on hold, but she'll make him see us.''

''Make him?''

''She nudges him into doing what's right for the company, and he's smart enough to respect her judgment.''

''This isn't company business.''

''Close enough. If he killed David, it'll reflect on the company.''

"You're trying to say she thinks he's innocent, even though a homicide detective wants to talk to him."

"Right."

"Since she doesn't suspect him, you don't, either?"

Tessa examined his tone for signs of contempt toward the untrained. She found none. "Lynn probably sees more of Hugh Carlson than his own wife does."

"You said she likes him. She wouldn't suspect someone she likes of doing what the killer did to David."

"Just like me?" she said.

He nodded.

"But we're smart enough to be afraid when someone acts like a killer. Maybe it's not in Hugh." She couldn't think like a murderer, and she didn't want to think like a detective. "Are you expecting him to confess when we tell him we want to take my case notes to Weldon?"

"I just want to see his reaction."

"Turn here." She pointed to the road that fronted Carlson's factory. The car rocked as Noah made the turn.

A thick forest of evergreens crowded them on the other side of the car. For the first time since she'd moved to Prodigal, the dark green woods seemed to threaten. She faced the brick-and-glass structure she knew as well as she knew her own home.

Noah slowed as they neared the gate. "This is a game," he said. "Don't tell a possible suspect I'm coming with you. You don't want to put the killer on his guard."

It didn't seem real. "You honestly think one of these guys is the killer?"

"I'm willing to give them all an even break." He grinned at her, and she wondered who he was.

What kind of man could enjoy the hunt so much? They'd lost a good friend, and she'd never seen him more vulnerable than he'd been the past few days. She'd also never seen him more ruthless. "Noah, we lived with each other for five years but you're a stranger. I don't know you."

"Keely's death changed us." His grin slashed to a straight, tense line. "Losing her pared us down to the basics." He pulled into the back of the line of cars waiting to get into the factory. "Why the security?"

"Hugh convinced himself someone started the fire in the other building." She turned to face the windshield and the pale blue, rust-encrusted car in front of them. "What happened between last night and this morning, Noah? Why are you different today?"

"Do you want the truth?"

The fact that he asked scared her, but he went on.

"I had a lot of time to think after you went to bed. I almost asked you to stay with me. For the wrong reasons. You know I wanted you."

She didn't dare answer. She didn't know what to say, now that she had Maggie to think of.

"I think it's something about Maggie." He glanced at her, and she felt the movement of his head, the touch of his gaze as if he'd brushed her face with the fingers he wrapped around the steering wheel. "About you and Maggie together," he said. "I see what I lost, and I'm sorry we threw away what we had left."

What they'd had left was each other. She felt as if she were falling. Eighteen months after they should have talked, she didn't know what to say. Fortunately, their turn at the gate came next. The security guard leaned into Noah's window.

"Ms. Gabriel," he said, "Mr. Carlson asked me to have you call him before you went up."

She glanced at Noah, and hit redial on her cell phone. Carlson answered, instead of Lynn. "Hugh, this is Tessa Gabriel. As Lynn mentioned to you, my—Noah and I would like to speak with you this morning."

"I'm a busy, man, Tessa. I can't make time to talk to you today. And I really don't know what I could tell you. I assume this is about David?"

"About your files," Tessa said. "I'd like to discuss how much of your information you'd be willing to share with the police."

"The police? What are you talking about?" His voice rose.

"We'll be up in about ten minutes. I'd be glad to buy Noah a cup of coffee in the cafeteria if you need to prepare for us." Suddenly she was as curious as Noah about what Hugh Carlson might have to hide.

"Just come straight up, but I'd like to know when you're going to stop pushing me around, Tessa."

"This should be the last time." She hung up and glanced at Noah, startled to find him smiling.

"Good work," he said.

"I'm in control with this stuff. It's my job." But she liked the pride in his voice. She'd never been sure he knew she was a capable lawyer.

"You weren't so willing to manipulate before."

Her pleasure faded. He glanced at her as he turned down a lane, looked for a parking spot. Suddenly he moved, and his big hand on her thigh spread warmth up and down her leg.

"I meant it as a compliment," he said.

She fought an urge to wriggle away from his splayed fingers. Being manipulative didn't sound so good to her. "You never saw me at work before," she said.

He pulled away, obviously looking backward over their five years together. "Is that true? I saw your office."

"From the doorway. But you never asked me about work, and you didn't come to court for any of my cases." She twisted her neck, tense, and pretty sure they should be talking about Hugh Carlson, not each other. "Not that I asked about your job that often."

He turned the car into a space. "You think we lived with each other for five years in total silence."

"I don't remember what we talked about before Keely died. After, we didn't say anything."

His eyes looked empty as he glanced from her to the building. "We should go in."

"As soon as Keely comes up you don't want to talk."

"It's the worst possible time." He turned his vacant gaze away from her. "We're trying to catch a killer."

She opened her mouth and licked her lower lip, holding back with frustration. But she'd thought the same thing. She opened her door and yet couldn't stop herself from trying again. "I know it's the wrong time, but I want to find a way to seal off the past and turn to the future.''

"Seal it off? It's part of who we are.''

"The best part?'' she asked. "Of either one of us?''

"Maybe not, but I don't want to forget.''

Suddenly she was hot in the numbing cold. She'd been angry with him for eighteen months because he'd hidden in his job to keep from remembering. But if he didn't want to forget even those horrible days after they'd lost Keely, he was braver than she knew how to be.

CHAPTER EIGHT

TIGHT-LIPPED, Noah followed Tessa into Carlson's antiseptically neat brick-and-glass building. A tall, middle-aged woman met them at the revolving glass doors. Tessa introduced her as Lynn. She shook hands with Noah and then took them to Hugh Carlson's private elevator.

Silence accompanied the whirring machinery that hauled them up the four floors to Carlson's suite. Lynn showed them into Carlson's wide-open office, where the florid man offered them plush chairs.

Noah walked where he was told, sat where Carlson suggested, but in his mind he kept straying back to what he and Tessa had said to each other in the car.

He made himself listen as she once more explained she wanted to pass her case notes to Weldon. The other man folded his hands on top of the polished cherry desk, his posture claiming ownership.

"First," he said, clearly delivering a rehearsed speech, "you and David cost me a fortune forcing me to follow every code any legislator in the state of Maine ever dreamed up. Oh, I know you and David meant well. Your firm made sure I got a good factory out of the deal, but now you think I was so pissed off, I—what?—had him killed?"

The mockery in his tone was a bogus effort to make

the suggestion sound ludicrous. He was belligerent, and he'd thought out his arguments, but he didn't look guilty.

Nevertheless, his word choice interested Noah. No one had suggested he might have "had" David killed. Noah hadn't even considered a hired killer, because David's death had been so savage, as if someone had paid off a long-held vendetta.

But Carlson was a big wheel in this part of the state, and he might know where to find a killer who performed custom hits.

"Don't eyeball me like that, Detective."

The man's booming voice probably intimidated some people, but Noah had heard and disproved better stories. "What made you think of hired killers, sir?"

Carlson froze, his brain clearly working overtime behind watchful eyes. Finally he leaned back, with studied indolence. His chair screamed in protest, and he grinned at the sound, slapping both hands to his voluminous belly. "I wouldn't look so good chasing a guy around with a big knife."

Tessa's arm jerked, as if she couldn't stop herself from reacting. Noah covered her hand with his.

"Sorry, Tessa." Hugh Carlson turned a remorseful look her way.

"What made you think of a knife, sir?" Weldon hadn't released that information.

"People talk in this town. What else are we going to do in all this snow?" Carlson tilted his head in a gesture that could have been a nod or a challenge. "What kind of weapon was it?"

Noah studied the man's face. Not a drop of sweat

shone anywhere on his shiny, pink flesh. His smile seemed natural. His voice remained steady. Carlson wasn't afraid of betraying himself.

But was he arrogant? Or innocent?

"Chief Weldon hasn't told either of us what the weapon was." Tessa didn't mention she'd seen the long butcher knife. She passed Carlson the notes she'd taken from his case file. "Take a look at this. I'm planning to fill Chief Weldon in on the clients we had problems with." She glanced at Noah as if she was looking for his agreement. "We think he's having a hard time focusing on the real killer, so I'd like to clear up his suspicions."

"You're suggesting I'm the killer." Carlson set the papers on his desk, carefully stacking the two sheets.

She leaned forward and plunged in. "I don't think you're guilty, and frankly, Weldon seems to consider me his favorite suspect."

Surprise dented Carlson's armor. "You were David's best friend."

"If I clear myself, and anyone who had a beef with David, maybe he'll start looking in the right direction."

"I spoke to him before you arrived." Carlson rose from his chair and planted himself in front of the floor-to-ceiling window. "I called him after you called, and he says I don't have to tell you anything."

Noah waited for Tessa, but when she straightened, swiping at the hair that fell across her forehead, he took over. "We aren't questioning you. Tessa's given you a list of the facts she wants to pass on to Weldon so you can tell her where you disagree. If you ask her not to explain the differences you had with her firm on this job, Weldon may think you're trying to hide something more incriminating. And you'll have tied Tessa's hands—she won't be able to explain the situation to him."

Carlson frowned. "Don't think you can scare me into some sort of admission."

Most innocent guys didn't think in terms of admissions. "I'm making certain you understand."

Carlson glanced at Tessa. "You know David and I disagreed, and I got plenty angry with him."

"But threatening to get us disbarred isn't the same as killing him. I know."

"And I was at the service when your house got shot up."

"If you hired a killer, you might have hired him again to fire at the house." Noah pushed the papers at the other man's clenched fist. "Take a look at these notes, and then tell Tessa if she needs to add or delete anything."

The heat came on while they waited for Carlson to decide. Against its soft whisper, he opened his fists and pulled the papers toward himself. "I'll look at them. You two want to wait outside?"

"I think we'll wait here." Tessa's wry tone surprised Noah. "We should discuss anything you want me to take out, and if you get rid of us, you won't let us back in. You'll just shove the pages at me through Lynn."

The other man's mouth curved in a smile. "You're right." He opened his desk drawer and took out a pair of rimless reading glasses, which he settled on his nose. "But I wonder if you're going to get someone in trouble." He peered over the glasses. "You're looking at other clients, as well, aren't you?"

"You were our first stop," Tessa said.

"And I'll bet I can guess who's behind lucky door number two and number three, but don't tell me. I'll look forward to the surprise when we all decide to fire you at the same time."

"Your prerogative," Tessa said, as if she didn't care.

Noah gazed at her. Her business had to provide for Maggie now. His ex-wife had turned into an actress, and she put on a good show.

Carlson read swiftly. While they waited, Tessa walked to the window, turning her back on both of them. Noah resisted a physical compulsion to follow her.

"This, Tessa." Carlson pointed with the nib of his pen. She came back to lean over his shoulder. Noah looked away from her, disturbed by the dark hollow between her breasts thrusting against her pale blue sweater. "Where you talk about the survey," Carlson said. "I don't know why you have to go into my argument with David over who we should hire. It's not code, and I wouldn't be human if I didn't want someone I knew and trusted to do the survey."

"True, but David thought we should get three surveyors, and you only wanted the one who'd most likely do the work in your favor. He didn't want you to look as if you'd bribed your way into this building if your neighbors tried to take you to court."

"I just wanted the land everyone in this town has accepted as belonging to my family for three generations."

Tessa hypnotized Noah with her concentration. She nodded as if she'd heard Carlson's claim before. "If you notice, I went on to say we'd all reached an amicable compromise."

"But not before you made me seem petty."

"Write what you want me to say, and I'll say it." Her impatience peeked through. "I just want this to be over."

"You didn't mention the bonuses I gave you both."

As she reluctantly curved her mouth, Noah found himself smiling with her. "I didn't want to tell Weldon I'd donated it to the Children's Fund. He might think I was trying to bribe Child Protective Services."

"You don't think much of him. He's got good credentials." Carlson stood as he spoke on Weldon's behalf. "If you think he's so bad at his job, why didn't you speak up before he took over?"

"He hadn't accused me of murder then."

The other man smirked. "Accusing someone other than me doesn't make Weldon a total idiot in my book."

Their camaraderie provoked an ugly undercurrent of jealousy that was almost as unwelcome as Noah's physical response to Tessa. Carlson was her client. And maybe her friend. Noah stood, too, feeling as if he had to hold his own.

Carlson came around his desk, ushering Tessa in front of him. "Make those changes—take out the surveying argument and add the bonus, and I'm fine with what you have." He urged them both toward the office door.

Noah let himself be led again. His instincts, completely clouded now and totally unreliable, told him this man could not have killed David.

Only a lunatic would worry about exhibiting his good humor and generosity when a possible life sentence might be hanging over his head. And Carlson wasn't a lunatic. Or at least not more of one than any big fish in a small business pond like Prodigal, Maine.

Carlson herded them through his door and then pressed both hands to the frame. "Lynn, our guests are ready to leave, if you'll take them down."

"No." Tessa shook her client's hand and then waved Lynn off. "We'll be fine. I know the way, as long as the elevator isn't locked. Thank you for your time, Hugh. Thanks, Lynn."

"Anything to clear up this mess and get Prodigal back to normal." Carlson released the door frame and took his mail from a box on Lynn's desk. He began to sift through the envelopes. "Murder hurts business."

Tessa smiled as they left the office behind. "We're one task he can check off his to-do list."

She pressed the elevator's button. The doors opened, and Noah waited for her to precede him inside the small, paneled cabin. He took her hand as she would have pressed the lobby button.

"See?" she said, misunderstanding his need to have her alone. "I told you he was innocent."

"I'm not ready to clear him entirely." Tonight he'd take some time to make his own lists, of what they knew and what they were guessing. "He might have killed David if the building had come in late."

Tessa shook her head, in charge again with her job. Noah liked the attitude on her.

"Late would have been the architect's problem." She tapped her index finger against her chin. "Although Hugh would have blamed us for hiring the wrong firm."

"Tessa, don't forget what he said about someone being hired to kill David."

A hint of fear darkened her eyes, and he stroked her shoulder, sliding his hand beneath her jacket. "I'm sorry," he said. Her warmth connected with his skin through the soft sweater. "I didn't mean to scare you." He had to straighten up and quit thinking about Tessa, rather than the murder that had brought him here.

"I don't think—" She broke off. "You saw Hugh. He's no actor."

"I'm saying a lot of killers seem sane until you get a confession. Stay on your guard until Weldon investigates him. He can request copies of Carlson's phone records, even his e-mail accounts. I can't do that."

She moved away from him and punched the lobby button, staring at her own image in the reflective door. "I don't want it to be someone I know."

The elevator jerked a little and began to descend. Noah watched his ex-wife. What did she see in her fuzzy reflection? She'd always worried about her weight, but her delicious curves rendered him tongue-tied and incompetent. He turned his head, just far enough to catch her worried expression.

He looped his arm around her shoulders, keeping his hand on the rough weave of her coat this time. She neither moved nor spoke, but, with her stillness, she accepted him.

A strand of her hair brushed his cheek. He closed

his eyes. Her scent evoked memories of dark nights. She might have insisted on undressing with the lights out, but once she'd let him take her in his arms, she'd been all generosity. She'd once convinced him forever existed.

His heart began to pound. He still wanted her. He wanted her with a desperation he'd never known, but she'd made his temporary position in her life crystal clear.

Knowing where he stood with her, he should have moved away. He didn't want her to know he still cared for her, and he hated the idea of her finding out he was scared of losing her again. He couldn't let himself look weak in her eyes.

The second the doors opened, he stepped out and immediately saw Weldon and his youngest deputy waiting outside the revolving doors.

"What now?" Tessa asked.

In thick navy nylon coats and their regulation caps, wreathed in the steam of their own breath, the men pushed away from the marble wall that surrounded the building.

"Wait." Noah reached for Tessa's hand.

"Something's on his mind. Could he be planning to arrest me?"

"For what? You're innocent," he reminded her. "Look at the envelope in his hand. I'd say he wants to show you something." Still he held her back. "We can call your lawyer."

She parted from him again. "I don't care what he's found. I've done nothing, so he can't incriminate me." She pushed through the doors, her head high.

Weldon was already opening the envelope when he nodded a greeting at Noah.

"Why are you waiting out here?" Tessa asked.

"We didn't want people to think we'd come to arrest Hugh Carlson."

"But you don't mind pinning me down in the doorway?"

"What choice do I have, if you two are trying to do my job? When you decided to talk to Hugh Carlson, you fired up the gossip mill."

Noah silently cursed himself. Weldon was right. If Carlson turned out to be innocent, he'd owe the man an apology for making it look as if they'd interrogated him.

"Chief, we're getting nowhere with all the games. Why don't you listen to us for a change, and we'll try not to step on your toes." He glanced at Tessa for confirmation, and she shrugged.

"Anything to make you see I'm your least likely suspect, Chief Weldon."

The policeman looked doubtful, his deputy, even more so.

"If you're innocent, why didn't you cooperate from the start?"

"You didn't want cooperation. You wanted me to confess, just because I found him and we disagreed at work occasionally."

"And carrying on your own investigation?" the chief said.

"We aren't," Noah cut in. "You heard about Tessa's problems with a few of her clients. When you didn't look at them, I asked her to give me some information on the ones who'd been dissatisfied."

"I had to get their permission to share my files with you," Tessa said.

Weldon braced his free hand on his holstered gun while he weighed their explanation. Finally he finished pulling a photo from the envelope. "I came to ask Tessa if she's seen this man." He turned the picture her way. "Have you?"

Noah peered over her shoulder at the grainy likeness of a male in classic burglar's attire—black slacks, sweater and knitted cap. Wraparound sunglasses hid half his face. It would have been laughable if not for the long knife he was already brandishing as a weapon.

"That's our office." Tessa spoke low in her throat, in a voice he hardly recognized. "He's standing outside David's door."

"We got it off the security camera. I've been passing it around your building, but no one recognized him."

"Are you sure it's a man?" she asked.

Weldon took a closer look at the photo. "You think it's a woman?"

"No." She shook her head, miserably pushing the picture against the policeman's chest. "I don't know who it is, and I don't want to look at it."

"Once more." Weldon held it up and waited until she complied. "Do you know him?"

"I don't think so." She shook her head. Noah moved closer, but he stopped when she stiffened. "There's something..." She looked up. "I don't think so. I mean he's a tall, rangy guy. He looks like a lot of men I know."

"I have to ask you." For the first time, Weldon seemed reluctant. "You didn't hire him?"

Rage flashed in Tessa's eyes, but she kept to their truce. "I loved David."

Noah slid his arm around her waist, and she leaned against him. Pride tightened his arm around her. They must be getting somewhere if he'd offered the right comfort at the right time.

Weldon showed him the picture. "I don't expect you know him?"

"No." But he studied the man's clothing, looking for labels or anything else that stood out, something they could check further.

The police chief plucked off his sunglasses and rubbed his eye with his thumb. "The thing is, we had a report of this guy driving down your street yesterday, Ms. Gabriel. One of your neighbors thought he looked suspicious and phoned minutes before Mr. Worth called us."

Tessa's indrawn breath hissed. Noah stroked her arm. "It's okay," he said, but then he turned to Weldon. "Obviously, you need to find the money to station someone outside her house."

"My budget won't allow it." Weldon's temper kinked a little. "You have no idea what it's like to run a department in a town this small."

"I know we need to keep Maggie and Tessa safe."

At the mention of the baby's name, Tessa grabbed Noah's sleeve and turned toward the parking lot. "We should get back to her."

"Wait." Weldon unzipped his jacket and pulled a sheet of paper out of the inside pocket. "This is a copy of a warrant to search Eric Sanders's house. My other deputies are already started, and I don't want to meet up with the two of you there. You can leave Ned Swyndle alone, too. I already established his alibi.''

Tessa stumbled, and Noah caught her elbow. "A warrant?" she said.

"I have been doing my job." Weldon's sarcasm simply wasted time. Apparently, he thought so, too. He went on. "You both seem to forget how much gossip goes around this town. I knew about your clients, Tessa, and Eric harassed you. I had probable cause, and I would have taken action sooner if you'd come to me."

"Why didn't you look at him first," Tessa asked, "instead of concentrating on me?"

"Because his problem's with you, not David." Weldon tucked the paper away again. "If David had found you instead of the other way around, Eric would have been my first suspect."

Noah didn't want Tessa thinking about that. "Did you show the photo to the Worths yet?"

Weldon nodded, and Tessa stared at the other man. "You didn't," she said. "You've probably scared them half out of their wits."

The policeman shook his head. "I don't think so. They didn't recognize him, so I left. I would have gone on to Sanders's house, but I had to chase you down."

Tessa burned him with an angry gaze. "Eleanor can't keep a single secret from Maggie. She's like an emotion conductor, and I don't want her to scare the baby."

Noah held her long enough to ask Weldon one

more question. "You're forwarding that photo to other jurisdictions?"

"From here, north to Canada, and south to Virginia. We'll find him."

"Boston's the closest large city for him to get lost in," Noah said. "Although if he's been paid, he's probably already gone. I'll call and make sure they give the search an extra push."

"Thanks." Weldon tipped his hat. "Good to work with you."

Dumfounded now, Tessa was still glaring at the other policeman as Noah turned her toward the parking lot. "It's a boys' club," she said.

"Not exactly." But he could have handled the situation better from the moment he'd come to town. "Maybe a contest that wasn't working for either of us. I thought it was time for a change of tactics."

"All right." She walked at his side, but when they reached the car, she looked up at him, her eyes brighter than he remembered, her smile softer than he dared believe in.

She curved her hand around his throat, and her bare fingers set a fire beneath his skin. She pulled his head down, so she could kiss his cheek.

With the tiniest movement, he could have taken her lips beneath his. He ached for the texture of her full mouth. He longed for one taste of her, one breath filled with her heat.

Terrified he'd frighten her away with passion so furious and impatient it startled even him, he let her take the lead. His muscles ached with the strain of not reaching for her, but he accepted the tender touch of her kiss at the corner of his lips.

"Thank you for putting us all on the same side," she said.

He could have admitted Weldon had wanted to work with them or he would have made it harder. But he was still just a man. If she wanted to be grateful, he was willing to be thanked.

She kissed him again, a fraction of a frustrating inch closer to his mouth. "I know he was in the mood to cooperate, but I was so angry I wouldn't have made the effort."

She caught him by surprise, offering a glimpse of the funny, generous wife who'd turned his dreams to sleepless nights. Her husky voice raised a shiver that nearly dropped him to the sidewalk. While he ached to wrap himself around her in front of Hugh Carlson's entire complement of employees, she slid into the car.

He shut the door and stumbled to the driver's side. His own harsh breathing echoed like tearing paper in his ears.

With one touch of her lips, Tessa had healed his hurt heart. For the first time since the day a judge had declared their divorce final in court, he couldn't make himself stop wanting to hold her.

He'd find a way to make her remember when they hadn't lived separate lives. They'd been one, a passionate sum of two incomplete human beings who'd loved each other completely.

TESSA BARELY KEPT HERSELF from stroking her mouth as Noah drove through the quiet, icy streets. She'd meant to thank him, the way she'd have thanked David, or any other friend who'd helped her.

Instead, she'd kissed his cold, chapped lips and

barely stopped herself from sinking into the shelter of his hard body. He'd even made her forget her urgent need to reach Maggie.

"Tessa?"

"Hmm?" She kept her eyes on the snowy road, wary of letting him see how much she needed to touch him again.

"I think we've both forgotten our access to technology. You have your cell phone. Call Eleanor."

"Jeez." She flipped the phone open and dialed. In moments, Joe answered.

"We just saw Chief Weldon," Tessa said. "Everything all right there?"

"We didn't recognize the man in his photo, but he took it pretty well."

"I mean, are you all—is Eleanor all right?"

"She's fine, Tessa. What are you trying to ask me?"

His attitude was slightly "don't worry your pretty head." Tessa tried again. "I was afraid Eleanor might be nervous about a killer roaming my street."

"We talked it over. We think he's probably long gone by now. He'd have to know someone would see him in such an outlandish getup. And a stranger would stand out here as much as a guy in a disguise."

He had a point. "So Eleanor and Maggie are fine?"

"Perfectly. Take your time. Everything going well?"

"Great," she said. "We had a talk with Weldon. Noah seems to have bargained a truce."

"Good. Maybe he'll start doing his job. I promised Eleanor I'd bring in some firewood. Talk to you later."

She hung up, but stared at the phone. "That was weird."

"What?"

"They've decided the killer must have left town because people here would have noticed him. Joe said to take our time."

"Maybe he and Eleanor are doing some wishful thinking. I don't intend to let Weldon stop his patrols yet." He turned at a corner. "Could you call his office and ask them to send you a copy of the photo? If they have e-mail, have it sent to your e-mail address. I'd like another look at it in case I missed something, and you could look again, too. You were right about it looking like a lot of tall, lean men, but something looked familiar to you."

The deputy on duty promised to e-mail the photo, and she spelled out her e-mail address. Hanging up, she finally risked a glance at Noah. He tried to smile at her, but his mouth remained a straight, unforgiving line.

She refused to jump to conclusions. He'd tensed against her when she'd kissed him. She hadn't mistaken his awareness of her, and he wasn't angry. Not now, anyway.

"I wish we'd worked together after Keely died," she said.

"What do you mean? Worked on what?"

"If we'd talked to each other, if we'd tried, even a little. I walked away, telling myself your feelings had changed, but now I think I was guessing at what you felt."

"My feelings changed? After Keely died?"

"I knew you blamed me." Again she couldn't look

at him—couldn't stand to see the old accusations in his eyes, so she turned back to the frozen sky. "I understand. It's the frustration. Someone has to be at fault."

"I didn't blame you." He reached for her hand.

She wrenched it away, fighting hot tears that stung her eyes. "I thought we were different today, that we could finally be honest with each other, but if you still can't—"

"Wait," Noah said. "I can't talk to you around Maggie and the Worths. We need privacy."

He jerked the steering wheel, and they skidded across the left-hand side of Prodigal's main street. Noah cut the engine as they neared the curb outside Jimmy's Italian Bistro. Tessa eyed him, startled into listening.

"Come inside with me." He reached for her hand, and this time she made herself take his troubled, tired expression at face value rather than assigning hidden meaning to his feelings. "We need to talk and I don't want you to freeze in the car."

"I have some things to say to you," she said, "and some questions to ask." She opened her door and met him at the front of the car.

Heat hit them with force as they entered the restaurant. A young blond woman greeted them with a wide, practiced smile from behind her podium.

"We'd like a private booth if you have one," Noah said.

"Yes, sir." A cynical smile curved her mouth as she recognized Tessa. "Afternoon, Mrs. Gabriel. Sorry to hear about Mr. Howard."

"Thank you." Tessa'd had no idea so many people

thought she'd been having an affair with David. No one bothered to hide salacious interest now, but she didn't care. She had nothing to prove, except that she could actually speak though grief swamped her every time she thought of him.

The other woman pulled two menus from a slot and led them to a dark booth in the restaurant's far corner. "Plenty of privacy here. I'll send Louise to take your orders."

"Not yet," Noah said, but then he softened his tone. "Thanks. We'll call when we're ready."

Tessa took off her coat and hung it on a peg drilled into the side of the tall wooden booth. Noah did the same as she slid into the side hidden from the rest of the restaurant. Noah sat beside her, stopping her breath.

"What do you mean I blamed you?" He sounded angry. "I never blamed you. I was the one who checked her last. I'm the one who didn't notice anything was wrong with her."

She ignored his antagonism and simply absorbed the words that freed her from months and months of shame. If he saw nothing to forgive, maybe she wasn't guilty. She wrapped herself in feeling nothing—no guilt, no rage, no pain. As if the freedom to feel just "normal" were a warm blanket Noah had wrapped around her after she'd crawled in from a blizzard.

But then she heard the rest of what he'd said, that he'd been the one who should have known Keely was in trouble. She finally saw his guilt, a twisted reflection of her own.

"Neither one of us could have saved her."

She'd said so over and over, a million times, since that horrible morning, but she'd never believed until now. Until Noah's forgiveness had eased her pain, maybe cleared the fog a little so she could see Keely's death, and the death of her marriage, as they'd really happened.

"We both blamed ourselves because we thought someone should have saved her," she said. "But we've both been wrong."

In his eyes, she saw only darkness and grief, pain she knew intimately. She forgot about protecting herself. She forgot that Noah had let her down.

She understood what had happened now.

Taking his hand, she pulled his arm around her shoulders, and scooted as close to him as she could get, surrounding herself in his scent. This close to him, she sensed time slowing down.

She had time for second thoughts, which she resisted. If she didn't face the past, she'd never learn to live with it. "We should have found a way to stay together, to talk to each other about what we felt, but we couldn't. We've been standing still since she died, Noah, and we should stop. For Keely, if not for ourselves."

He didn't answer. Was he so determined to hold on to his self-control? She cupped his chin and turned his face, terribly aware of the scratch of his beard against her fingers.

"You helped me. Let me help you."

Everything happened at once. With a groan, he lowered his head until his face pressed against her hair. His weight pushed her into the edge of the table, but she welcomed the slight discomfort. It reminded her they were both real, both still alive and able to feel, both together.

Noah put his arms around her, inch by inch, as if he could barely make himself move, but then he was holding her so close she could hardly breathe. He shook as if he were crying.

She froze, unable to turn, unwilling to believe Noah knew how to cry. Though she'd resented him for not needing her, she'd admired his strength. Could she endure tears from the strongest human being she'd ever known?

She struggled to loop her arms around his neck. If he needed her to survive tears, she would. "I let you down because I couldn't stop being hurt myself long enough to care for you." Her own regret choked her.

"You didn't let me down." Muffled in her hair, his voice shook as violently as his body.

She leaned back to look at him. His face was hard with the effort to keep himself from crying. His eyes, reddened and hollow, seemed like a stranger's. Tessa stroked his unruly hair. The familiar, silky feel of the dark strands reminded her this was Noah. This man had been her husband.

"Let's get out of here," she said.

"I'm all right." His irascible tone pushed her away.

"I'm not." She didn't intend to let him slip away until they settled their broken marriage once and for all. "I'm trying to be honest. I'm scared and lonely, and deep down, I don't know if I'll ever really believe I didn't do something wrong that made me lose both of you."

A muscle flexed in his jaw as he stared at her. Heat

swept her, a flush that felt both familiar and dangerous. She imagined kissing that small jerking muscle, but not to comfort him. In the tight circle of his arms, she began to remember desire.

She'd never managed to resist desire for Noah.

"I've been able to read your mind from the first moment you ever looked at me." He wasn't bragging—he sounded sorry. "I never told you. I didn't want to intrude."

Surprise made her laugh. She couldn't lean away and she didn't want to. She stayed in his arms and didn't care that half of Prodigal might eventually stroll past their booth.

"What are you seeing?" she asked.

"You still want me. We can't touch each other without feeling that, but you don't want to." He stopped, and reluctance shadowed his face. "This is nice for today, and you're glad I don't blame you, but you don't trust me."

"You're right." Why pretend? "I needed your attention. You needed success. I needed a marriage, but I didn't know how to make one."

Noah let her go, and she felt cold until he stood and grabbed her hand. "You're right," he said. "We do need privacy." He dragged money for the hostess from his pocket and tossed it on the table without looking.

Tessa didn't look back, either. She just snatched both their coats off the peg and followed him out of the restaurant, past the startled woman who'd seated them.

"Thanks," Noah said.

"We have to get home," Tessa added.

He turned to her as they stopped to put on their coats outside. "You always care what people think."

"You never do." She tried not to resent him for it.

"Where can we go?" He buttoned his coat, his blunt fingers already turning pink with cold.

When she didn't answer, he turned to her, the wind blowing his hair. She liked the look of it, longer—less in control. "Your room will be empty tonight," she said.

He froze. "Maybe I can't read your mind."

"I want to talk." About the lives they'd thrown away. She wanted to know if they'd ever had a chance. Had they always been too different to survive?

He looked away from her and then back, obviously twisted by emotion that didn't sit easy with him. "I've been trying to find words to ask you..."

Flecks of ice couldn't cool the heat that nearly melted her. "Maybe we finally want the same thing," she said.

CHAPTER NINE

WELDON'S YOUNGER DEPUTY ROSE from his parked
car as Noah pulled into Tessa's driveway. Clenching
his fists around the steering wheel, Noah cursed under
his breath. He'd been a cop for as long as he could
remember, and that part of his life had been more real
than anything since he'd lost his family. But today,
for the first time, he wanted to turn the car around
and take Tessa away.

He couldn't go, and she couldn't leave. Maggie and
her grandparents were waiting inside, and who knew
what was really at the bottom of all this?

"Weldon and his men are starting to follow us,"
Tessa said. "What do you think he wants?"

"Let's go see." He yanked the keys from the ignition.

She got out on the other side, stuffing her bare
hands and her gloves in her pockets. The deputy
joined them.

"Chief Weldon asked me to meet him here with
both of you."

"What did he find?" Noah moved between Tessa
and the road, protecting her from anyone who might
drive by.

"I'm not sure why Chief Weldon assigned me to
you and Ms. Gabriel, sir." The deputy moved to

Tessa's other side. "But he asked me to stay until he could get here to talk to you."

Suddenly Tessa bolted away from both of them, skidding up the slippery sidewalk. As she slammed through the front door, he knew what had frightened her.

"Maggie." The little girl's face swam in front of his mind's eye, her innocence a possible challenge to the maniac who'd killed her father. He grabbed the deputy's shirt, all but dragging him toward the house. "Did something happen in there?" He felt as if his frozen feet slipped a step for each stride that took him toward the wide-open door.

"Everything's fine inside the house." The deputy sounded as if he was choking, and Noah let him go with a shove.

As Noah stepped on the rag rug just inside the door it slid out from under his feet. He slammed into the wall, taking a quick survey of the empty living room as he regained his balance.

Fear made him clumsy. His mind seemed to work on two planes. "Tessa!" Logically he knew they were fine. The deputy would have known if something was wrong. Weldon wouldn't have sent him here blind if Maggie was in danger.

But deep inside, Noah was still the man who'd lost his daughter, who'd pulled away from Tessa because he hadn't ever planned to be this afraid again. Not even for her.

He hauled himself up the stairs two at a time, gripping the rail. The second he burst onto the gallery, Tessa came out of her room, cradling Maggie in her arms.

Noah grabbed his knees, gasping for air, fighting panic as he stared at the woman and the baby who'd made him feel again. Maggie didn't really want to be cradled. She flailed her arms and legs, trying to escape Tessa's tight embrace.

"She's all right?" Already controlling his breathing, he tried to look careful and capable. He just wanted Tessa to know she could depend on him.

"She's fine." Tessa pressed her cheek to the protesting child's head.

"Well, I'm not." Eleanor smoothed her hair as she popped out of the room. "What's going on here, Tessa? You scared us both, grabbing Maggie out of her crib. I know you're in charge around here, but have a little consideration."

Tessa's mouth tightened before she turned a steady gaze toward the other woman. "I was worried about her," she said, "and she shouldn't be playing in her crib anyway. She's too big to be cooped up."

"Joe only put her in there while I was in the shower."

Noah studied Maggie's perfectly dressed grandma. She must have just finished her shower. "Where is Joe?"

"He went to fill the car with gas and buy an evening newspaper." She crimped her white, lacquered curls. "We thought we might have dinner out tonight. Can we bring you two anything?"

"No," Tessa said.

Faint color in her cheeks reminded Noah of their plans. "I'll go down and see what Weldon wants."

Tessa turned her head, and understanding flowed from her to him. At last they were in this together.

"I still don't understand why you were worried,"
Eleanor said. She peered over the gallery as if she
expected Prodigal's police force to show up in the
open door. The deputy appeared on cue. "Did Weldon find something else?"

"When I saw him—" Tessa nodded toward the
deputy, rubbing her chin on Maggie's head, as the
baby calmed "—I thought Weldon must have sent
him because something had happened here."

"Oh, no." Eleanor's soothing voice faded as Tessa
led her back inside the room. Noah met the deputy
midway down the stairs and left the other man no
choice but to turn around.

"I don't believe we've met officially." The deputy
held out his hand at the bottom of the stairs. "I'm
Tom Davis."

"Tom." He shook the younger guy's hand. "I'm
Noah Gabriel. You want to tell me what this is
about?"

"I honestly don't know, sir, but the chief is on his
way. He'll explain as soon as he gets here. My job is
to watch the premises."

"To make sure we don't leave, or to keep someone
else out?"

"Both, I assume."

The deputy seemed to be telling the truth. Grilling
him wouldn't get them anywhere. As long as Tessa
and Maggie were safe, Noah opted to wait for the
chief. "Come on into the kitchen. I think we might
find some coffee. I could use it after the cold outside."

He found the sugar and cream Tom required, and
they were finishing their first cups when the doorbell

rang. Tessa must have been waiting for it. Her foot-steps pounded down the stairs.

Noah, shadowed by their new bodyguard who armed himself with his coffee cup, reached the door just ahead of her. Lifting one brow, she stood aside when Noah opened up for Weldon.

"What's wrong?" Noah asked.

The chief shook his head. "I have some news, but I don't think anyone's in immediate danger."

Tom lifted his coffee cup. "My fault, Chief. I think I scared them half to death."

"Sorry." Weldon looked apologetic. "I should have explained a little better."

Noah offered the chief a seat on the sofa. "Tell us now."

"I bring nominally good news." Weldon glanced at his deputy's cup. "Taking a break, Tom?"

"Sorry, sir." He spun toward the kitchen to return his mug.

Weldon unzipped his coat and stood in front of the couch, waiting for Tessa to sit first. Noah sat at her side. He slid his hand down her back, lingering over the light strands of her hair and her taut muscles.

"I believe I've taken David Howard's killer into custody," Weldon said.

Tessa gasped, and tears spilled out of her huge eyes. Noah pulled her close.

"Who did you arrest?" he asked, frustrated at be-ing out of his jurisdiction. At the very least, he'd like to feel a little more faith in the chief's abilities. "How do you know you got the right person?"

"Eric Sanders." Weldon watched Tessa stiffen as if he'd hit her. "My deputy called me just after I sat down with Hugh Carlson, who appears to be totally clueless about the murder. What I have to say about Sanders isn't as pleasant.''

"We'll take the truth." Tessa laced her fingers through Noah's, her grip like a claw.

Weldon went on, looking doubtful. "We found certain personal items of yours in Mr. Sanders's house, Tessa.''

"What personal items?'' To his complete amazement, Noah managed to sound calm. He'd like to drive over to the jail and remove the man's windpipe.

Weldon glanced at him, but then focused on Tessa. "He'd stolen some of your mail. Catalogs, if you can imagine, a bill or two, letters from your parents. We haven't opened them because he didn't, but we'll have to keep them for evidence.''

"He stole my mail?'' Tessa's grip slackened. She shook her head slightly. "That's a little creepy, but it sounds like some sort of fixation, not a precursor to murder.''

"I wish he'd stopped at your mail,'' Chief Weldon said.

Cold rage broke a sweat on Noah's upper lip. He knew what came next before the sheriff continued.

"Once my deputy found letters addressed to you, he took a sharper look at that rabbit warren of a house Sanders bought. When he got to the closets, he found articles of your clothing, feminine things, a slip, a camisole, all neatly folded into a gym bag—'' He broke off, his gaze on Tessa's pale face. "That's when he called me. Suffice to say, Sanders used plenty of your belongings to feed his fixation.''

"My perfume." She straightened, as if a wire from the ceiling held her.

Weldon sat forward. "We found a bottle. What brand?"

Noah answered, "Changeless Joy." His voice shook. His knees locked, as did the rest of his body, with ineffective rage.

"I bought three bottles before I finally realized something was wrong." Tessa looked up at Noah, her face open and vulnerable. "I thought I was setting it down somewhere—at the office, or in the store. I usually do my shopping during my lunch hour."

"He must have sprayed it on your clothing," Weldon said. "I noticed it because my wife uses the same kind. He kept the bottle under a sink in the guest bathroom farthest from his room, but we could smell it in the closet."

"He wanted to believe she used it for him." Noah considered punching his fist through the nearest hard object. "He left it in the other bathroom to put it out of sight, so he could pretend he wasn't spraying it himself."

Tessa swallowed. Her throat made a sound that wasn't a whimper, wasn't even fear. But she was scared. He knew by the way she edged closer, by the fingers that bit into his skin. Horror darkened her green eyes. "I'm glad you changed the locks."

"He's a nut, but I won't let him get to you," Noah promised with ease. He'd make sure Eric Sanders never came near her again. "I want to talk to him, Weldon."

"Not a chance. You're not in charge here, and I'm

not letting you kick the crap out of this guy so you can feel better while you screw up my case."

"You found him because of Tessa."

"And I'll question him without the benefit of your biased experience. This man probably killed one of Prodigal's prominent citizens. No way am I losing a conviction because you're pissed he stole your wife's underwear."

"You've got me wrong. I just want to be sure. What else do you have on him? Did he try to give you an alibi?"

"I think there's a problem," Tessa said. "Did you bring the photo from my office?"

Weldon unfolded it from his inside pocket. Tessa took it to her desk and switched on the lamp. "I don't think this is Eric."

Weldon got up and Noah went with them. "He could have hired a killer as easily as anyone else," Weldon said.

"This wasn't a hired gun." Noah leaned over Tessa's shoulder. "Whoever killed David wanted him to suffer. He killed with rage. I wish I'd gotten a better look at Sanders during David's service."

Weldon leaned in as well. "What's wrong with that picture?"

"I don't think Eric is as tall as this man, and I'm sure he's not this thin."

"The guy's got muscles. Eric works out."

"This guy doesn't work out. He's just lean," Tessa said.

"You can't know that," Noah slid his finger down the photo. "He's covered, head to toe in clothing."

"But you can tell."

"That's not good enough, Tessa." He turned to the chief. "Did you fax the photo to Boston yet? I know someone who can analyze weight and height."

"All right." The chief looked doubtful. "But how likely is it—"

"I've known Eric for over a year. He's never been violent, even when he was most angry with me."

"How much violence do you need to see before you're convinced, Tessa?" Weldon peered from one to the other of them before he settled his gaze on her again. "The man's been breaking into your home to steal your most personal possessions."

"But catching him was too easy." She lifted both hands. "If he'd killed David, he wouldn't have hung around in his house with my underwear. He might be sick, but he doesn't want to be tried for David's death. At the least he'd have thrown away my stuff."

"He was jealous of David Howard. You've heard of 'if I can't have you, no one will'?" Weldon tugged at his collar, clearly uncomfortable with what he'd seen that day. "Sanders is a big fan of that philosophy, especially where you're concerned."

"It's still circumstantial," Noah said.

"It might be circumstantial in a city the size of Boston, but you two are suggesting we suddenly have a stalker and a killer." Weldon shook his head. "And these two separate criminals were after two best friends?"

Noah shrugged. "Tessa doesn't believe Sanders is capable of killing."

"He's a neat freak," she said. "You've been in his house. He hoards stuff, but every surface is spotless. You said he even folded my lingerie. He couldn't have caused the gore I saw in David's office. He would have been covered in blood himself. And if he had done it he would have been sick afterward."

"Neat freaks occasionally lose their will to keep clean." Weldon folded the photo. "Especially when they want to escape from a murder scene."

"What about David's place?" Noah asked. "Remember how clean it was? What if cleaning is part of his MO?"

"But why would he kill David?" Tessa asked. "He stole my things. He wanted to see me outside of work. Why would he kill David?"

"Because you turned him over to David," Noah said, "and David had your friendship. From his point of view, David stood in his way."

Weldon signaled his deputy to follow him. "I'll double-check his alibi, and I want to talk to him again. You won't believe this, but someone in the judge's office alerted Sanders's lawyer about the warrant, and the attorney got to him before we did."

Behind him, Joe Worth walked into the room. Tessa jumped. Even Noah caught his breath. The other man had made no noise, opening the door.

"Did you say you found David's killer?" Joe asked.

"I believe so, Mr. Worth. I'm going to question him now." Weldon walked around David's father-in-law.

"Fine," Joe said. "You've arrested him?"

"Not exactly, sir." Weldon avoided Noah's gaze and started through the open door.

"I'll walk out with you." If even Weldon wasn't sure enough to arrest, they still had plenty of problems. He glanced at Tessa, but she'd turned to Joe, resting her hand on his shoulder.

"Let's update Eleanor on the latest news."

Noah followed the two policemen outside, waiting until he shut the door before he spoke.

"You haven't arrested him. You don't think it's going to stick."

"As you mentioned, I need to check his alibi. I'd like something that ties him to the murder scene." Weldon put on his cap. "But he's our guy."

His arrogance hit Noah the wrong way, but he'd rather not antagonize the man and get himself and Tessa ousted from the loop again. "Until you're positive about Sanders, I'd like you to continue the patrols."

"I intend to, but have a little faith. I'm not an idiot, and I believe there's worse to Eric than we've seen so far. I'll make him confess, but I won't let up on any protection I can offer you."

Noah couldn't blame him for wanting to solve the crime committed in his own backyard. "Thanks. And you'll let us know what you get out of Sanders?"

"I'll call you as soon as he confesses."

"Why weren't you keeping a better eye on him? He's been stalking Tessa."

"You know the law. I couldn't act until he did something overt." The chief stepped into a fresh batch of swirling snow, but looked back. "I thought he was just a nut I'd inherited from Sheriff Patterson, one more problem, like the way Patterson handled the Joanna Howard case."

Noah eyed him closely. "What about Joanna Howard?"

After spreading hints like election posters for three days, Weldon suddenly clammed up. Tom put on a poker face. At last, Weldon shrugged.

"She was high when she drove into that telephone pole. I have no real proof except the rumor of an altered autopsy report and a gut feeling that my predecessor was forced to resign because he'd gone along with David Howard's plan to keep his wife's drug use a secret."

"Gut feeling?" Noah doubted the other man's suspicions.

"You never follow your gut?"

He trusted his more than he trusted Weldon's. "That's not enough to convict, either. Have you investigated at all?"

"I called a dealer Mr. Howard defended. He swears he's cleaned up, doesn't know anything about Mrs. Howard's habits." Weldon turned away.

Tom paused to shake Noah's hand before following his superior. Noah watched the two police officers head for their cars.

"Weldon, what does your gut tell you about Eric?"

"It doesn't make sense that a town this small could hatch a murderer and a deviant at the same time."

He was right, but maybe Eric and the real killer, if he wasn't the one, hadn't thought to time their crimes.

Noah swore. He'd give a lot for five minutes with the pervert who'd stolen his wife's underwear.

THAT NIGHT, Tessa prodded the fire dying on the hearth. One charred log broke apart, spraying sparks and flame. From the floor above, footsteps and soft thudding told of her makeshift family settling in for bed. She glanced nervously toward Noah's room, noting faint smoke stains on the blue-and-white delft tiles that surrounded the fireplace.

Noah wasn't part of her family, but he seemed to be planting himself here. Those reckless moments in the restaurant replayed themselves in her head, a swift, terrifying movie that almost felt as if it had happened to someone else.

They'd come closer to each other in those few crowded moments than they'd managed in a shared home in a shared bed in the months between their daughter's death and the day she'd told Noah she was leaving. Why had they taken so long to talk?

She rubbed her forehead. Why start working at their relationship now? What were they salvaging?

Since Noah and the Worths had moved into her life, she'd realized how alone she was. And when she stopped to think of what it meant to raise a child by herself, she still wondered if she was up to the job.

Single women had been parents long before she'd found herself taking a crack at it. And she had to consider Maggie before she made any reckless decisions with Noah.

He'd come to Prodigal now because she'd asked him. He'd helped her, and if Eric Sanders was the killer, it was time for him to leave.

She just wanted to know, before she let him go, why they'd failed so badly at their marriage. She'd pretended for a year that her marriage was completely in her past, but she couldn't keep it there.

Tessa swallowed, pressing both hands against the hearth tiles. She could march up those stairs, knock on Noah's door and talk to him about the reconciliation that had been on the tip of her tongue in the restaurant.

Or she could hide down here and pretend nothing had changed between them. Send Noah back to Boston and the job that still felt like an adversary.

She picked up a fresh log and then shoved it onto the dying embers. For the past eighteen months she'd told herself Noah had deserted her before she'd left him. The story had justified her actions, but she refused to lie to herself or to make him look less caring than he was. If she hadn't mattered to him, he would never have come to Prodigal.

A familiar, uncertain, needling voice whispered from the depths of doubt she'd held about her own worth since childhood. Maybe Noah's guilt had driven him this afternoon. She hated the idea of him thinking he owed her.

Overhead, he opened his door. And stopped. As if he wasn't sure what to do next. She knew exactly how he felt. She didn't want to hurt him again, and she didn't want to expose herself to being hurt. And then there was Maggie, who still missed her "Da."

Noah started down the stairs and Tessa released a breath she hadn't known she was holding. If he could face her, she'd make herself face him.

With honesty.

He was three steps down before she saw him, his black hair damp, his hawkish face drawn tight with the same apprehension that clenched her stomach.

"Is Maggie asleep?"

"In my room," she said.

"Eleanor and Joe?"

"They wanted an early night."

He nodded, his relief palpable and comforting. "Are you still up for a talk?" he asked, the expression in his eyes making him more vulnerable than she'd ever seen him.

"I'm not sure we should." Clasping her hands behind her because she couldn't stop them from shaking, she turned her back to the fire. "We're both looking for a second chance."

He kept coming. "Would that be wrong?"

She tried to be careful. "If we're making decisions because we're both getting attached to Maggie, and we both think she and I might be in danger, it's wrong."

He studied her as if she were a suspect. Suddenly he crossed the room in four long strides, reaching her before she took a full breath.

"I can't give up on you again," he said. "Ever since Weldon left, I've been seeing what might have happened if you'd stumbled in on Eric in David's office."

She just couldn't see Eric as the killer type. "I still don't think—let's not borrow that trouble. The outside world apart, what do you see us saying to each other to make our past right?" She slipped her fingertips inside her back pockets. The better to keep her hands off her ex-husband.

Noah looked down at her, his eyes darker than any coals in the fire. The slope of his full lower lip reminded her how good he was to kiss, but then tension drew his mouth tight.

"I'm sorry," he said. "First I'd say I'm sorry for pushing you away." Easing closer, he crowded her.

She borrowed some of his courage and made it her

own, relaxing her hands at her sides. "I'm starting to
think we've apologized enough."

"Tessa." Her name became a prayer. He ran his
index finger along the fall of her hair, following its
path with his dark gaze until he reached her neck. Her
heartbeat combined with his pulse, and both seemed
to race beneath her skin. "I never meant to hurt you."
His warm breath brushed the strands of her hair.

"I left you." Until tonight, she'd always insisted
she'd left because of him. "I gave up first."

A faint smile turned him back into the Noah she
knew, the man she'd loved before they'd lost Keely.
"Thanks for trying to let me off the hook, but we
both know you told me you were leaving long before
you went."

She leaned her face against the fingers that still
rested on her throat. "I always wondered why you
didn't notice."

He slid his hand to her shoulder, his gaze catching
hers as his thumb probed the hollow of her collar-
bone. "I noticed, and I missed you. I should have
told you how much I missed you instead of signing
those damn divorce papers."

"Maybe I shouldn't have sent them." A short
breath escaped her. "I was angry that you didn't
come after me, but I should have talked to you before
I filed. What would you have said if I'd asked you
for the divorce?"

"Back then, I don't know. I wasn't capable of rational thought for a while." He leaned down until his
lips moved against her forehead with each word he
spoke. "But if I had it to do over now, I'd try to
explain. Work is safer than actually making an effort

to live with someone I couldn't stand to lose. And I lost almost everyone who mattered to me.''

His husky voice and his closeness confused her with images that flashed before her eyes, the rise and fall of muscles in his hip and leg when he bent over her, the up and down of his chest as he breathed beneath her, the perfect fit of his lean, long body to hers.

"You make it sound as if you're cursed, but your mother's fine. And I'm okay."

"I don't believe in curses." He pressed his mouth to her temple. She couldn't mistake his intent or the sweet pressure that began to build in her at such innocent contact. "But I wonder if I'm allowed to love. My father was my favorite." He broke off. "I've never admitted that to anyone. He was always so tall, Tessa, and to a boy, such a tall man looked powerful. I had to look up at him. He looked strong without trying, and he never made mistakes. He was my hero. My mom was scattered, and she didn't seem to notice she had that crazy Einstein hair. Or that no one ever saw red like that in nature. She dressed like an MTV queen, and my friends made fun of me when they saw her. I felt guilty because it was easier to love my dad.''

"Easier," Tessa said. "But you love her. I know how much you love her, and she knows, too."

Noah caught her face between his hands. "You're sidetracking me when we should be talking about us. I've distanced myself from my mom and from you because I'm terrified of losing you both. I'd give anything to bring Keely back, but after she died, I knew I wouldn't survive if something took you away from me, too." He grimaced, and the lines that scored his face hurt her terribly. "I thought I could keep you both safe if I didn't show you how much you meant to me. As if I could fool the curse I don't believe in."

Tessa closed her eyes. She couldn't judge his actions. She'd made mistakes of her own. "I'm familiar with curses. I thought I lost Keely because I had a moment's misgiving when I got pregnant. Instead of fighting to stay together, you and I got scared and lost each other."

"Maybe temporarily," he said. "Weren't we bargaining for safety?"

"Protecting ourselves?"

"I think so." His thick tone worked strange magic on her. He moved closer in a dance that made her fully aware of his body and the need he no longer bothered to hide. "What do you think, Tessa?"

How could she think with his smell, familiar and yet indefinably different—more precious because she'd gone without him for so long—filling her senses? "I agree I'd rather give something up than have it taken from me, but I don't want to be the kind of frightened woman who could half kill us both with a bad bargain."

"I suspect I dealt first." He kissed her other temple, his lips lingering, teasing.

The touch of his mouth made her feel hollow inside. Needing to be closer, she curved her hands around his hips. The texture of his rough denim jeans anchored her to reality. If she didn't stop soon, her body would be making this decision.

"Stay with me," Noah's lips brushed her ear. "Let me try again. Let me be the man you need."

His voice sang in her head, defeating caution.

She'd managed to take Maggie into her life and into her heart. Why couldn't she consider a future with Noah if they both wanted it? "Why would this time be different?"

"This time we'd take care of each other."

Pain caught her by surprise. How many nights had she clung to him, wordless with grief, until she'd realized he couldn't comfort her?

"Maggie deserves stability."

"I'm serious about trying again, and I'll do what it takes to fix what went wrong between us before. I'm not looking to make any more regret."

A nuance of their failure seemed to have escaped him. "What happened between us wasn't all your fault, and you can't fix our relationship all by yourself, either. We'd have to learn to live together again. With Maggie."

Hope lightened his gaze. He traced the line of her rib cage as if he were relearning her. "Tell me what you're willing to do."

"We live in different states." And she'd already started over once.

Pulling her so close she had to time her breathing with his, he shook his head, and his chin brushed her hair. "That's easy. Come home."

She pressed her hands to his chest. "I have a firm to run and a child to support. Maggie's grandparents are here. You could move."

He went utterly still. "And my job?"

She shifted her glance from his. "I know Prodigal isn't Boston, and your job was always the one that came first in our family, but I owe David a family for Maggie. Maine needs policemen, too."

He laughed, but she wasn't joking. "And what about Weldon, Tessa? Should I take over his job as the local law?"

"Just come to Maine. Somewhere, a position would open for you. I'm not even sure I could live in Boston again. I left because of the memories." She cut herself short, light-headed. He was part of those memories she'd fled. "Are we really talking about a reconciliation?"

"I wouldn't have asked you if I wasn't sure." Lowering his head, he took possession of her mouth, and she took from him in equal measure. He tasted of the past, but he made her believe in the future.

He slid his hands down her shoulders, following the curve of her breasts. She ached with need. Loving habits were hard to break. It was her last thought as she set fire to the walls she'd built between them.

CHAPTER TEN

"WHAT ABOUT MAGGIE?" Tessa fumbled for the words in a haze of desire that almost made her forget she was committing more than herself to Noah.

When he lifted his head to look at her, his pupils were large and round, and he didn't look as if he'd understood the question. Or maybe even English.

She smiled, her faith in him inching back. He wanted her, and he knew she came with a baby now.

"I'll be her second father if you'll both have me." He kissed the corner of her mouth, but then his gaze grew hard as if he were remembering the circumstances that had brought them here. "Not that she has much choice."

"Don't think about work." The last thing Tessa wanted to talk about now was murder. "I'm asking you if you can love her as much as you loved Keely."

"I'll learn. You're learning. I can."

She'd prefer wholehearted acceptance—love that already startled him with its intensity as it did her, but Maggie would make Noah love her, too.

He pushed her hair back from her forehead and then kissed the skin he'd exposed. "I thought of Maggie, Tessa."

She pressed her head against his chin. "I should go check on her."

"Now?" He pulled away, doubt narrowing his eyes. "Are you running away from me?"

She twisted her head from side to side, as awkward as the shy, uncertain virgin she'd been when she'd met him. What came next? Was he asking her to make love with him, or was he asking her to consider the possibilities? The physical commitment came hard for her, because she'd never made it without knowing she was in the relationship for the long haul. And that had been with Noah.

"I won't back down unless you tell me we're making a mistake." She held his gaze. "But I trust you'll talk to me this time if that happens."

"I don't want to make the same mistakes. I don't want to lose you again."

Her heart pounded like a jackhammer. Her legs felt infused with jelly. She longed to wrap herself in Noah's arms, but she still didn't know what he wanted for tonight, and she didn't know how to ask. She started for the stairs.

"Tessa."

At his bewildered tone, she turned, too relieved to hide the joy that felt as if it were shooting from her body. "Yes?"

"When I asked you to stay with me, I meant starting now." He looked as doubtful as she felt. God, they'd been hard on each other. Noah without self-confidence was a horrific sight to behold.

"Tonight?" she asked, letting herself believe.

"Yes, but you should get Maggie's monitor."

"I will." She was glad Noah had thought of it. "I'd like to take a shower, too. I could come to your room after."

"We could share a shower."

Heat raced up her throat and across her cheek-bones. They'd never bathed together. In their most passionate moments, she'd momentarily managed to forget she was the short, round disappointment whose mother had surprised her with fad diets. But tonight she was too nervous to feel that kind of passion.

"Maybe we could try that sometime." She tried to sound casual while she fought a stray fear that he'd confused her with some other more fashionably thin, daring woman he'd met after she'd left Boston.

"You look scared, Tessa." Crossing the room, he gently grasped her upper arms. His gaze apologized as if he'd done something wrong. "I don't want to force you to sleep with me if you need time to be sure."

This more perspicacious version of Noah reminded her she'd hurt him, too. "I'm positive." She tiptoed to kiss him. Immediately he cupped her head, and she opened his mouth with hers. The sound he made, deep in his throat, excited her. She traced the straight line of his teeth with her tongue, wanting more, needing more of him.

She splayed her fingers across his chin, rubbing his lower lip with her thumb. He nipped her with gentle teeth, and she shivered, pressing closer, nestling his arousal against the softness of her belly. But when she shivered at so much power, just for her, he slid his hands down her waist and set her away from him. After he let her go, she felt cold.

"Don't wake Maggie, but hurry. Okay?"

She didn't even bother to answer as she rushed up the stairs.

NOAH BRUSHED his teeth for the second time and stared at himself in the bathroom mirror. What should he do—take off his clothes and wait for her in bed, or keep on anything that covered his erection and try to make her believe he wasn't as randy as a teenager on his first date?

He'd been away from his wife for too long. He was fighting a less than civilized compulsion to prove she belonged to him again. What he really wanted was to belong to her. He turned back to his room and shut the door, rubbing his hand across his mouth.

He hadn't had a drink in four days, but he'd suddenly kill for a beer. Bad sign. He'd better lay off the beer for a while—until, in times of need, it didn't seem like an old friend.

Narrowing his eyes against the harsh overhead light, he turned on the bedside lamp and then went back to flip the switch beside the door. Better. She'd like that.

Tessa hadn't turned on her shower yet. He could just picture her stuck like a statue to the middle of her floor, convincing herself she was making a mistake.

They hadn't decided where they'd live. He hadn't agreed to move here. She didn't have all the answers yet.

Neither did he, but the one he needed tonight was Tessa in his arms.

He grabbed sweats, a T-shirt and a towel and headed to the guest bathroom. A quick, cold shower couldn't hurt. It didn't help, either, and when he turned off the water, Tessa still hadn't turned hers on. He dressed and toweled his hair. And when he opened his bedroom door, he found Tessa, curled up in the armchair, a lavender silk robe covering every inch of her body from her neck to her toes.

He searched the room for the baby monitor and found it on the nightstand. "Did you turn that on?"

She nodded.

He tried to grin. "That takes care of the important stuff. I didn't hear you turn on the water."

"I hurried once you got in. I'm not sure about the hot-water supply." She stood, and the lavender that turned her eyes a deep dark green also swathed her voluptuous curves in seductive silk.

She tied his tongue, but not long enough. "You're beautiful." Smooth move. Original, and stirring, too, if he correctly read the somewhat nauseous look she turned his way.

"You don't have to do that," she said.

"Do what?" Tell her how much he wanted her? The robe was more revealing than anything she'd owned when they'd been together. Had she grown up since she'd left? Did she finally understand he needed her—not some doll-like ideal of beauty her mother had imprinted on her? He went to her, but he didn't touch her.

He didn't dare, because once he did, he wouldn't be able to stop or think. She still needed him to think.

"I know I'm okay to look at," she said, "but you don't have to say I'm beautiful. I could lose a few pounds, and I haven't had a haircut in about six months. I still don't do manicures, and I'm too practical to pay for a pedicure."

She twitched her hem aside, revealing bright red toenails that made him laugh.

"You've forgotten how I loved watching you do your toes. It was foreplay."

"Because you have some sort of gymnast fantasy, and you liked seeing me with my knees up to my chin."

Not exactly. She performed her self-pedicure at night after she'd showered and dressed for bed. Feeling all possessive of her as she'd curled up in his T-shirts to paint her toes, he'd seen more of her body than he often did when they'd made love.

The tension that made even stray strands of her hair quiver in time with her pulse told him she wasn't ready to hear that confession.

"Come to bed." As they walked together, the silk caressed her as he longed to do. Her nipples hardened, and so did he, all over again.

He bent to pull back the sheets, and then he shucked off his T-shirt. Tessa's hands, on his back, startled him. He stood still, while she stroked his muscles, sliding her palms in ever-widening sweeps from his shoulder blades to the small of his back. Nerve endings flashed urgent messages all over his body.

He reached for her, finding her forearm with his hand. She leaned into him. Silk and flesh, lush curves pressed against his skin, as she traced the outline of his rib cage. With one hand, he pulled her around him, reluctant to break contact.

He caught her face in his hands, and she opened to him. He kissed her, holding nothing back, taking from her, learning the taste and the feel of her mouth as if he'd never known her before.

She tiptoed to reach him, but the difference between their heights kept him from feeling enough of her against him. He lay down and pulled her onto the cool sheets at his side.

Her gaze melted as she tilted her head back. She breathed in, and he followed the rise of her breasts with his gaze and his hands. Her nipples teased him. He kissed her again and again, whispering her name, until she pushed him away to explore the lines of his face with her fingers.

"I think I'll die if we don't make love," she said in a voice so soft he prayed he wasn't indulging in another fantasy. When she unknotted her robe, he knew he must be dreaming.

He rose on one elbow above her, and she drew him closer. Her silk lapels had parted on beautiful, creamy flesh that begged for his touch.

Spreading his fingers against the web of bones beneath her throat, he opened the robe farther. She grew shy for the first time, and she turned her face into his shoulder as he dipped his head to the luscious hollow between her full breasts.

He waited for her to change her mind. Each breath she took lifted her closer to his mouth until he couldn't wait any longer. He opened his lips on her breastbone and kissed a slow path to her navel.

She tasted faintly of soap. Against her skin, he licked his lips. "You were in a hurry. You still use the same brand." He licked again, rimming her nipple and then covering the peak. "Mmm, better without the soap."

A sound half moan, half a chuckle, vibrated against his mouth. He closed his eyes. He'd wanted her so long, needed her so badly. If he was dreaming, he prayed he wouldn't wake until he'd forgotten the past and remembered only making love to his wife.

He slid his hand between the sides of her robe and parted the cloth to caress her belly, the jut of her hip. He knew her body as well as his own. Except she had become more vital to him than the air he breathed or the nourishment of food and drink.

Suddenly Tessa pressed her hand to his chest to hold him off. He braced himself on his elbow again, and she sat up, not looking at him as she reached for the lamp.

The robe fell off her shoulder. He ran his hand over her skin, beneath the silk, dipping to bare her back. "I'm hungry for you," he said, and then he asked for what he wanted. "Don't turn it off."

She pushed the switch.

"Tessa?"

Her stillness refused him, but she didn't lie down again.

"Please," he said. Only she would ever make him utter that word. "Turn on the light. Let me see you."

"I can't." Her voice, stretched as thin as her nerve, made him want to protect her from the taunts that had shamed her. Lucky thing her parents were out of the country. He'd like to talk to her mom about true parenting.

"Let me see you," he said again. The yearning of all their years together made him speak. "I want to watch you make love to me." He tried to tug her back, but she resisted. He tightened his hand on her shoulder. "You carried my child inside your body. One look at you, and I forget what I'm doing here.

Don't you know I want every inch of you? I've always wanted you.''

She waited so long he thought he'd lost her again. But finally, she leaned away from him and a switch clicked and soft light formed a circle on the bed. A circle that held them both as one.

Tessa eased onto her back and rolled toward him, her hair catching in silk as she shrugged out of the robe. The wariness in her eyes brought a lump to his throat. After everything, she actually thought he was capable of pretending.

Her courage humbled him. She could doubt her own beauty and yet uncover herself for him simply because he'd asked her to.

He looked his fill, tracing the delicious curve of hip to thigh, smiling at the pleasure that slipped between her lips in a soft moan. She caught his hand, when he ran his finger across the pale triangle at her pelvis. Her skin, pale against his darkness, was softer than he remembered. She reminded him of love and the child they'd made together. She was more precious to him than he'd remembered.

He looked into her eyes. As she gazed back her alarm began to fade. He smiled in surprise. Who'd known a woman's trust could give a man such power?

A secret promise of intimacy curved her mouth, and she took his hand and placed it on the slope of her breast. Her nipple prodded his palm, and he forgot how to breathe.

"What's next, Noah?" She leaned toward him, pressing a kiss to the corner of his mouth. She traced the seam of his lips with her tongue and rubbed her nipple against him.

He kissed her back and cautioned himself to go slowly.

They'd been apart for a long time. He wanted her to remember their private reconciliation with joy. Fighting a selfish urge to roll her beneath him, he lowered his head and opened his mouth against the underside of her breast, teasing lightly with his teeth. Her groan lost itself in his. Her satisfaction weakened him with his own need.

He didn't give a damn about a judge's ruling on their former marriage. He was making love to his wife, the only woman he'd ever truly wanted, the woman who would carry their other children and make a family with him and Maggie.

She was sustenance after deprivation. She was rain after a drought. She was love after loneliness that even now taunted him from the memories of eighteen months of empty nights.

And she arched against him, her body an invitation to hurry.

"Tessa, I meant to—" Offering her other breast, she interrupted his proposal to take her slowly. All but drinking from her body, he thrust against her thigh, unable to hold back. "I thought we'd take our time," he said, kissing where he could reach her, hungry for any taste of her skin.

"I can't." She opened her legs, reaching for his hips. "We'll talk about time later."

"I wanted this to be for you." She was ready. He couldn't stop himself. She took him inside her, and as she caressed him, he gritted his teeth, fighting the inevitable just long enough to give his wife equal pleasure.

"This is for us," she said on a broken note that shattered as her body took his to the deepest joy he'd ever known.

Her way was infinitely better than his.

TESSA OPENED HER EYES and looked for Noah. He'd turned his back on her in his sleep. She cuddled into his warmth and listened. Not a sound came from the monitor behind her.

Thank God for babies who slept through the night.

But maybe Maggie wasn't sleeping.

The thought dragged her upright. She curved her knees to her chin. She'd taken so long coming to Noah tonight because she'd been reluctant to leave the baby alone. But she didn't want to teach Maggie to be afraid, and her urge to overprotect might scare a growing girl.

Nevertheless, as she listened to the silent monitor, she had to admit she couldn't quit being who she was cold turkey. She had to make sure the baby was all right.

Creeping from Noah's bed, she snatched her robe off the floor. She belted it at her waist before she opened his door. The house was quiet, too. They hadn't managed to waken Joe and Eleanor.

Good.

She eased her own bedroom door open. She'd adopted a night-light rather than the lamp she'd left on the first night she'd had Maggie with her. Even the dimmer light offered enough illumination for her to see the baby's stomach and chest moving up and down.

She was breathing. She was alive.

Tessa braced herself for the usual wave of relief. As always, she rocked on her feet, unable to believe she was so lucky. She'd left the room, and Maggie was still sleeping—not hurt, not dead.

A hand flattened against her back. She immediately recognized Noah's touch and his smell. She smiled, happier than she'd believed she could ever be again.

"She's all right?" he said against her ear.

She nodded and turned him toward the door. Noah let her push him. She smiled again, feeling utterly feminine. He'd let her push him when they'd made love, too.

She'd enjoyed feeling in control, not worrying about how she'd looked. Noah seemed to like the way she looked. Believing him, after all these years, had been something of an aphrodisiac.

His slow, loving pace had frustrated her. She'd needed him to destroy her, to fuse her old self with the new woman who believed he wanted her. In the end, they'd destroyed each other, rocking together until the last pulsing vestiges of their lovemaking had faded to lovely echoes of feeling. They'd fallen asleep, wrapped up in each other.

She shut the door behind them, but then Noah turned her and she let him lead her back to his room.

"I hope you had enough sleep." He was already pulling the robe from her shoulders.

Turned out, she wasn't completely convinced yet. Without thinking, she lifted her hands to cover herself, but Noah pulled them away, tripping as he tried not to step on her feet. He took her not to the bed, but to the window.

When he opened the curtains, she drew back, but

Noah maneuvered her gently into the light. "I've wanted to see you like this since the first time we made love," he said, "with the moonlight painting your skin."

"And the neighbors taking pictures?" She tried to make a joke of it, but his frank passion made her forget all the good-girl teachings her mom had ever offered her. And her cautions about being such a short girl for so much weight.

She was the woman Noah wanted. For him, she'd dance nude in the near darkness that still held too much light for her taste.

"Let the neighbors find their own women," he said. He ducked his head to kiss her, lifting her out of the paltry body that kept her here on earth. She opened to him, offering all she could find of the finest parts of herself, the love that no longer seemed to need proof of an equal measure of his devotion. Trust that made her lift her arms in the moonlight.

"Too late for showing off." He smiled against her mouth, scooping her close against himself. "I need a close-up view now." Just then, headlights slashed the window and Noah turned her away from the glass. "The police," he said.

"They promised to patrol. I'm glad, for Maggie's sake."

"I don't understand why you're so determined to believe Eric didn't kill David."

"If he's not the guy in the picture, he's not the killer. I've seen Eric at his worst. He'd barge in. He'd call and list the reasons he was the man for me, and he'd send me details of his bank balance, but I can't see him getting violent.''

''He stole your panties.''

She shivered. ''Leave it to you to state your case in blunt terms. I want to get sick every time I think of him in here, rooting through my things, and I'm not about to let myself imagine what he might have done with them. But I can't believe he's capable of stabbing David like that. Why would he if he's after me? It would make sense if he'd come to my office to kill me and David had interrupted. But you've often said yourself, whoever killed David meant to kill him.''

''No one else makes sense, Tessa. This bad guy knew David. No stranger would attack a man with so much vindictiveness.''

''And the picture?''

He shook his head. ''I don't know. I didn't get a good enough look at him. Weldon doesn't seem as reluctant as you to think it's Eric.''

Tessa had another reason. She still wasn't satisfied that they'd put away the drug dealer possibility. Her promise to David nagged at her conscience. Someone high on one of the drugs Joanna had been unable to resist might do that much damage and not even know about it later. What if Eric went to prison because she didn't want to tell anyone the truth about Joanna?

The drug industry was limited in a town as small as this. Weldon could easily find and question the known dealers, and if she spoke up, he could start with Hank Sloma.

Where did her loyalties lie? With David in the past,

even though he might have been wrong to swear her to secrecy? She had to think of Maggie first. If a dealer was that angry with Joanna's family, he might eventually get around to being pissed off at her baby.

"I have to tell you something, Noah."

He stepped back from her, and suddenly she felt naked. Skirting him, aware he was about to be furious, she reached for her robe again.

He turned with her. "Do I want to know what you need to say?"

"It's about Joanna."

He came to her in one step, and she dropped the robe. "Weldon told me what he thinks, but you know the details?"

His relief took the wind out of her sails. "That came out easier than I expected."

He didn't seem to think she'd made a joke. He grabbed her forearm. "Where did she get the drugs?"

"I don't know. If I did, I'd have checked it out myself."

He tightened his hand. "I'll bet you would have, without telling me. You'd risk your life and Maggie's future because you don't want to involve me. Maggie needs you to be more responsible."

"You're not hearing me." She denied his ridiculous accusation. "How much more involved could I beg you to be? I promised David I'd never tell anyone. I walked in on him after her funeral when he was flushing her drugs down their bathroom toilet, and he begged me to help him make sure Maggie never found out."

"She's a baby. By the time she grows up no one will care how her mother died."

"She'll care, and Joanna loved her. She would have stopped using if she could have, because of Maggie." Tessa shrugged, grief for David and Joanna sweeping her with an even stronger determination to protect their child. "Besides, Prodigal is a small town. People care for a long time."

"Did she die owing someone money?"

"That's the only conclusion that makes sense to me." She pulled out of his grasp. "I tried to pump Eleanor for information, but she thought I was accusing Joanna of stiffing me on a loan."

Noah considered their options. In the dim light, his expression grew hawkish again. He was a hunter on the trail of his favorite prey. "I think we have to ask Eleanor and Joe flat out. If they're hiding anything, because they're ashamed, they could be in danger next."

"They were here when the house was shot." It was a relief to share her real suspicions at last. "And everyone knew I'd be at the service."

"But 'everyone' might logically have assumed you'd take Eleanor and Joe and Maggie, too." He took her hand and rubbed his fingers over the skin he'd treated roughly. "I'm sorry. I didn't mean to hurt you."

She nodded. "It's all right. Let's just make sure Maggie's safe from any crazy who might have a grudge against anyone in her family."

"I'll help investigate, but that's what we're doing for Maggie. For us, I have to believe you trust me,

Tessa, or I'm going to wait for you to leave me again.''

"I left because I couldn't reach you."

'Did you try?'' he asked.

She took a deep breath. Not wanting to be in the wrong, she had one answer, but it was a lie. "I didn't try hard enough. I'm trying now."

"That's all I'll ask." He turned to the bed and lifted the sheets, but all the passion had left his gaze.

"You're angry with me?" she asked

"Wary," he said. "But I'm telling you so. That's a start, isn't it?"

"I don't know what to say. We aren't going to argue?" Shouldn't they at least talk until they reached an understanding?

"You sound as if you expect me to leave you this time."

"I want you to care. In fact, I don't intend to lie down beside you in that bed again if I don't believe you care."

He muttered a word she couldn't understand as he reached for her. This time he was gentle as he pulled her close. He brushed his lips against hers, teasing until she had to wrap her arms around his neck and urge him to deepen the kiss. When at last he raised his head, she hardly remembered what had upset her.

"I care, Tessa. And you care. Every argument doesn't have to be an ending."

She kissed him, claiming him. He wanted to belong to her. Together they fell onto the bed, but Noah lifted his weight off her.

"Make me believe again," she said.

"All right, but remind me to call Weldon in the morning."

She laughed at the concept of having to remind Noah to do police work. Then his mouth on her breast made her forget everything....

CHAPTER ELEVEN

A STATIC-LACED GURGLE on the monitor woke Noah while Tessa still slept. When they'd had Keely, they'd had a deal—first one who woke got up with her. Because of that old habit, he reached over and turned off the monitor.

Tessa muttered in her sleep. He couldn't understand what she said, but her smile suggested repletion. Grinning with pure happiness, he dressed as quietly as he could.

Maggie was bouncing in her crib when he opened the door. She stopped in midsong, clutching the crib rail to eye him with cautious welcome.

"Morning," he said. "What say we clean up and find something to eat?"

"Eat." She liked that word. It set her bouncing again.

She was more of a morning girl than Keely had been. She chattered nonstop in her own language, requiring only the occasional grunt from him as he changed her diaper and dressed her in the overalls and sweater Tessa had laid out on the dressing table.

Happily swinging her arms in an apparent demonstration of something she felt he needed to know, she let him carry her downstairs, and then beat a tattoo on his back as he started cereal and dished up the rest of some disgusting goo in two jars Tessa had left in the fridge.

Maggie only proved obstinate when he offered her the first spoonful of cereal. She slammed her hands onto the table and closed her mouth. But her eyes sparkled naughtiness at him and he had to laugh.

"Are you playing games, or do you hate this stuff?" He glanced from her to the spoon, and she pushed his hand toward his own face.

"No, thanks," he said. The cereal didn't smell that bad, but it looked like wallpaper paste. Keely had eaten it cheerfully.

He tried again, and Maggie shook her head, pressing her lips together in a tight seam.

He pried a little cereal out of the spoon and then dipped the tip into the fruit. When he offered it this time, Maggie partially opened her mouth and then leaned forward to snap up the mixture.

"Careful. Tessa will have my hide if you hurt yourself on the spoon."

Feeding her went pretty well after that, though Maggie seemed sure he needed to join her in a bite or two. He offered her the spoon to hold, and she liked the process even better as he helped her feed herself. He managed to get close to the bottom of the bowl by leaning toward her as if he planned to take a bite, as well, from the spoon in her cereal-smeared fist. He loved her delighted giggle as she ate the cereal to keep him from having it.

Suddenly the door opened, and Tessa came in, yanking a sweater over her head. A quick glimpse of pink flesh pressed against pale blue lace struck him silent and lustful. Her grin, as she popped her tousled blond head out of the top of the sweater, intimated she'd performed the show for his benefit.

"I can't believe you did that with Eleanor and Joe in the house." He also couldn't believe how deeply he didn't want anyone else seeing her nearly undressed.

With a pleased smirk, she ignored his complaint. "I called the D.A. and made an appointment to talk to her about drug activity in town."

"When?" He didn't like the idea of her going out without him. If she was right about Eric, someone who liked a big knife was still roaming Prodigal.

"I'm supposed to meet her in about twenty minutes at the coffee shop across from the courthouse. Could you look after Maggie?"

He stared at the baby, who waved her cereal spoon at him as if it were a semaphore flag. "Yeah." He wiped a glob of cereal and fruit off her chin. Meanwhile she grabbed his hand for a quick gnaw that left a deposit of cereal on his fingers and in his palm. "This stuff really feels repulsive." He took a deep breath, guessing he was about to overstep their new limits. "Be careful. Make sure you're not followed. Do you have your cell phone?"

"You don't have to worry, Noah. I'm scared. I don't want anyone shooting at you and Maggie or Eleanor and Joe, or my house. I certainly don't want to be shot. You don't have to remind me to take precautions."

Grinning at her predictability, he nodded. "That's what I thought you'd say."

She scooped her hair over her shoulder as she leaned down to kiss his cheek. "Sorry. I overreacted.'' Straightening, she wiped a spot of cereal from her nose. "Maggie's food is—aromatic, too.''

Hearing her name, Maggie cooed, making them both look her way. With a guttural sound that appeared to be language to her, she offered Tessa a spoonful.

"You've got her feeding herself?''

"She seemed to want to. She's pretty good.''

"And you're going to clean the fallout, right?'' Tessa stroked the baby's hair and then gripped his shoulder, her smile open and yet a little anxious. "I am sorry about snapping at you. I know you're concerned.''

"Don't apologize. We have to learn how to live with each other again, and we've changed in ways we might not have if we'd made our marriage work.''

"What do you mean?'' She let him go as if he'd accused her of something.

"You're still determined not to need me.'' He offered a confession. "And I need to believe you do.''

Tessa bit her lip, already swollen from the hours he'd spent kissing her as if he'd never touch her again. "I do need you,'' she said. "I just forgot I'm allowed to again. We can't change overnight.''

He turned to Maggie. He'd changed. Where he'd felt grudging affection for her before, Tessa's acceptance had freed his feelings for the baby. He wanted to do right by her. He wanted to be a father who might make up for the loss of David.

Maggie beamed at him and pushed her spoon his way, whacking him with it and leaving his face full of slimy oatmeal.

Her laughter, at his expense, was one of the

sweetest sounds he'd ever heard. He turned back to Tessa, plowing the cereal off his cheek with his fingertips. "I think we have to make this work together."

Tessa shook her head at him. "When she grows up, I'll have to thank her for showing me the key to your heart is in a bowl of tepid oatmeal."

"It's her arm," he said. "With that strength, she'll be the first female pro pitcher."

"Yeah? Too bad she's too young to use her arm to help you chisel the cereal off my floor, and you'd better get moving. I don't want Eleanor to think we're sloppy around here." At the kitchen door, she turned back, frowning. "Noah, keep a close eye on Maggie while I'm gone."

What a crazy thing to say. But he chose not to overreact.

SUNLIGHT ON CRUSTED SNOW blinded her. She slipped on her sunglasses as she turned out of the driveway. The streets were clear, two lines of black pavement between the dirty brown snow that had piled up beneath passing cars.

As soon as she pulled away from the house, she scooped her cell phone out of her pocket. She still remembered Lucy's phone number. She'd wanted to dial it often enough in the past eighteen months.

Noah's mother took her time about answering, and when she said hello, she sounded as if she might still be asleep. She had to say hello again before Tessa found the will to answer.

"It's me," she said. "Tessa."

"Dear God."

Tessa smiled at the joy in Lucy's voice. "Does that mean you're glad to hear from me or you wish I hadn't called?"

"About time you called—nothing's happened to Noah?"

"No." She hastened to reassure his mother. "He's at home, looking after Maggie, David's daughter."

"I'm so sorry to hear about him, sweetie. Are you all right?"

"I'm getting there. Now."

"Meaning my son has something to do with your improvement?"

"I think so. He said something this morning that made me think I should call you."

"I've been browbeating him for months to make you call. What was the magic word?"

Tessa laughed. "He said we have to make this work."

"Make what work?" Lucy sounded anxious.

Tessa felt almost as wary, but she refused to back down. "I'm not sure yet, myself, but I thought we'd need our family while we're working."

"I'm glad, Tessa. I've missed you."

"Me, too, but Lucy, I just didn't want you to feel uncomfortable with Noah."

"No matter what happens between you and my son, Tessa, you're my daughter. Don't forget that again. I lost you *and* Keely when you left Noah."

Her simple statement struck Tessa like a sharp blow. "I never thought…"

"We don't have to dwell on it, but don't cut me out of your life again."

"Why didn't you tell me?" Tessa asked.

"I'm thinking this is the first day you could hear me and believe how much I love you."

Tessa nodded and then remembered Lucy was on the phone and couldn't see her. "You're right." Noah had given her the confidence to believe in love again.

Suddenly a male voice spoke in the background, and Tessa burst into laughter. "Is that Mr. Davis, Lucy?"

"I'm afraid not. Mr. Davis got too possessive. You know I can't stand that in a man." As she seemed to have turned her face away from the phone, Tessa assumed Lucy was talking to her early-morning visitor. Lucy had her own quirks after losing her husband at such a young age. Noah had viewed her fear of commitment firsthand.

"I should let you go."

"For now," Lucy said. "But I'd like to see you."

"As soon as we find out what happened with David."

"I'll hold you to that promise."

"I love you, Lucy."

"Love you, too, sweetie. Call me soon."

Tessa folded the phone shut against her coat. She'd bet Lucy called Noah before she got home.

In the square downtown, work went on as usual. Bundled-up tourists wandered in and out of the antique shops. Local citizens, less bundled but more serious of expression, made their way in and out of the business offices. Everyone eventually trekked to the doughnut maker whose wares were known and most greatly admired from Boston to Bangor.

Tessa found a parking spot just off the square and walked around the corner to the courthouse. As she crossed to the coffee shop, Jill Dayton, Prodigal's D.A. waved from inside the wide glass front doors.

Tessa hurried inside, clutching the sides of her coat together against the cold. They took a table, and a server came to settle silverware and coffee cups in front of them. Tessa hadn't slept much the night before, and she asked for a double shot of espresso. When they were alone, she leaned across the table.

"Thanks for making time to see me, Jill."

"I'm grateful someone's willing to talk about drug use in town, and you're an attorney. You have access to the people who can change things around here. I don't think we have many offenders, but one child buying drugs is too big a problem for me."

Tessa sat back. "I hope I didn't mislead you, because I'm not sure what I can do to help you."

"You handled family law in Boston. What happened?"

The answer was too private, but Tessa was getting used to baring her soul. "My daughter died. SIDS. I couldn't face families without her."

Jill seemed willing to respect the pain behind her clipped response. "But you know what these families face when their children get involved with drugs?"

"I'd be glad to help, and I promise I'll do whatever you ask of me, but right now, I have to ask you an awkward question. The answer might be in David's files, but I haven't had time or access yet to go through them, and you know what goes on in this town." She couldn't mention David's client by name. "You may not understand what I'm trying to say, but can you think of anyone who'd be willing to kill if a customer didn't pay up?"

Jill sat forward in her chrome-plated chair. "Are we talking David Howard? I heard rumors about Joanna, but never David."

"What do you think?"

"They'd try to scare someone, but murder?" The other woman plucked at her auburn braid. "These are small-time guys. They like the money and the monopoly they have in such a limited area, but I don't see anyone killing a customer."

"How about killing someone else, as a warning to other customers?"

Jill shook her head, but then she seemed to reconsider. "I guess times and drug business could change, even here in Prodigal." She pulled her napkin over and fished a pen out of her purse. "Give me your number. I'm going to check anyone David defended and I'll move out from there. I think I should warn Weldon to keep looking outside his holding cells."

"You'll have to beat my ex-husband to the punch."

"What do you mean?"

"I told him about this last night, and he's planning to talk to the chief today." Tessa thought of her broken promise, of the friendship she'd had to betray. "But you're right about talking to Weldon. Can you ask him to keep any investigation quiet until he has some evidence?"

Jill looked up, her pen poised, suspicion imprinted on her face. "Keep what quiet?"

Tessa licked her lips. It was one thing to tell Noah, but a stranger? And Jill would see to it that everyone in Prodigal with any power found out that

Joanna Howard had fallen prey to drugs again before she died.

Tessa smoothed her fingers across her own napkin. Letting people see David's wife as an example furthered Jill's own plans for stopping the problem, but Tessa couldn't forget what David had reluctantly admitted—that Joanna had mistaken Tessa for a rival, in her depression after Maggie's birth.

"Keep what quiet, Tessa?" Jill said again.

"Joanna." Saying the name put both her friends in the past. Promises that might hurt Maggie weren't worth keeping now, and she hadn't come between David and Joanna. David had loved his wife.

She opened her purse and slipped a business card out of a pouch. "This has my phone numbers on it. If you find out anything, you'll call me?"

Jill nodded, studying the card. "I'll start with a quick search on David's cases. He argued Hank Sloma's case against me."

"And what did you think? Was Sloma guilty?" She wished she'd asked David that question at the time.

"I didn't agree with giving him probation, but he hasn't taken a step wrong since David got him off."

Tessa glanced at the other woman, a little peeved. "David didn't 'get him off.' He did his job, and he was an honorable man." Jill widened her gaze, and Tessa remembered the D.A. didn't share her deep grief. "Sorry. I just miss him." She closed her purse. "And I need to talk to Joanna's parents before you get in touch with Weldon."

"No problem. Why don't you call me after you talk to them?"

"Thanks."

Jill glanced at her watch. "I say we get that coffee to go."

Tessa nodded and signaled their server. "I need to stop by David's house and pick up his mail before I go home, but I should be able to call you within a couple of hours."

"That sounds good."

Tessa put on her coat and paid for the coffee. She and Jill shook hands at the door, and she started across the street to find her car. As she reached the sidewalk, she looked up and saw Noah striding toward her. Noah, with his coat rounded and a tiny pink knit cap rising out of his lapels.

Maggie.

Tessa hurried to meet them. She stopped at Noah's side, the better to lean around him and view Maggie's somewhat tipsy smile of greeting.

Noah hefted the bundle strapped to his stomach. "I thought you and I might drop by Weldon's office and explain about the Sloma kid."

Tessa kissed the baby's forehead. "With Maggie?"

Noah offered her a rueful smile. "Might as well use any leverage we have. He's going to be angry we held back, and since I can't think of a reason to blame him, I thought he might be calmer in front of Maggie."

"Do you care? I don't think of you as someone who worries about what other people think."

"I'll see his point this time."

She nodded. Noah remained a cop, sticking with his brother police. "I need to ask him if I can pick up David's mail anyway."

"Do you want to carry the baby? You'll be a less likely target with her in your arms."

She laughed shortly. "Thanks, but I suspect you'll be his first concern—a lawman intruding on his turf—and believe me, nothing appeals as much as a man with a baby."

"Not to another man." Noah looked ludicrously appalled.

"Call it an extra bonus for me, then." Grinning, she took out her cell phone again. "But I still think he'll be calmer if you come bearing a baby." She opened the phone and tapped in Jill's phone number.

"Who are you calling?"

"The D.A. She promised to hold off on calling Weldon until I had a chance to warn Eleanor and Joe that he'd be looking into Joanna's accident again. I'll let her know we're going to visit Weldon and that I'll be a little later than I planned talking to the Worths."

Weldon was as furious as Tessa feared, but as Noah had predicted, Maggie softened his reaction. He allowed himself only one, "I knew she was using again" and even with that, he eyed Joanna's child with empathy.

"One other thing," Tessa said as they turned to leave Weldon's office.

The police chief looked at her as if she were a week-old chunk of muddied snow that had stuck to his boot. "What now?"

"I need to pick up David's mail. He may have bills I should pay. It's not part of your crime scene, is it?"

"Do you have keys?"

She nodded, holding up a ring. "We kept a spare set for each other."

"You have more on that than I have. I'll need you to leave these."

Noah leaned down as they left the room. "Sometimes when he talks to you, I think I could help him form a more respectful attitude toward the public."

"Big talk from a guy with a baby strapped to his heart."

He arched an eyebrow. "I'm serious, Tessa. I'd like to take him apart when he goes at you."

"I could tell, but you said yourself, I should have spoken up earlier."

"What I say and what he says are two different things."

"You're both arrogant enough." She nodded to the deputy behind the front desk and pushed the door open to let Noah and Maggie pass through. "And I can take care of myself. I appreciate your protectiveness, but I wonder if you're trying to make up for lost time."

He stopped on the sidewalk. "What if I am?"

She met his gaze. Last night had changed things, but how much? They'd vaguely discussed the future, but already things were turning sticky between them.

"I called Lucy," she said.

"I know. She told me."

"You don't sound pleased." She faced him anxiously. "Should I have waited?"

"I'm glad you called her, and so was she."

"But something's wrong." She tugged at his arm, leaning into his body. "You don't have to make up for the past, unless you want me to, as well. Let's call it even and try to make a clean start."

"I thought we were," he said. "You're the one suggesting I shouldn't worry about you."

She nodded hesitantly. "I'm sort of glad you care so much, but I don't like feeling hemmed in."

He looked uneasy, as if he were on shifting ground. "Maybe I'm trying to care for you now with all the wrong moves."

"Your moves are okay." She rubbed his shoulder, warming with memories of the night before.

"I wonder." Last night obviously didn't occur to him. "It's in my nature to stake out boundaries."

She shivered, not necessarily because of the snow-kissed air. "You should get Maggie home, out of the cold."

After a second, he shifted the baby a little to the side and leaned down to brush Tessa's lips.

"Don't pull away, Tessa."

"It's in my nature to avoid staying where I'm not wanted."

"You were always wanted."

"I want to believe you, but I couldn't tell then." She kissed him, forgetting they were on the street in the middle of her new hometown. Maggie's giggle broke them apart. Tessa leaned away, regretfully, wiping lipstick from Noah's mouth. "I'd better go."

"You believe me now, Tessa? I'm trying to convince you I'll stay involved."

"If you don't find something more important to do, I'll eventually trust." Was it now or never with him? "If you can wait for me."

He kissed her again, reassuring her. With a brief sensual smile, he smoothed Maggie's cap as the baby cooed at a fluttering piece of newspaper. "Where did you park?"

"Behind the courthouse, but don't come with me. It's too cold."

"You aren't going to David's house alone. I'll follow you in the car, and we'll go in together."

"You aren't bringing Maggie," she said.

"Then don't go inside. Where's his mailbox?"

"Out by the street, but I thought I'd make sure nothing's spoiled in the fridge, see if his pipes burst during the storm the other night."

"The fridge and the pipes were fine yesterday. Pull up, and take out the mail. Do not go in that house by yourself."

"Why would someone kill David and then hang around his house?"

"I'm not trying to manhandle you, Tessa, but I can't just go to your house and hope you show up later." He stopped when Maggie slammed a mittened hand against his mouth. "And neither can she," he said, his voice muffled.

She relented. They both had a lot to learn about being together again, and she'd worried often enough about him not coming home that she got his point.

"I'll check the mail from my car. You take Maggie home where she'll be safe." She kissed the top of Maggie's cap and then pressed a kiss to the corner of Noah's tense mouth. "I'll see you later."

"Call me when you pull away from the house."

"Okay." He had a lot of rules. They might be sensible, but they still felt stifling.

To Noah's astonishment, he managed to persuade Maggie to take a nap. With Keely, naptime had often been fight time.

Eleanor and Joe were sharing lunch in the kitchen when he went downstairs. She'd put together a salad, and they'd warmed up leftover chicken to make sandwiches.

"Smells good," Noah said from the kitchen door.

"Oh." Eleanor turned. "We heard footsteps upstairs. I thought it was Tessa."

"She'll be home soon. She had to—" He caught himself before he spilled Tessa's guts. He wouldn't mind explaining about Weldon and the D.A. and the new investigation that might include Joanna, but he didn't want Tessa to think he was acting for her because he thought her incapable.

She was anything but. He wished he had gone to court before, to watch her work. She was good. Confident.

"Had to what?" Joe asked.

"Pick up David's mail and a few other things." He poured himself a mug of coffee and joined them at the table.

"What's she going to do with David's mail?" Joe asked.

"I guess she wants to pay the bills."

"Doesn't it bother you that your wife was so close to another man?"

Noah stared at Joe. "What are you talking about? You didn't believe the gossip, too?"

"Of course not," Eleanor snapped, "but we didn't like hearing it, either."

"As long as we all agree it meant nothing." He stared them both down, more glad than ever that he was going to be around to back Tessa up. "Maggie's a sweet baby." He changed the subject. "She went right down for her nap."

"Being out in the cold probably made her tired," Eleanor said. "You dressed her warmly?"

"Head to toe. Only her face was uncovered, and she had that in my chest most of the time. She liked being out."

"But she's probably not used to it. David had her in day care." Joe coughed, a scoffing sound. "You know how that is. Why would they bother to take the children out into the fresh air?"

He was full of surprises today, but who could blame him for resenting the son-in-law whose will had left Maggie to someone else? "You would have liked to have seen more of her?"

"I'd like to have seen her spend less time in day care. She could have been with us more often."

"David's been busy these past months. He had to shoulder the errands Joanna used to do around the house." Eleanor sounded defensive again. "Besides, you can see he wouldn't want to be away from his daughter."

As they both still hated being parted from theirs. Noah understood that bitterness all too well. He pushed his chair back and dumped his coffee into the sink. Glancing at his watch, he wondered why Tessa was late calling.

"Excuse me," he said. "I want to take a look at Tessa's computer."

"What do you hope to find in there?" Joe asked.

"I'm just going to look at the notes she made again." Actually, the computer sat in front of the bay window in the living room. He could keep a casual watch for her from the desk.

"Joanna always wanted us to buy a computer," Joe said.

"She thought we could talk each day through that electronic mail," Eleanor said. "I wish I'd let her set it up for us now. She wanted to so much."

Nodding absently, Noah went back to the living room. He booted the machine but leaned into the window. Up and down the street, a few cars were parked. None moved, and Tessa didn't pull up. He checked the time again, his stomach starting to clench. A few more minutes, and he'd have to call Weldon and then prepare to face Tessa's wrath.

While Eleanor and Joe began to clean the kitchen, he stayed at Tessa's desk. But when he opened her word-processing program, he found an odd file name in the list of files she'd recently used. It was called "Financials D."

David's financials?

He hesitated a moment. Opening it would definitely be crowding Tessa. But hadn't she asked him here to help find David's killer? This might point him in the right direction.

He couldn't help himself. He clicked on the file's title.

A screen flashed up, listing income and outflow. Several checks for a "Mr. Sloma" and another entry for "Sloma, supplies" made him flinch. Why would David record drug and paraphernalia buys? And why would he buy drugs at all? Tessa insisted that only Joanna had the problem.

Obviously she'd recently looked at this file, but

she'd decided to keep it from him. If this was evidence, it was key.

He stared at the screen, thinking fast. If David had been in trouble with the dealers both he *and* Joanna had used, his death was no longer a mystery.

A slamming car door dragged Noah's gaze to the window. Tessa climbed out of her car. Something about her expression pulled him from his chair. As she stared at an open letter in her hand, he crossed the room to open the front door.

She looked up at him, her gaze intense. "I have to talk to you."

"Okay."

She lowered her voice. "Where are Eleanor and Joe?"

He nodded toward the kitchen.

"Maggie's asleep?" Tessa asked.

"For about twenty minutes."

"Come outside."

He grabbed his coat. As he pulled it on and shut the door behind himself, he remembered the gloves that must have fallen to the floor. He rammed his hands into his pockets.

"What's wrong? Something in that letter?"

"I know I shouldn't have opened it, and I never would have normally, but it's a bill from an attorney I know, Simon Gould. He's a family lawyer, Noah." She glanced back at the house as if she expected a crowd of cops to pour out of it and arrest her.

He stared, fascinated by the play of her long straight hair over her shoulders, but he couldn't read her mind now. "So? I'm not seeing the problem."

"Family law. I specialized in family law until I

came here. David must have consulted this guy on something he didn't want me to know about."

"Maybe he felt you were too close. He had some private questions to ask someone else. Just as you wouldn't ask a doctor who was also a family friend to treat some embarrassing condition."

"But what was so embarrassing?" She waved the letter and envelope. "I wonder if he wanted Eleanor and Joe to have custody if something happened to him."

Noah frowned. He was nearly as attached to Maggie as Tessa. The possibility of giving her up already hurt too much. "I guess," he agreed, "but why?"

"Because of Joanna's death. He may have felt family was more important than Eleanor and Joe's ages."

"That doesn't make sense unless something changed. David didn't get the letter seven months ago when Joanna died. It was delivered to him this week. He talked to this attorney recently."

Her haunted gaze wounded him. "It would make sense if someone threatened him. He'd be thinking about repercussions. Maybe he realized how much Eleanor and Joe want Maggie to be with them. For all we know, he may have changed his will to leave them as her guardian and me as the backup."

"We're groping in the dark. Didn't you agree to make sure they stayed close to her?" He cared too much. He couldn't be objective. Nothing made a whole lot of sense about David's death. "We have to talk to this guy."

"He won't break David's confidence. He can't."

"But you know David's executor can ask him to waive privilege. Who's the executor?"

"The attorney who set up his will."

"Why not you?"

"I didn't want access to his estate. I never really believed it would come up, but I assumed that if it did, I'd just petition the executor for anything Maggie needed."

"You know his name, though?" At her nod, he turned her back toward the house. "Let's call him and then ask Gould for an appointment."

"I have to tell Eleanor and Joe that Weldon knows about Joanna's drug use."

He felt for the older couple. "Do you think they knew?"

Tessa shook her head, her face drawn. "Even if they did, I don't believe they could have admitted it was true." She leaned into him, and he put his arm around her. "I'd hate having someone make me look at losing Keely again, and you know they'll relive her death. How many times have you gone over every minute of that morning we found Keely?"

"We?" He glanced down at her in surprise. She really hadn't blamed him because he'd walked into Keely's room and found her by himself. "You were still in bed. I was the one who saw her first, the one who should have—"

She pulled him around to face her. "I thought it was the same as if we both did."

"Not if you've been living with it for eighteen months." Surprise widened her eyes, and that reaction stunned him.

"I didn't understand," she said. "That day in the restaurant, I thought you were guilty the way I was— out of frustration, because I should have found a way to do something, but you're serious. You think you should have been able to save Keely's life. Why didn't you tell me?''

Words wouldn't come at first. He didn't know how to admit weakness when she needed him to be strong. But, as he remained silent, her face went blank and she pulled out of his reach.

"I did tell you, in a way, as best I could." He'd never admitted the depth of his guilt to anyone—and most of all, not to Tessa. "I couldn't talk to you, because I thought you held me responsible. I couldn't risk hearing you say the words out loud."

"Noah." She lifted her hand to his face, and he noticed she'd lost her gloves also. Her fingers were cold against his cheek, but her gaze warmed him. "What you said at Jimmy's Bistro—about not blaming me—I believed that, and I felt better for the first time in months. We both have to believe we couldn't have saved her. It was a horrible tragedy, but it's time we learned to survive."

Touched by her hell-bent expression and her offer of absolution, he pulled her hand to his mouth. "We made a mess of things when we should have taken care of each other." He kissed her fingers with gratitude, trying to warm her with his body heat.

"It's not too late." Her smile was a secret they shared, based on trust they'd begun to build. She turned toward the house. "I'd better go inside and talk to the Worths."

He caught her hand. "I found the file on your computer." He didn't wait for her to ask. "The list of payments to Sloma."

She stared at him, convincingly confused. "Payments? For what?"

"For drugs, I guess." He watched for her reaction, but she seemed as surprised as he. "Maybe that's just what we're supposed to think."

"What are you talking about?"

"Has anyone else used your computer?"

"David, occasionally. I don't even look at the file list, but I would have thought all the other files I'd used—for Carlson and Eric and Mr. Swyndle—would have been more recent than the one you're talking about if David created it. Do you think he might have been listing information he'd found on Joanna?"

"I think we should let Weldon have access to your computer, and I'll make sure he gets an expert in to examine the file."

"You don't think someone broke into the house?"

"We have to assume so," he said. "We were all out yesterday."

With a shiver, she tucked the attorney's letter in her pocket. "Maybe you could call Weldon, and then I think we should talk to Simon, whether he'll give us any information or not."

"I'm right behind you." He meant it more than he'd meant even their wedding vows. No one would get at her or in her house again as long as he was around. And he was here to stay.

Opening the door, she looked at him over her shoulder, with startling seriousness. "I'm counting on you." She paused for a moment. "And we're bringing Maggie with us. Eleanor will offer to look after her, but I'll feel a lot safer if she's with us."

"Yeah," he said grimly, aware that Eleanor and

Joe seemed to want more from their relationship with Maggie than they were telling Tessa. "She'll have to understand after we explain we may have had an intruder."

CHAPTER TWELVE

NOAH OFFERED to help Tessa tell Eleanor and Joe about their talk with Weldon, but she thought it was best to do it on her own. She wanted to save them from any more pain than they had to endure and they might prefer a smaller audience as they tried to get used to the idea of having Joanna talked about.

Facing them on her own was easier said than done, though. She stood at the kitchen door, her heart pounding in the top of her throat. She didn't want to tell them.

When she finally opened the door, Maggie's grandparents were sharing a cup of coffee at the kitchen table. Eleanor seemed to see bad news on Tessa's face.

"What's happened? Is it Maggie?"

"No." Her heart went out to them. How long before a bereaved parent stopped anticipating the worst? "I had to talk to Sheriff Weldon today, about some information David asked me to keep quiet."

She waited, giving them a chance to leap to the right conclusion, as if that would be less painful. Joe seemed to get it first.

"It's about Joanna?"

Tessa nodded. "I don't know how to tell you."

"Quick and merciless works best," Joe said, clenching his hands on the sides of his chair.

Eleanor sat still, looking stunned. Then she stood so abruptly her chair turned over behind her. "What about Joanna?"

"Just after her funeral I walked in on David flushing some drugs down the toilet. At first I thought they were his, that her death made him want to forget, so he'd started taking them." She'd understood such a depth of despair.

"Don't tell me he blamed them on my daughter," Eleanor said.

Tessa bit her bottom lip, unable to go on.

"Whose were they, Tessa?" Joe was relentless.

Tessa lifted Eleanor's chair and laid her hand on the other woman's shoulder. "I knew, really. David had never touched drugs. He was so horrified at what they'd done to Joanna, I don't think he'd have been capable, but he didn't want Maggie to know about her mom."

"Joanna learned her lesson," Eleanor said. "She didn't take drugs after she left the rehabilitation center. She had too much to live for—her daughter, parents who adored her."

"And her husband," Tessa said, meeting Eleanor's bitter gaze. "David loved her, too."

"David let her believe he couldn't choose between you and her." Eleanor pulled away, and Tessa rubbed her palms together, feeling a sting where she'd touched Joanna's mother.

"He didn't, Eleanor. David loved only Joanna. I don't know why she would have believed anything else, and I know David pulled away from me before she died and after. He didn't want her to be confused about which of us he loved as his wife.''

Joe came around the table. ''Try to understand, Tessa. We lost our daughter and David, and we're angry. When your daughter died, didn't you want to blame someone?''

''I blamed myself.''

He nodded. ''Because you should have seen the problem. We feel the same. We're searching for answers, just the way you have. And we're doing our best to live.''

''But you don't think David would lie about Joanna?''

''No,'' he said, his tone firm. ''But why don't the police know for sure what happened? Why does Weldon insist Joanna was under the influence?''

Tessa glanced at Eleanor, reluctant to hurt her further. ''David bribed the former police chief to cover it up. That's why he left office. He's not working in Presque Isle. He's hiding out, probably praying Weldon won't be able to gather enough evidence to prosecute him.''

''Why didn't this come out in the newspapers?'' Joe demanded.

''Because of Joanna.'' She shrugged in frustration because she couldn't do anything to help Maggie's trembling grandmother. ''According to David, the editor figured he and Maggie had already suffered enough, and Joanna was his friend, too. He dropped the story.''

''It's not true.'' Eleanor pushed away from Joe to stand on her own two feet.

''I'm sorry, Eleanor. I'd give anything to avoid telling you all this, but I'm afraid Joanna might have made someone angry." Tessa softened her tone. "We have to think of Maggie and of you and Joe. I don't want someone to hurt you. That's why I asked if anyone talked to you about Joanna's bills. I was trying to find out if the dealer she used threatened you."

"No—because you're wrong, and the police are wrong. You just believed David, when he should have been the one you doubted. He was using those drugs—not Joanna—and he must have felt guilty, maybe even afraid, because he had Maggie on his own, so he was throwing the drugs away."

Tessa had no hope Eleanor would believe anything she could say. The other woman couldn't face the truth, and Tessa empathized with her. Nevertheless, she had to warn them about the possible intruder, too.

"I have to tell you one other thing. Noah found something on the computer—a file that doesn't belong to me—and we think someone must have broken in. He's calling Weldon right now."

"Great," Joe muttered.

"But you should stay alert if you're here by yourselves." She caught a quick, remorseful breath as Eleanor glared at her with soulless eyes. "Noah and I have to take Maggie out for a little while, but I'm going to call a locksmith before I leave, and arrange to have the locks changed again."

"As if I'd care if someone broke in now," Eleanor said through tears. "I'd welcome anyone who could put an end to this evil."

Her plaintive need stopped Tessa in her tracks. Impelled to offer comfort, she gently rubbed the other woman's back.

"I loved Joanna, too, Eleanor. David made me promise never to tell anyone, but I had to because of you all and Maggie."

Eleanor turned her face into Joe's chest, and Tessa's hand fell to her side. His mouth drawn with sadness, Joe simply nodded toward the kitchen door. Tessa took his hint.

The pain in the kitchen practically pushed her out of the room, but she found Noah at the computer. He turned and his reassuring smile helped.

"You couldn't do anything else." He looked back at the screen. "Come look at this file," he said, low voiced, "just to make sure you haven't seen it before. I told Weldon we'd drop a copy by his office."

She peered over his shoulder, her mind with the couple in the other room. "I don't think they believed me."

"I've seen it before. They need time to absorb the truth." He eyed the text on the monitor. "I don't understand this file, though. Leaving it for us to find is such an obvious mistake."

"What do you mean?" She didn't even recognize the names that didn't have to do with Sloma.

"If David were in with these guys, he wouldn't leave evidence like this lying around, and if someone broke in here and put this on your computer, it's too obvious to believe."

Behind her, Eleanor's voice rose every so often, not loudly enough for Tessa to understand what she said, but enough to intimate angry grief.

Tessa pressed her hand to Noah's shoulder, taking comfort from her right to touch him. He covered her hand with his and stood. His glance, slipping from her face to the closed kitchen door, looked uneasy, too.

"The worst part is not knowing what to do," he said.

"Joe waved at me to leave them alone."

"Have you talked to David's executor yet?"

"I left him a message he hasn't returned."

"Why don't I dress Maggie, and you call this Simon." He snatched a piece of paper from the printer and took a floppy disk from the computer. "Let's give them some privacy."

"You've had to tell people stuff like this before, haven't you?" She'd never realized how much it hurt to shatter another human being's illusions.

He nodded. "Not my favorite part of the job, though I always come away determined to find the scum who caused it."

"Maybe we're getting close to this guy." She touched the paper in his hand. "If this is a mistake, someone's getting desperate."

"You told them to be careful while we're gone?"

"Mmm-hmm, but that reminds me. I need to call a locksmith."

"We won't wait for that. We'll stop at a hardware store on our way home, and *I'll* change the locks again. Tessa?"

She looked at him.

"Did you happen to ask Eleanor and Joe if they left off the alarm when they went out yesterday morning?"

"No, but I'm thinking I should have it replaced. It's obviously easy to defeat." She went to the keypad. "It looks fine, and I know I set it last night."

"Let's change the code again." Noah circled her, folding the sheet of paper. "I'll get Maggie."

Tessa persuaded Simon Gould's assistant to make an appointment for them on short notice after his regular office hours. She wanted to look in on Joe and Eleanor again, but they were quiet in the kitchen. And they probably would have come out if they'd wanted company.

Tessa wished again that she could have made any other decision. Maybe Joe could be a little stiff now and then. And too often Eleanor tended to remind Tessa that they were Maggie's blood relatives. But Tessa already accepted those small hiccups in their changing relationship as the price they had to pay to build a new family for Maggie.

Upstairs, her door opened and Maggie let out a cheerful whoop as Noah carried her, bundled again for outdoor weather, to the stairs. "We'll take my car," he said. "I left her seat in it."

They wrestled a wriggling Maggie into the seat, having both grown unfamiliar with babies and confusing straps. Maggie seemed to want to play. She arched her back and giggled at their efforts until Tessa began to sweat, even in the cold.

"Was Keely this difficult?" she asked.

"I don't—" His silence startled her and she looked at him.

"What?" she asked.

"That's the first time we've talked about her in a normal way." He shook his head, and his hair brushed the car's gray roof. "I feel sad, as if we're putting her behind us. And I don't remember if she fought being put in her car seat."

"She'll always be part of us." Their serious voices had distracted Maggie, and she unbowed. Tessa snapped the restraining belts into place without a second to lose. "But I think we're doing Keely's memory a disservice, still fighting the fact that she's gone. She was a happy girl, and she made us happy. We've been sad and angry for longer than we had her."

Dismaying her, Noah's eyes seemed to fill with moisture. His mouth worked, but he didn't speak. Instead, he leaned across Maggie's kicking feet to cup the nape of Tessa's neck.

His kiss was the absolution she'd offered him earlier, and a wish for the future. Hope she wanted to share with him.

"I'd like us to make the most of our good memories," he said.

Maggie stuck her snowsuit-covered foot between them, and uttered a question in her own language. Laughing as her heart raced at the promise of a future with Noah, Tessa leaned down and kissed the bridge of Maggie's nose.

Then she straightened and kissed Noah again. He opened her mouth with his, brief but possessively thorough. Tessa pulled away, her head swimming.

"We should go." She caught Maggie's waving foot. "I don't want to leave the Worths alone too long, and they might feel better if they spend some time with this crazy girl."

Noah grinned, a guy in charge of his family again. He liked being in charge, and she saw no reason to burst his bubble.

The temperature must have risen during the day. The tree-lined streets were wet but bare of snow.

They went to Weldon's office first, where they all studied the file while Maggie played with the deputy's handcuffs. Weldon had arranged for an expert from Augusta to come take a look at Tessa's computer, but due to fresh snowfall in the capital, he wouldn't be getting out of town until tomorrow.

Shadows began to gather as they drove to Simon Gould's office on the outskirts of town. The Maine forest edged closer out here. Tessa shivered.

"I must be getting paranoid. It seems as if we understand less, and I'm getting more scared as time goes on."

"I won't let anything happen to you or Maggie."

She turned, smiling gently. "That's a heroic promise, but we both know even you can't stop someone who's serious about killing."

He stared out the windshield. "My talents lie in catching them afterward," he said. "But this is different. I won't lose you now."

Unspoken between them lay the future, but Tessa was too aware of mistakes she'd made in the past. Noah had talked about being certain before he'd asked her about reconciling, and she needed time to be sure she wasn't going to let him down before she made promises. Deep in thought, she almost missed their last turn, into a small office park.

"There," she said. "He's at the far end, in the back."

"How do you know this guy?"

"I asked him to look over the papers we drew up for Maggie's guardianship."

Only three cars remained in the parking lot this late. Noah nosed his car between two of them, and then Tessa took Maggie from her seat. Simon met them in his reception area.

"Hello, Tessa," he said. "I've been meaning to call you. This must be Maggie." He chucked the baby under her chin and didn't bother to wipe off her drool. "She's grown since I last saw her."

Tessa jumped in with both feet. "David didn't bring her when he consulted you last?"

Simon's expression flattened.

"Maybe we should talk in your office," Noah said.

"Good idea." Simon led the way past his assistant, who nodded at them all as she put on her coat.

In his office, he offered them a large, leather sofa, where Tessa loosened Maggie's snowsuit and peeled off her cap. Noah sat beside her and the baby while Simon took the leather armchair.

He crossed his legs. "You know I can't tell you much."

"I hoped you could give us a lead." She turned to Noah. "This is my—my—this is Noah Gabriel. We were married before I came to live here."

"Yes, I think David mentioned Noah, and, of course, the town's awash in gossip. You're a cop, aren't you?"

"I have no jurisdiction here," Noah said, "but David was our friend, and I want to know who killed him. Tessa found your bill in his mail." He fished the envelope from his inside pocket and held it out. "Naturally, we'd like to know if you can tell us anything that might lead to David's killer."

Simon widened his gaze, looking mystified. "That, I know nothing about."

Tessa glanced at Noah impatiently. He was usually

much more subtle. "Maybe you could put me at ease about something else. Did David come to see you about Maggie?"

Simon uncrossed his legs and crossed them the other way. "I can't answer that."

Fear took Tessa's throat in its clammy hand. "Should I expect another will to show up? Did David change the provisions he made for Maggie?"

Simon hesitated, his gaze moving between her and Noah, finally resting on the baby. "I can tell you I produced no paperwork for David, but I can't say anything else, Tessa."

"Simon." She knew it was unethical, but she couldn't help herself. Resorting to flat-out interrogation, she leaned forward.

"Wait." Noah rested his hand on her arm, holding her back. "You can't force the man to break privilege, but look, Simon, if David knew that Tessa was taking care of Maggie, would he be pleased?"

Tessa eased into the back of the sofa as Simon's mouth curved in a big grin. "Good question," she said, eyeing Noah with gratitude.

"Perfect question," Simon said. He caught Tessa's gaze, with meaning in his own eyes. "And David would be delighted."

"Thank God." She cupped her hand over the familiar shape of Maggie's head, and her heart melted. She'd have forced herself to turn Maggie over to Joe and Eleanor if David had wanted her to, but she wouldn't give Maggie up to anyone with a whole heart now. She was learning to be a mother again, at this baby's small hands.

"I'm glad I could help." Simon stood. "But now

I need to go home. My son has a hockey game to-night, and I have to admit, David's death has made me more cognizant of my own family's needs. I'd hate it if I was gone, and they hardly noticed. Funny how you let yourself get so busy, when you're prac-ticing law to keep families together.'' He held out his hand to Tessa. ''But you know all about that.''

She shook his hand. ''I do,'' she said, not looking at Noah. They'd both been distracted before. How would that be different now? After they found out who'd killed David, they'd go back to their regular lives. Would they forget their good intentions in the first week of rushing from appointment to crime scene to day-care center? ''Thank you, Simon. I can't tell you how you eased my mind.''

He caught Maggie's hand between his index finger and thumb. She cooed at him, and he fell under her spell, too. ''I can guess,'' he said. ''Take good care. Call on me if I can do anything else.''

''I'd like to know exactly what you discussed with David,'' Noah said, but Simon snapped his mouth shut, and Noah lifted his hands in acquiescence. He shook with the attorney, as well. ''Thanks for seeing us.''

Simon stood with them while Tessa dressed Mag-gie in her snowsuit again, but he seemed relieved to lock the office door behind them.

Outside, the sun had disappeared, and icy darkness had taken its place. Tessa and Noah wrestled the baby back into her car seat and scrambled into the car themselves.

''I know you're relieved,'' Noah said, ''but if he

didn't talk to David about Maggie, why did David consult a family lawyer?''

Tessa threaded her fingers through her hair. The wind had knotted it, and it kinked painfully. "I don't know. Maybe David had another client who wanted some help on a family matter. I've had that happen since I came here."

"What did you do?"

She held her hands out to the heating vents, toasting them. "I referred them to Simon."

"But you didn't talk to him yourself?"

"I would have if the client had asked me to."

Noah glanced at her in the dim dashboard light. "Didn't you and David discuss the cases you worked on separately?"

"Mostly. Sometimes we were too busy. He never mentioned Simon." She peered into the back seat. "Maggie's asleep already."

"Remember how Keely used to fall asleep the second we started the engine?"

She nodded. How she missed her daughter, but the pain was different now, blunted by acceptance. "Noah, I'm grateful you came. Being with you, working with you to keep Maggie safe, I finally understand we can't bring Keely back no matter how much we refuse to move on." She allowed herself a brief smile as she swung around to look at him. "And I only feel faintly guilty."

"You talk as if we won't be seeing each other." He turned the car onto a narrow street, remembering the way without her help. "I don't want to leave you again, Tessa."

"But one of us would have to make changes. Big ones."

"So we'll find a compromise if we want to try again."

If. Not a reassuring word.

He slid his hand possessively across her thigh. "I mean it," he said.

"I know you do. For right now. Turn there, into that strip mall. See the hardware store?"

"I see." He parked the car at the curb in front of the store. "You think I'll change my mind about us once I'm not afraid someone's going to kill you?"

"You're a bright guy, Noah. You haven't wondered if we've been good together because of the situation?"

"You're the one having second thoughts." Frustration laced his voice. "You didn't doubt us this morning."

"You'll have second thoughts when you have time to think, and I know how we were before."

"But neither of us wants to be like that now." He put the car into Park. "What happened to trusting me?"

"I don't understand why you're better at trusting than I am."

He shook his head. "Because I never wanted you to leave in the first place. I thought we'd find our way back to each other."

"Without ever talking about Keely, about where we went wrong?"

"We're talking now, Tessa." He slid his hand over her shoulder, down the jut of her breast and around her back to pull her close. "All you have to do is commit."

She wanted to when he touched her as if she belonged to him again. She kissed him, taking her time, relearning the shape of his mouth, the tortured rasp of his breath as she aroused him with her tongue and her need. At last, he lifted his hands to her face, his grip hot and desperate as he pulled back.

"You're going to get us arrested." He sucked her lower lip into the moist warmth of his mouth. His slight tug seemed to reach all the way through her body.

She arched toward him, peering at the hardware store's lights. "Why are we here?"

"We'll go inside in a second, if you stay on your side of the car." He reached for her top coat button, but then backed into his own seat. "Who's not committed?"

She ran her hand over the only part of him she could reach, his slanted thigh in tight jeans. He lifted his leg and pulled her hand higher but then pushed her away with a rueful grimace.

"Do you want to take Maggie out?" he asked.

"No. We'll wait in the car. Just leave the engine running."

He studied the darkness outside the car. "I don't know. You can't see anyone from here. It's too dark."

"A second ago there was too much light. How long will you be?"

He regarded her as if she was his wife, and she laughed. They might work this out after all.

Once at home again, Tessa hopped out of the car.

She opened the back door and pulled a sleepy Maggie from her car seat. As the baby rubbed her face, Tessa cuddled her against her own chest, as much out of the cold as she could manage. Noah came around and added his body to the shield for Maggie.

Still she woke fully by the time they reached the house. Noah opened the door for them, and Tessa laid the baby on the sofa to take her snowsuit off.

"Wonder where Eleanor and Joe are." Noah looked up at their closed door and then went to the kitchen, shrugging out of his own coat. He peered inside. "Not in there."

"They must be in their room."

She was right. Joe opened his door and came out, looking tired, holding a piece of paper. "I thought I heard you. Noah, I took this message for you while you were gone."

Tessa's heart slowed, but then began to race. "From Weldon?"

"From some guy in Boston. I didn't quite get his name." His gaze skidded over Tessa's face, as if she was responsible for the grief she'd unwittingly caused him and his wife. "He said they have a lead on another guy—a Frank? Frank Edison?"

"Frank Eddings?"

Joe brought the slip of paper down the stairs. "Eddings sounds right. That's all I got, I'm afraid. Maybe you should call."

Noah pushed back his sleeve and looked at his watch. "My shift is off duty, but I'll try to reach Baxton." He turned to the kitchen. "I'll call from in here."

Tessa watched him go, wary, because this was their

old pattern, but he'd insisted she trust him. She was willing to try. She looked at Joe, trying to duck his biting gaze at the same time. "How's Eleanor?"

"Better. How are you? I know telling us and Weldon wasn't easy after you promised David."

She paused, her hands full of snowsuit and wriggling baby. Joe's eyes were careful now. He was trying to make room for her. "I didn't want to badmouth Joanna, either."

"We know that. We just, well, I'm sure you understand. You've lost a daughter."

"If I'd known she was using drugs again, I would have tried to help her."

"I don't want to talk about that. Eleanor and I have decided to talk to Weldon about what he knows before we reach a final decision on what Joanna was doing."

Noah returned, saving Tessa from searching for an impossible response.

"I couldn't get a straight answer from the night shift," Noah said. "I have this case in Boston. A woman named Della Eddings and her children. Her husband has been threatening them, but they were safe as of yesterday afternoon. No one's talked to her today, and no one in the office knew anything about Frank. They just said Baxton was looking for me, that he absolutely had to talk to me today. I tried his home number, but he's not there, either."

"Can't you call him tomorrow?" Tessa asked.

Joe cut in. "If it was this Baxton who called, he said it was urgent, and he said it was about this Eddings guy. Baxton wanted you in front of him then and there."

Noah stared at the older man. "That sounds like him."

"Oh, no." The words escaped Tessa. She knew what came next. After all his trust talk, he was walking out, handing her the answers to all her fears about their so-called future.

The determination in Noah's gaze left no room for doubt about his plans. "I have to find out what's going on," he said.

"I'll take Maggie and leave you two alone." Joe scooped up the baby and started for the stairs.

"Joe." Noah stopped the other man. "Could you replace the locks for me? And Tessa, you change the alarm code again and set the system the second I leave. I'll make sure Weldon parks someone outside this house tonight."

Tessa wasted no time being shocked. She'd half anticipated this call—not the specifics, but the type of call—an emergency only Noah could resolve. And Noah believed his own press.

"I'll change the locks," Joe said. He swiveled his head toward Tessa, his gaze reassuring, clearly calling a truce. "He has no choice, and you'll be fine with Eleanor and me."

"You don't understand, Joe." And he wouldn't be able to persuade her Noah wasn't making a bad decision. Shaking, she turned to her ex-husband. "Think of what you're doing," she said.

"I'll be upstairs." The older man turned away again, tall, but hunching over the baby in his arms as he climbed. "I need to check on Eleanor."

"Thanks, Joe." Noah gazed after him, as if he were evaluating Joe's possibilities as a bodyguard.

Then he caught Tessa's gaze. "Try to hear me. You're in no more danger than you were that first night when I went back to get my things."

"You've put me on the back burner too many times." She pushed her hands through her hair in despair. "Do you think you can run down there and fix things overnight? You can't, and you know it. If they haven't arrested him, you'll have to find him. You won't be back tomorrow. Lie to yourself if you have to, but you aren't fooling me."

He took a step closer, but they didn't touch. She wanted to touch him. She wanted to beg him to stay with her, but not even begging would change his mind. She knew him too well.

"Tessa, if I can find this man, I can save someone from being killed instead of cleaning up the mess after. And I'm a good detective. If they have a lead on him, I'll find him."

"I'm asking you to choose us and let someone else save the day."

He challenged her with a frighteningly detached gaze, and she realized he had to distance himself or he couldn't do the job. "Do you feel threatened?" His arrogance almost knocked her off her feet, and she suddenly knew how suspects felt when he interrogated them. "Right now," he said, "if we take the precautions I've suggested, will you feel safe tonight?"

"Yes, except when I remember someone may have come in here and put a file on my computer." She wasn't about to admit she felt safer when Noah was with her. Not now.

"I swear I won't go unless Weldon promises one

of his deputies will stay on duty outside. And if Joe changes the locks and you set the alarm, you're going to be fine until I come back.''

She started to turn away, but he caught both her arms. ''If you were in trouble, and I couldn't get to you, and the police told me I couldn't take action against the person threatening you until he'd hurt you or our child, I'd want a cop to be as desperate to keep you alive as I am to make sure Della Eddings doesn't become one of my cases.''

When she thought of a woman in jeopardy from her own husband, Noah made sense. She wanted him to stay because she needed him to prove he cared for her. Her priorities were immature when she thought about Della Eddings.

''But what about tomorrow? What if you don't find him tonight?''

''I'll come back by tomorrow afternoon. And I'll call the whole way down to Boston. If I find Baxton or Della, and they don't have anything on Frank, I'll turn around.''

She nodded, grudgingly, shamed by her need to come first with him. He was doing the honorable thing. ''Call me the second you find out what's going on.''

''I will.''

He packed swiftly for one night, stopping every few moments to speed-dial Baxton and the woman in trouble.

Tessa tried not to hover. She took sheets and pillowcases for four from the dryer and began to fold them, but she knew part of her self-confidence would leave with Noah. And his urgent need to put someone else before her and Maggie had shot her confidence in them all to hell.

Tessa was lifting her hand to knock on Eleanor and Joe's door as Noah came out of his room, his bag gripped in one hand.

"What are you doing?" he asked.

"I'm late feeding Maggie."

"I'd like to say goodbye to her."

Letting Maggie get used to Noah was a bad idea, but she nodded and knocked on the door. When Eleanor invited them in, Noah followed her. Sprawled on the bed, Joe looked up from his newspaper. Eleanor and Maggie were sharing a rocker and a big storybook. Maggie looked up from Eleanor's lap and clapped her hands.

"Time for dinner," Tessa said.

"I lost track." Eleanor rose, tucking the baby into the curve of her arm. "But I'll feed her, Tessa. Joe tells me you're leaving for the night, Noah?

"I'll be back tomorrow." He moved to her side to stroke Maggie's cheek. Then he leaned down and kissed her and she yanked his hair, but Eleanor carefully set him free. She nodded to Joe and they left the room together.

Tessa started to follow them, but Noah caught her arm. He waited, obviously to let Joe and Eleanor descend the stairs and cross the living room. "I don't want to leave you angry."

"I am," she said. "Maybe I want too much from you because you were so distant before, but I have to know I can count on you."

"You and Maggie matter most to me. If I honestly thought someone was coming after you tonight, I wouldn't leave you, but how would we both feel if I stayed here, and something happened to Della Eddings?''

Damn him, she believed his press, too. "How am I supposed to risk letting another woman get hurt if you can help her?''

Concern replaced his arrogance. ''I wouldn't risk you, Tessa.'' His tone, unbearably tender, stroked her nerve endings, lulling her into a false sense of trust.

Maybe she had to be responsible tonight. Maybe she was destined to love a man who would never put her first, but she didn't have to like it.

"You should go. The sooner you go, the sooner you'll be back.''

He cupped her face in both his strong, capable hands. He kissed her, gently at first, barely touching his lips to hers, but then, as if he couldn't help himself, he nudged her mouth open. With a groan he pushed his hands beneath her sweater, kneading her bare skin.

"I'm not running out on you.'' He buried his face in her hair. "If I can get to Eddings before he hurts Della, I can save a life instead of investigating a death. Think of her children.''

"I am thinking.'' But she wanted him with her, and she couldn't help feeling he should turn Della Eddings over to someone else. He confused her this close, with his arousal nudging her belly, his heat bathing her in pure need. She arched into him, sighing as his hands traced a hungry path beneath her sweater. "Don't you take chances with this guy, either.''

He looked down at her, tracing the curve of her waist. "You forgive me?''

"I'm trying."

"I'll be back before anyone here knows I'm gone."

Wrong promise to make. He'd disappeared too many times. She backed away from him and pushed her hands into the pockets of her jeans.

He stared at her so hard she felt as if he was touching every line on her face. "Set the alarm," he finally said, and then he spun on his heel and was gone.

Tessa stood perfectly still until the door closed downstairs. Then she sagged against the nearest wall, her heart pounding.

She didn't allow herself to mope for long. She had an alarm to reset and a baby who was at least an hour late with her evening routine.

While she deciphered the directions for changing the alarm code, Eleanor finished feeding Maggie. Tessa called the monitoring company to be sure they called the police if the alarm went off-line during the night, and then she folded another load of the baby's laundry while Joe occupied her and Eleanor cleaned the kitchen.

Then Tessa collected Maggie and took her to her room to run a bubble bath. The baby danced in Tessa's arms as the bubbles piled on top of the water.

Laughing at her excitement, Tessa wrestled her diaper off and dipped her in. Maggie immediately began to scissor her arms and legs through the suds. The door opened behind them, but Tessa was too busy keeping Maggie afloat to turn around.

"Tessa, Joe and I were thinking maybe we should go home tonight—and you and Maggie can come with us."

CHAPTER THIRTEEN

ELBOW DEEP IN SUDS, Tessa looked up from Maggie's bubble bath. Maggie puffed a snowball of suds in her grandma's direction, delighting Eleanor, who knelt at the end of the tub.

"What do you think?" she asked, scooping up suds to blow Maggie's way.

"Why do you want to go?"

"I'm uneasy," Eleanor admitted, "after what you said this morning. I know we have the police outside, but what if you were right about someone breaking into the house? It could happen again."

"I changed the alarm and I've set it, and the security company is monitoring. We're fine." Tessa turned on the water and adjusted its temperature. "I'm going to rinse Maggie now."

She turned on the shower and Eleanor helped her hold the baby upright while she sprayed the soap bubbles.

"We could bundle her into her pajamas and snow-suit and just set off. In forty-five minutes, we'll have disappeared." Eleanor held out Maggie's towel and helped Tessa wrap the baby in it. "Say you'll do it, just to ease my mind."

"But you don't have a crib."

"Sure we do, and a supply of diapers and food. We kept it all for Maggie's visits."

"What do you think of our plan?" Joe asked from behind them.

Tessa looked up to where he leaned against the doorway. Hesitating, she sat on her heels so she could see his face. "I'm not that impressed with my security measures. And maybe we would have the advantage if we leave the place where everyone expects us to be."

"Just to ease Eleanor's mind," Joe said.

They must have talked it over pretty strenuously if they both described their plan the same way. "We'll have to let Noah and the police know," Tessa said.

"Fine." Joe was already heading for a telephone, his long stride easier than she'd ever seen it. He must have been as worried as his wife. "I'll make the calls. You ladies get the baby ready to go."

Tessa dressed Maggie and then Eleanor took her off to her room, while Tessa packed a diaper bag and a few of her own things. She looked around the room, strewn with Maggie's belongings.

She couldn't think of anything else she or Maggie might need for one night at the Worths'. She grabbed a notepad and scrawled a note for Noah in case he missed Joe's phone message, and then she paused on her way to the Worths' room to slip the message under Noah's door.

Eleanor met Tessa in the hall with Maggie cuddled, grinning, against her shoulder. Tessa laughed at the baby.

"She thinks we're starting an adventure," Eleanor said.

"I think she's planning how to make us pay for totally messing up her bedtime tonight."

"Maybe a little of both, but she'll fall asleep in the car."

Resisting a yawn until her eyes watered, Tessa remembered why she and Noah had enjoyed so little sleep last night. "I hope she sleeps when we get there. Forty-five minutes to your house?"

"As long as the snow holds off and we don't run into traffic." Eleanor spared an arm to hug Tessa. "Thanks for doing this for me. I'll be so grateful to sleep in my own bed tonight."

Her happy mood convinced Tessa the relatively short trip was worth it. As Eleanor sailed down the stairs, Joe came in from the cold, stamping his feet.

"I've warmed up the car. You ready?" he asked them.

"Did you talk to Noah?" Tessa grabbed Maggie's snowsuit and cap from the sofa, but Eleanor took it and began to put it on the baby.

"I left a message on his phone. Apparently, he was trying to reach Boston when I called, but I also talked to the deputy outside, and he radioed Weldon. We're just outside his jurisdiction at home, and he wants to leave the deputy here to make sure no one breaks into the house again, but he's arranged with our police to send someone to watch our house."

"Sounds good."

Eleanor rose from stuffing Maggie into her snowsuit. "I'll let you take her, dear. You're already better than I am at talking her into her car seat."

Joe opened the door and then picked up Tessa's bags. "I put ours in the car already," he said.

Tessa stopped to set the alarm, for all the good it seemed to do. Maggie might have been looking for an adventure, but her idea of fun didn't start with the dreaded car seat. By the time Tessa strapped her in, Joe and Eleanor were waiting in the front.

Tessa spread her hands like a calf roper. "Done." Slumping, she yanked her coat open. "Fighting her is hot work."

Joe chuckled as he maneuvered his big boat of a car in a U-turn. Tessa caught a quick glimpse of the deputy as they left her house behind.

"You don't have to entertain us with small talk," Eleanor said over her shoulder. "Just lean back and enjoy the ride. I may sleep myself."

For forty-five minutes? Tessa held back a laugh. The night was still in its infancy, and second thoughts about leaving the safety of her home began to pick at her. But Maggie reached for her with both hands and a mournful cry, and she leaned over the car seat, wrapping the baby in a warm hug. Before she knew it, young night, short drive and all, she was asleep.

FOR ABOUT AN HOUR, Noah managed to persuade himself he'd done the right thing. He kept trying to reach Baxton and Della on the phone, but he got only answering machines. He called the station again. No one there had heard from Baxton yet.

During the second hour, Tessa's voice in his head grew too firm to ignore, asking him to choose her and Maggie over his job. How many detectives in his office would have dropped everything to find Della Eddings?

Noah believed that Tessa and Maggie would be

safe tonight, but maybe their physical safety hadn't really been the point.

He'd wanted to do the right thing for Della. Her children had clung to the back of her jeans in a row of three the day she'd come to his desk. She'd sworn her husband was going to kill them all if someone didn't stop him. Noah and Baxton had introduced her to people at the agencies that could help her, but they hadn't been able to arrest her husband. Finally, when he'd brandished a gun at her on the street across from her office, Baxton had agreed to let Noah enjoy a man-to-man with Frank.

But Frank had made other plans. He'd disappeared as if he scented the law on his ass. And Noah and Baxton, on their own time, had spent the past three months searching for him.

Tonight Tessa's last caution to be careful had quenched the fire in his belly. For the first time in his professional career, he wanted to turn a job over to someone else. What would happen if he did? Someone else would find Frank Eddings, leaving Noah free to take care of the family that had begun to feel like his own.

A little over an hour would take him back to the house in Prodigal.

He called the office one last time and spilled his guts to the duty lieutenant. Pitching a battle, which he spiked with the information that he couldn't find Baxton, who must be out looking for Della, he persuaded the duty guy to arrange an unofficial posse. Then he asked for a report when they found Baxton and Della, and he turned the car around.

Snow began to fall again, outside Portland. Noah

had to slow for it and the occasional plow. He considered calling Tessa, but he wanted to see her expression when she saw him, to make sure she understood what he meant by coming back. He wanted a future with her, and he was willing to change to make it.

With the snow and the slower traffic, he passed the Welcome To Prodigal sign just before eleven.

His cell phone rang. He picked it up and flipped it open. Before he could say hello, Baxton was yelling in his ear. "It was a damn false alarm."

"What was?" Noah asked.

"I had a call this afternoon, an anonymous tip, but the guy asked for me, said he'd heard we were looking for Frank Eddings, and that Frank had a gun, and he planned to pay his wife a visit today."

"Where have you been since then?"

"Looking for her. I finally found her in Atlantic City, gambling with her mother. I've had her apartment watched all day, and no one showed up. I think someone played us." He finally stopped. "Maybe it was Eddings, himself."

Noah shook his head in the silent car. "I don't know, but I'm glad Della and the kids are all right. Can we use this to get someone assigned to her case?"

"Not ethically." Baxton barked a laugh that was sadly devoid of devotion to ethics. "But I'll see what I can do. Where are you?"

"Didn't you hear I turned around? I'm about five minutes from Tessa's house."

"Well, don't bother me any more tonight. I've got

to find a way to pay for the man-hours you racked up, calling out the cavalry."

"Thanks, Baxton."

"Yeah. Sometime early next week, let me know when you plan to come back to work." And Baxton hung up as abruptly as he'd started speaking.

When Noah turned onto Tessa's street, the house was so dark it looked empty. A twinge of uneasiness made him hit the brakes, but Weldon's deputy was just where the chief had promised he'd be. Noah parked behind him and got out of the car.

The guy didn't move as Noah approached. Great— Prodigal's finest had fallen asleep on the job. But when Noah came level with the car, he saw the deputy's head, pressed to the window in a pool of dark moisture.

"Damn." He drew his gun and ran for the house. Just in time, he realized if he kicked in the door, he could get Tessa and the baby and the Worths killed.

He eased around to each of the windows. No movement at all. When he'd circled the house entirely, he kicked in the door, swearing his frustration as the wood splintered and the alarm began to scream. No one moved anywhere.

He took the stairs at a dead run but found all the bedrooms empty. Where the hell were they? Kidnapping didn't seem like this killer's style.

Tessa's room looked as if a cyclone had hit it, but that might have been Maggie's influence. The Worths' room looked as if no one had ever stayed in it. All their clothes were gone. What kind of a killer stole an elderly couple's clothing?

He went back to Tessa's room. Nothing. No note.

No real sign of a disturbance. He had to get help for the deputy and alert Weldon to his failure as a guard. And he had to fight off the bone-crushing knowledge of his own failure until he found Tessa and Maggie.

Passing his own room, he kicked the door wider.

And saw a square of white paper on the dark floor.

He snatched it up. In Tessa's handwriting, he saw the words. "We've gone to Eleanor and Joe's house." And she'd penned a phone number that he dialed as he launched himself down the stairs.

No answer there. Not even an answering machine. "Damn, damn!"

He dialed 911 and explained the situation to the operator as he snatched up the plaid blankets Tessa left on the couches and ran from the house.

Noah's cell phone rang as he eased the deputy's car door open. Weldon shouted his name before he could get the receiver to his ear.

"The alarm company called, and I just got your 911 call, too. What the hell's happened?"

"Your deputy is out cold, and Tessa and the Worths are gone. Send the paramedics." Noah dropped the phone and gently slid the deputy onto his back on the car's seat. He covered him with the blankets and waited impatiently for the paramedics. He couldn't leave the deputy alone.

He reread Tessa's note and dialed Weldon's office back to ask for an address for Joe and Eleanor. Had they been jumped as they'd left the house?

He doubted it. The deputy wouldn't have rolled down his window for a stranger. He would have been leery of anyone who didn't belong in Tessa's house.

Noah turned his head toward the house's open

door. A moment, just before he'd left tonight, re-played in his head.

He'd been trying to persuade Tessa he wasn't aban-doning her. Joe, climbing the stairs, had argued on his side. Noah had looked up and finally noticed how tall the older man was. How lean. For a second, Joe had reminded him how frustrated he'd felt at not be-ing able to get another good look at Eric Sanders so he could compare him to the man in Weldon's photo of the killer.

Evidence began to stack up in Noah's head. Some-one had wanted him out of the house tonight. How many times had he called Baxton about Della Eddings from Tessa's phone? Someone who'd overheard him checking in with Baxton could have called in a tip to get him out of the way.

And the file in Tessa's computer had been too easy to place there. Maybe someone who was supposed to come and go in Tessa's house had inserted the com-puter file and called Baxton. Joe could easily have persuaded the deputy to roll down his window. Roll-ing it back up and then shutting the door on a bludg-eoned man would have been child's play for the per-son who'd killed David.

More afraid than he'd ever been in his life, furious that he'd been so distracted with his own feelings for Tessa, he took down the address Weldon's other dep-uty gave him.

At last sirens sounded in the distance. Weldon pulled up first, the paramedics just behind. Once the deputy was being treated, Noah went to the chief's car.

"It's Joe," Noah said. "Or maybe he and Eleanor

are in this together. It must have something to do with Joanna. I'm on my way."

"Did you call their local law enforcement?"

"Everything just fell into place. I'll call them now."

Weldon nodded. "I'll call, too, and explain. You might get more cooperation."

"Tell them I want to try to talk to Joe or Eleanor first. If I don't let them know I've been here, they may think they're in the clear."

"What if they've already killed your ex-wife?"

A cold chill went through him. "I don't think so." Maybe he was fooling himself, but he had to hope. "They'd want to get Maggie to their house, and Tessa goes with Maggie. They love the baby. They'll try to part her from Tessa without violence."

"You've tried to call them already?"

"Yeah, but they didn't answer."

"It's snowing. They might not be there yet. Try them again, so I can tell the chief to stay out if you talk to them."

Noah frowned at the other man. "Send him in if he sees Tessa's in trouble."

"I'm not a hick, Gabriel. I thought we established that."

Noah dialed the Worths again. On the third ring, Joe answered, sounding plain scared.

Noah nodded at Weldon and took a deep breath. If he screwed this up, Tessa could die. "Hi, Joe. I changed my mind and turned around. I'm almost at the Prodigal turnoff, but I've been calling Tessa's house, and I finally realized you all must have left."

"Yeah." Joe's breath was audible. "Eleanor felt

nervous staying there when someone might break in, so we called Weldon and told him we were coming up here.''

"Quite a drive in this weather, wasn't it?''

"We slowed down when we hit the snow. Why don't you go on to Tessa's house, and we'll see you tomorrow?''

"Nah. I just want to make sure everything's okay with you all and the baby, and it's not that far. I'll come on over if you give me directions.''

Joe faltered again. Noah only prayed he wasn't prompting the other man to kill Tessa and run for cover. "Will you put Tessa on the phone?''

"She and Eleanor are tucking Maggie into bed. Why don't I have her call you?''

"Okay.'' Noah had a brainstorm. "But tell her to keep trying if I don't answer. I'm going to call the chief up there and have him send a patrol car by.''

"Weldon was supposed to do that already,'' Joe said.

"Good. They should be outside your house before I am,'' Noah said with relief. David's killer wouldn't have kept lying about the police if he didn't think there was a chance no one had found the deputy yet. Noah took Joe's reluctant directions and hung up.

Weldon was already dialing his own phone. "Give me five minutes,'' he said. "I'll explain what we need, and then you call and tell them what you want them to do.''

"Thanks.''

He flew through the snowy night, cursing his own idiotic mistakes. He'd die before he'd lose Tessa and Maggie.

He followed Joe's directions, swearing he'd kill the other man with his bare hands if Joe had sent him on a wild-goose chase. But Joe had managed to pull off a vindictive, well-planned murder. He wouldn't throw his near escape away for one less night with Tessa and her detective ex-husband.

What had driven Joanna's parents to such a murderous rage? He intended to find out and stop them before they killed his wife.

His phone rang again. He flipped it open and Tessa's voice filled him with relief he couldn't show her.

"I'm so glad you turned back," she said.

"Tessa, concentrate on what I'm about to say. Don't change your expression—don't move a muscle—are you standing where Joe and Eleanor can see you?"

"Yes," she said.

"Turn around, as if you're just looking at something nearby. Touch it as if it interests you."

"Okay, sounds good."

"I don't have time to ease you into this, so hold on. At least one of them killed David, and I think they planned to kill you tonight. When you can get away from them, go to your room. Take Maggie with you, and lock yourself in."

"How long will you be?"

"Less than thirty minutes, but I'll shave off the seconds where I can. I need to get to you."

"Yes."

"I love you, Tessa. Now hang up before we look suspicious."

He felt as if he were abandoning her again. But he

couldn't keep her on the phone. Joe and Eleanor would know they were caught. He called the number Weldon had given him and arranged to keep Chief Tinsley's men out of Joe and Eleanor's sight unless they heard signs of a struggle.

This time, when he got off the phone, he focused on what came next—on destroying the man and woman who wanted to kill Tessa.

All his adult life, Noah's only goal had been to get killers off the street. But tonight he had a new goal, one that brought him supreme and terrifying anticipation.

The second he'd heard Tessa's voice, known he could still save her, he'd become the kind of human being he hated and hunted.

He couldn't count on the courts. He couldn't even count on himself not to make mistakes. There was only one way he could make sure the Worths never had a second shot at killing Tessa.

He intended to kill them.

TESSA LAY IN THE DARKNESS, Maggie nestled close to her side. She'd already dressed the baby in her snowsuit again. She didn't dare make a sound.

As far as Eleanor and Joe were concerned, she'd suddenly grown so tired she had to lie down so she'd be awake later to talk to Noah about what they should do next. That ridiculous nap she'd taken in the car supported her story.

She surrounded Maggie with pillows and eased off the bed. Crossing to the window, she hoped to see Noah down below.

In the darkness, alleviated only by the glow of the

light outside the garage, she saw no movement. Was anyone out there? She looked back at Maggie, feeling reckless for standing ten feet away from the baby— as if something might happen. But she didn't want to wake her until she had to. Eleanor would be in this room like a shot if Maggie made a sound.

Tessa had to get her out of this house. Eleanor and Joe weren't going to give up their grandchild without a fight. Maybe Maggie was the reason they'd begun killing after Joanna's death, but Tessa would die for her, too.

A sudden flicker of movement caught Tessa's attention. Pressing her face to the window, she thumped her forehead on the glass. Outside, a man stepped into the open. She knew Noah without a glimmer of light touching him.

She clamped her mouth shut to keep from crying out. He'd come. He was going to help them. Nothing bad would happen now.

He lifted his arm, motioned for her to come down, and then stepped back into the darkness.

She whirled toward the bed, but then eased Maggie into her arms. The baby stretched, mewing a soft sound that wrapped Tessa's heart in a vise. She waited for Maggie to settle down and started for the door, but then stopped.

Only an idiot would unlock that door and leave this room without even the semblance of a weapon. She couldn't turn on the light, but she made a mental inventory of the things she'd brought along.

Hairspray. If she got close enough to spray it in Joe or Eleanor's eyes, she could run like hell. She eased to the bag she'd left on a chair beside the door and shifted Maggie so that she could hold the spray bottle and the baby. She twisted the bottle, so that if the baby grabbed it, the nozzle would be pointing out.

She cursed herself for choosing the environment over aerosol.

The lock made the faintest click as she turned it. She waited again, straining to hear any sound outside her door. No need to rush. She just had to get Maggie outside, away from her insane grandparents.

She moved into the hall, concentrating with all her might on keeping her footsteps silent. She stepped, rolling her foot from heel to toe, and waited. Another step, heel to toe. Another wait.

At the end of the hall, she faced a choice. A light still burned in the kitchen they'd used upon arriving. The living room Joe and Eleanor had left dark remained dark.

She'd seen the outline of a door on the living room's far wall. It would be farther from Noah than the kitchen, but she was willing to risk the extra distance if it was a room Joe and Eleanor rarely used.

She started again—heel to toe. Until she'd carried Maggie halfway across the room.

"Tessa, we know about you and David. Joanna told us." Eleanor's voice floated out of the darkness, a nightmare in the making that stopped Tessa dead. Eleanor had sat in this room, waiting. Knowing. "That's what made Joanna unhappy," she said. "Your affair with her husband drove her car into that tree. I wanted you dead for that, but now you're helping Weldon spread that lie about Joanna using drugs. You can see we have to kill you."

Horror crept over Tessa's scalp. "Joanna was

wrong about David and me. We were friends, and you killed him for no reason."

"I don't expect you to admit the truth." Joe spoke from somewhere between her and the door.

Tessa turned her head toward the sound of his voice, thinking fast. She could still reach the kitchen. That put her closer to Noah anyway.

"I don't want Joe to hurt you in front of the baby," Eleanor said. "In a way I've grown fond of you. I don't know how you could wreck Joanna's family— steal her husband, arrange to take her daughter and then start carrying on, within days of David's death, with Noah. But you love Maggie. I'll give you that."

"I do love her. And I won't let you touch her. You're sick, Eleanor."

"A sick woman can't plan with my wife's cunning." Joe sounded proud. "You seemed to forget we were in the house. We overheard everything you and Noah said—to each other—him to his office."

"I treated you as my family." Not that they seemed to mind killing family.

"You gave us everything we needed. That Sloma guy's name. Eleanor dictated that file to me. And then she knew Noah wouldn't be able to resist being the big hero for that woman in Boston, so she had me call Baxton."

"What's your role, Joe? You just do the stabbings?"

"And I used your flashlight on the deputy outside your house tonight. I'm still strong for my age. But maybe having a vendetta keeps you young."

If she thought too long about what he'd done to

David, she'd fall through the floor, and she might hurt Maggie on her way down.

"Tessa?" Joe's sharp tone implied she might have been trying to escape in silence.

Light flooded the room. Tessa, blinking, didn't dare move. They wouldn't set out to hurt Maggie, but she might wake in a grumpy mood, and Tessa didn't want to test Eleanor or Joe's patience with a crying baby.

"Give me my granddaughter." Eleanor stood, arms outstretched.

Behind her, along the wall, they'd hung all the pictures Noah had said were missing from David's house. Joanna smiled from the photos, and Maggie laughed. David had been blotted out. In each photo of him, they'd simply taken a marker and painted him out, then hung the photos as if they didn't see the inky blobs.

"What did you do?" Tessa breathed.

Eleanor glanced around. "He had no right to those pictures of my baby. Look how happy she was. He took her from us, and then he tried to take Maggie." She looked back, madness lighting eyes that had only glowed with warmth before tonight. "Just like you thought you could take Maggie."

Tessa backed one step toward the kitchen.

"Stop," Joe said.

"Give me our girl." Eleanor held out her arms.

Tessa backed up again, keeping them both in front of her. "I won't even let you hold her, after what you did to David."

"After what *you* did to him, you mean." Joe leveled a gun at her. "You stole him from his family. He thought he could keep Maggie away from us after

Joanna died. He hired that lawyer to tell us we might lose any rights to Maggie if we didn't stop telling her the truth about him.''

"She may be a baby, but she had to know the truth about her father," Eleanor cut in. "I'll make sure she grows up hearing the truth so she won't ever trust a man like David Howard."

"I killed him, and I won't mind killing you the same way." Mired in his anger, Joe didn't seem to notice his wife had spoken. "I want to see you suffer. When I think what you did to my daughter..."

"I helped her find treatment, and I would have helped her again, if I'd known." Tessa turned to Eleanor, moving ever steadily toward the kitchen. If Noah had seen the light, he'd know they'd been waiting for her. He'd come. "Eleanor, you're the one she didn't want to disappoint. She lied to you about David and me as an excuse—and if you knew she was using, you should have persuaded her to go back to the rehab center."

"She didn't touch drugs. She wanted to die because you started an affair with her husband while she was giving birth to his daughter."

At Eleanor's low, furious tone, Maggie jumped. Tessa arched her hand over Maggie's eyes, to shield her from the light—and to make it easier to grab the hairspray wedged between their bodies.

"Give me my granddaughter." Joe came at her. "I'm going to stop your filthy lying, and I want Maggie."

"Joe, wait. Don't hurt her in front of the baby."

"She's asleep, honey. She'll never know—"

Tessa took advantage of their concentration on each other to speed into the kitchen.

Behind her, the door burst open. Joe raced at her, waving the gun. Tessa snatched the hairspray bottle, prayed the nozzle was aiming at his face and sprayed. It hit him but hardly slowed him. A hand yanked her from behind, and suddenly Noah was in front of her.

He and Joe stood, toe to toe, gun to gun.

"I want to kill you, Joe. Please don't put that gun down." Twisted pleasure in his voice turned him into a stranger, and fear ripped through Tessa.

"I don't intend to give up," Joe said. "I was hoping you'd make it in time."

"No." Tessa reached for Noah's arm, but her hand didn't even cover half the girth of his flexed muscle, and he shook her off.

"Get out of here." His voice brooked no argument.

"If she moves, I'll kill you."

Tessa believed Joe. She didn't move.

"Think of Maggie," Noah said.

"They won't hurt her."

"You don't know for sure. Remember what they did to David, and get out of this house."

He turned his head as if to look at her, and Joe must have relaxed. In that instant, Noah moved.

And Joe hit the floor, his gun skidding toward Tessa. Eleanor dashed into the kitchen, her hands curled like claws as she went for the baby.

Noah pointed his own weapon at her. "Don't."

"You won't hurt me," she said.

"I'm dying to hurt you. For what you did to David, for the way you've made Tessa grieve. You and your husband deserve to die, and I'm sick of your kind."

Folding Maggie, restless, but still mostly asleep, to her breast, Tessa gasped a breath. "Noah, where are the police?"

"I sent them to the bottom of the driveway. They're probably rushing the hill." He cocked his gun at Joe. "They won't get here in time to save you. They'll wait for a signal as long as we're quiet, which means they won't come in until they hear me shoot you."

Tessa grabbed his arm again. "You can't."

"I'm not out of control." Terrifying satisfaction curved his mouth in a smile that left her aching to scream. "These two are lunatics. They're going to do a little time and get out. For all we know, they'll come after you and Maggie again. I lost my father. I lost my daughter, and for a while I lost you. Now I've found you and Maggie, and I don't plan to lose anyone again. I'm going to destroy the problem, Tessa. That's all."

"You don't have the guts," Joe said. "You actually believe in the system. You threw your life away. No one took anything from you."

Noah aimed. "Tonight I'm a man who finds joy in fixing my problem."

Tessa shook his free arm. "You don't know how to kill. You do your job because you still want to save your dad and Keely. You *have* saved Maggie and me."

"I don't plan to clean up after your murder."

Tessa stepped in front of him. "You'll have to shoot me first."

His beautiful mouth twisted with fury. "What are

you doing? They butchered your best friend. They want to kill you."

"I'm not going to lose you. Don't let them turn you into a murderer. Put the gun down and let the police take them. You come home with me and Maggie. Be my husband and her father—not a killer."

Hatred left his gaze, and love replaced it. Tessa nearly cried out in relief.

Behind her, Joe actually growled. She turned. On his feet again, he pulled a knife from his sock, like a damn B-movie villain. "I gave you a chance, Tessa Gabriel, but you didn't take it. Now, you die."

Noah fired and jumped to shield her at the same time. On her way to the floor, Tessa's only thought was to cushion Maggie, who finally woke and wailed in terror. Tessa found herself completely covered by a male body she would recognize if she didn't see Noah again for sixty years. She tensed beneath him as they both waited for the stabbing blade.

Nothing happened. The only thing she felt was Noah, protecting her with his own life.

She twisted her head, but Noah cupped his hand over her face as if he could shield her with a thin barrier of bone and skin. Through his splayed fingers, she watched Eleanor grab Joe's knife.

"The sirens, Joe," she said. "The police are coming."

Without making a sound, Noah uncoiled from the floor. Again, with movement so swift Tessa hardly saw what he was doing, he took the knife from Eleanor and threw it at the sink. Then he grasped the older man's wrists and pushed him to the ground.

"I want you dead," Joe shouted.

With a knee to his back, Noah cuffed him and drew his gun from the waistband of his jeans before Eleanor could take more than a few steps toward the sink.

"Don't," he said.

"Shoot. I have nothing to live for if I can't kill your wife."

"Don't say anything else." He shoved Joe and rose, planting his foot in the small of the other man's back. "If you can persuade him to shut up, he'll be better off, too."

Scrambling to her knees, Tessa unzipped Maggie's puffy snowsuit and checked her little body to make sure she hadn't been hurt when Noah threw them to the floor.

"May I hold her one last time, Tessa?"

Eleanor's pitiful voice dragged back all the pain Tessa had known at losing her own child. Eleanor would never see Maggie again, but the knowledge of how long never lasted weakened Tessa. Until she remembered how desperate Eleanor had been to destroy them all. With no hope of keeping Maggie for herself, what might she do?

Tessa climbed to her feet, balancing the baby. She carried Maggie, still whimpering, to shelter in the warmth of Noah's long, strong body. He wrapped his arm around her. His heart pounded like a jackhammer against her shoulder. His free hand clenched convulsively, biting into her waist.

The only risk Tessa ever intended to take again was the sure one of loving Noah. "I don't think so, Eleanor."

EPILOGUE

"COME LOOK," Lucy Gabriel said.

Dusty and hot, Noah and Tessa turned from trying to hook up the dryer vent. He glanced at his bride. A line of dust crossed her sweatshirt, from shoulder to waist. The people who'd sold them this house hadn't bothered to clean much before they'd left.

Tessa didn't mind. She said they had to claim every nook and cranny to make it their home. Noah doubted the need, but he didn't say so out loud. Tessa knew some things better than he did.

As if she felt his gaze on her, she looked up, and a soft smile begged him to take her mouth for the millionth time since their wedding the week before.

"Cut that out and come with me," Lucy said.

Grinning, Tessa grabbed a handful of his shirt, and they followed Lucy in her astoundingly pristine white caftan, into Maggie's playroom. Lucy had been unpacking boxes while Maggie had reacquainted herself with her toys and books. At the door, Lucy pressed her finger to her lips and pointed.

Though snow still lay high on the ground outside, sunlight splashed through the window to warm the mountain of packing paper and the baby curled up on top of it.

"She wore herself out," Lucy said. "She was tearing and inspecting and singing, and then all of a sudden, she climbed to the top and passed out.''

Tessa toed the bare, light pine floor with her filthy sneaker. ''Should we put her in her crib? She might hurt herself if she rolled onto this.''

''I'll take her.'' Lifting Maggie still felt awkward to Noah. He'd made himself forget what being a father felt like, but he cradled her against his chest, and she felt right in his arms.

Tessa linked elbows with his mom and they both beamed as if they'd created him from the ground up. He allowed them their moments of Mother Earth serenity. They liked to feel in charge.

The second he reached the hall, the phone shrilled from his and Tessa's bedroom. Maggie arched as if she were a cat about to fall, and then she screeched as if she knew she wasn't going to land on her feet.

''I'll get it.'' His mother flew past them, startling Maggie even more with her fluttery white dress.

With impressive outrage, the baby howled until he turned her to his shoulder where she got a better view of her new world.

''It's for you, Noah.''

He turned into the bedroom, using his knuckle to wipe away Maggie's tears.

''He says he's the mayor,'' Lucy whispered. She handed him the phone and took the baby. ''Offer him pizza and ask him to come help unpack.''

''Mom.'' He buried the phone in his sweatshirt. ''He's my new boss, and aren't you still dating—''

''I like Vermont.'' She winked. ''And after two days with the three of you, I'm thinking I might just take a whack at commitment if I found myself a nice, steady mayor. You'd better answer, son. He sounds anxious.''

She flitted away, and he reminded himself she'd been a good mom. She'd looked after the baby so he and Tessa could have a honeymoon, and he had plenty of time to caution her about influencing Maggie in adolescence.

He lifted the phone, but he'd barely said hello before the mayor, who'd labored hard to talk him into the job as Holden's Chief of Police, started filling him in on plans for his first day.

In fact, if he wanted to drop by this afternoon, they could start his paperwork.

They'd agreed on a couple of days to let Noah and his wife and child settle in to their new house. ''I can't come to the office today,'' Noah said.

''But I want to talk to you about a safety program for the high school. I thought we might include instruction for new-driver etiquette with our substance-abuse program.''

Noah glanced at the phone. If teenagers in Holden, Vermont, studied etiquette of any kind, they were kids like he'd never known.

''Oh, and by the way, welcome to your new hometown,'' the mayor said.

''Thanks.'' Paper rustled behind Noah, and he turned to find Tessa unpacking a box he'd set at the foot of their bed. He'd put Keely's pictures in that box. ''I have to go,'' he said, ''but I'll see you on Monday morning, and you can fill me in on the rest of my duties.''

He doubted his ability to stay busy in a town that was even smaller than Prodigal, but, as Tessa had pointed out after he'd almost killed Joe Worth, he might be due for a break from big-city crime.

He'd scared himself that day, thinking he could right all wrongs, win back all he'd lost, by destroying the killer who'd tried to take the most from him.

"I'll pick you up, Noah. You'll be lucky if we don't plague you with a parade—been trying to fill this post for nearly a year."

He should have held out for a higher salary. He didn't look forward to his wife being the major bread-winner again. "Thank you, sir. A parade would be uncomfortable, but we can talk about that safety program. I'll talk to you Monday." He hung up and took the top picture from Tessa, uncertain she was ready to see it.

"Where's Maggie?" he asked.

"Your mom took her downstairs for a snack."

"I hope they don't try to make s'mores in the fireplace."

"What is that?" She pointed to the picture frame upside down in his hands.

"A photo."

She shivered. "I still see those pictures at the Worths', where they'd colored David out. I think he avoided me, trying to protect me from them after Joanna died. Simon told me he'd said they weren't rational and he wanted their threats documented."

An echo of rage flashed through Noah's mind. "I wish he'd told you. We were lucky I turned back. Eleanor and Joe might have convinced Weldon and me that the 'bad guy' in the ski mask finally fulfilled his contract by killing you."

"You would have figured it out, but I'm glad you

came back." She tiptoed to kiss him, and he liked the thrust of her breast against his forearm. Too soon, she pointed to the photo again. "It's Keely?" she asked.

He nodded. "I put them away after you left."

"I couldn't look at my pictures of her after I moved, either." With sudden impatience, she peeled back the brown paper that covered the frame and turned the picture over. They both stared at their baby. Keely grinned at the camera, tufts of blond hair standing on end, a tooth peeking out of her mouth as she chewed a plastic giraffe.

Tessa laughed. "She was a mess, wasn't she?"

He smiled, too. Along with regret came a wave of happiness. They'd had her for a while and she'd been a joyful girl. He hugged his wife. "I guess we're taking her back in a way."

Tessa's eyes filled, but Lucy's voice lilted in the hall, and Tessa rubbed her sleeve across her face as Lucy carried Maggie into the room. Noah ducked the gummy graham cracker Maggie waved at him.

"What's up?" Lucy asked. She spied the picture. "Oh, you're back to unpacking. Hold on a minute."

She passed Maggie to Noah and bolted from the room, her spiky hair glinting russet in the afternoon sun. "She's mellowing," he said. "Lighter hair color, and she actually talked commitment." He handed Maggie the paper Tessa had torn off Keely's picture.

"She's found a steady?" Tessa asked.

"She's willing to consider our new mayor."

As Tessa laughed, Maggie dropped her cracker and tore the paper down the middle. With both hands, she shook it up and down, and then waited for them to congratulate her.

Tessa cheered and Noah kissed Maggie's proud little head. They were adopting her to make certain Eleanor and Joe had no legal rights to her ever again.

Suddenly Maggie caught sight of the photo in Tessa's hand. She leaned over Noah's arm to tap the picture's glass with a wet finger. "Baby," she said.

Tessa and Noah stared at each other. He burst into laughter. "Keely didn't talk at ten months."

Tessa grinned, setting Keely's picture on the mantel. "My mom's going to love her. She's already an overachiever."

Lucy burst back into the room, another wrapped photo in her hands. "I brought you a gift," she said. "I always meant you to have it, but the time never seemed right." She handed it to Noah. "This time I'm not waiting for you."

"Who is it?" Tessa took Maggie from him but hovered at his shoulder.

He already knew who he'd see when he unwrapped the picture. He stared at his mother, unable to move until she smiled and the years and her not-so-maternal habits, and their own unspoken, unshared grief fell away.

"Go ahead," she said. "Don't be afraid."

Nothing scared him now. He tore off the paper, which Maggie snatched out of his hand.

"Oh," Tessa breathed.

His father, in uniform, eyed him levelly from the frame. It was almost like looking into a mirror. He swallowed but couldn't dislodge the lump in his throat.

"You needed to see," Lucy said. "Because he's part of your family, as much as Maggie, as much as

I am. He was strong, and he made his own decisions, took his own risks. He loved you, son, and he would have chosen to drive on by that day if he'd known." Her voice broke. A tear, wrapped in mascara wobbled down her cheek. She reached for Maggie. "Let's take Grandma Lucy for a walk. What do you say?"

Tessa handed her the baby, but then grabbed Lucy and Maggie in a powerful hug. "Thanks," she whispered. "You're such a mom."

Beaming, Lucy spirited Maggie toward the door.

Noah finally found a word. "Mom."

She turned.

"I love you," he said. She just grinned and waved her hand over her head as she left them alone.

He set his dad's photo beside Keely's and turned to Tessa. For once she didn't stop herself from crying. "You talked to my mother," he said.

"But I didn't ask her to fix your problems with your dad. We aren't the only ones regretting lost time."

He pulled her onto the bed and cupped her head to lick a tear off her nose. "Thank you for moving here. I know you didn't want to sell the practice in Prodigal."

She leaned an elbow on his chest. "You and Maggie changed my priorities."

He caught her in another kiss, and she plunged her fingers into his hair, chasing shivers down his spine. She pulled away first to give the door a bemused look. "Maybe we ought to close that."

"Against Maggie? She'll just tear it down."

Tessa laughed, warming him with love and accep-

tance he'd never be foolish enough to take for granted
again.

"She's wily," he said. "I didn't even want to
know her once, and now she's got me grateful as hell
she's going to be my daughter."

"Ours," Tessa said. "Still Joanna's and David's.
We'll tell her how much they loved her, but she's
ours now, too."

Wallowing in family affection, he suddenly realized he had too much to do at home to think about
work on Monday. "Go shut the door, Tessa. I have
to call the mayor back."

"What's wrong?" She stood and pushed the door
shut, pulling down the shirt that had rucked up as
she'd lain on top of him. Her suspicious gaze reminded him they still had hurt feelings to soothe for
each other.

"I have to let him know I'll need a few more
days." He sat up and pulled her between his legs. As
he traced the vulnerable line of her lower lip with his
index finger, erotic plans for the evening flashed
through his mind. "Or as long as it takes," he said,
losing his voice to husky desire, "to remind you I'll
love you all my life, that I wasn't really living when
I wasn't with you."

Laughing with pure joy, Tessa yanked her sweatshirt over her head and pushed him onto his back.
Her generous kiss demanded response. "I have some
promises I'd like to make, too. Call him later."

With his arms full of half-naked woman, his plans
altered one more time. "I'd better ask for a month."

HARLEQUIN *Super***ROMANCE®**

One of our most popular story themes ever…

Pregnancy is an important event in a woman's life—
and in a man's. It should be a shared experience,
a time of anticipation and excitement.
But what happens when a woman is
pregnant and on her own?

**Watch for these books in our
9 Months Later series:**

What the Heart Wants by Jean Brashear (July)

Her Baby's Father by Anne Haven (August)

A Baby of Her Own by Brenda Novak
(September)

The Baby Plan by Susan Gable (December)

Wherever Harlequin books are sold.

HARLEQUIN®
Makes any time special®

HSRNM

If you enjoyed what you just read,
then we've got an offer you can't resist!

Take 2 bestselling love stories FREE!

Plus get a FREE surprise gift!

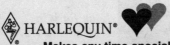

This is the family reunion you've been waiting for!

TRUEBLOOD
Christmas

JASMINE CRESSWELL
TARA TAYLOR QUINN
& KATE HOFFMANN

deliver three brand new Trueblood, Texas stories.

After many years, Major Brad Henderson is released from prison, exonerated after almost thirty years for a crime he didn't commit. His mission: to be reunited with his three daughters. How to find them? Contact Dylan Garrett of the Finders Keepers Detective Agency!

Look for it in November 2002.

HARLEQUIN®
Makes any time special®

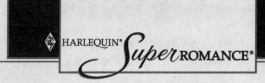

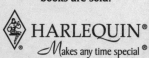

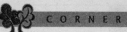

COOPER'S CORNER

The latest continuity from Harlequin Books continues in October 2002 with

STRANGERS WHEN WE MEET
by Marisa Carroll

Check-in: Radio talk-show host Emma Hart thought Twin Oaks was supposed to be a friendly inn, but fellow guest Blake Weston sure was grumpy!

Checkout: When both Emma and Blake find their fiancés cheating on them, they find themselves turning to one another for support—and comforting hugs quickly turn to passionate embraces....